THE DEVIL'S CONCUBINE

A NOVEL

Sebati Edward Mafate

Every Dream Has A Price...

"The Devil's Concubine," by Sebati Edward Mafate. ISBN 978-1-62137-892-1 (softcover); 978-1-62137-893-8 (eBook).

Published 2016 by Virtualbookworm.com Publishing Inc., P.O. Box 9949, College Station, TX , 77842, US.

DEDICATION

For my mother, Edith Kabutu Mwiya. Rest in peace, Mama. I love you always. And also to a special woman, Sharmalie Fernando, whose words, *"Follow your dream Sebati,"* still echo in my ears even after all these years.

ACKNOWLEDGMENTS

A lot of people have been pillars of strength in my life, especially during the dark days. It would take far too many pages to mention them all, but I am grateful for them all. However, the following are preeminent: Jim and Monica Langley, two wonderful people who opened their hearts and house to us when we had no place to go; Sharmalie Fernando, who encouraged me to follow my dream no matter the peaks and valleys that lay in the way; Don and Angelita Johnson; Maria Vaughn, a fellow writer whose dedication to her art is unmatched; Rob Sherman, Victor Monsour, Sepideh Haftgoli, Mara Lane, Daniel Haile, Mpho Mapoulo, Pastor El Clark, Dan Moore, Eric Hudson, and Cassius Latlhang; may you be blessed in whatever journey life leads you.

TABLE OF CONTENTS

PROLOGUE

THE BACK HOUSE of the witch doctor — known only as Baba Brima — was dark, even when dimly lit by the numerous candles. It was dark even in broad daylight, because the windows and all other crevices that let in the natural light were always covered, and in some cases permanently sealed. On this particular day, dusk was not too far off yet the orange glow of the sunset was almost imperceptible in the ominously dark room. On the walls hung an assortment of animal skins and ritualistic masks, horrifying artifacts that made each and every one of his clients shudder the first time they saw them. A large African drum was set at the corner of the room. The air was filled with incense, creating the eerie feeling that this was no ordinary room. It was a known fact that there were unseen presences in this room – the gods and other spirits of long-departed people.

Brima was seated on a stool. He was a middle-aged black man with gray hair and a pair of deep-set eyes. Seated across from him was a much younger black man, handsome, with dreadlocks. The young man had driven from Altadena,

California to the small town of Rosamond in the Antelope Valley. It was fitting that Brima would choose this place for his residence because it gave him the feeling that he was in some third world country, similar to the home he left some thirty years ago, even though one of the largest and most famous cities in the world, Los Angeles, was less than two hours drive away.

In between the two men was a small mat made from goatskin. On it were small bones, cowries, sea shells, and other such objects scattered around, suggesting that some sort of communication process with the supernatural was taking place. Raymond Pata, or Ray, as he liked to be called, was a young man of 25. He was spellbound, as he again shifted uneasily on his stool, wondering for the umpteenth time what pronouncements the witchdoctor had up his sleeve.

At last Brima broke the uncomfortable silence; they had been seated like that, without uttering a word, for close to five minutes.

"Are you sure you want to do this, Raymond Pata?" He had a very distinct accent from the islands in the Caribbean. And the fact that he had called Raymond by his full name did not escape the younger man, who winced briefly but quickly regained control of himself.

"Yes Baba Brima," Raymond answered respectfully. He had a similar accent, even though it was not as strong, revealing that the younger man had spent the majority of his adult life in the United States.

The older man considered this response for a while, as if he was uncertain of the next step. "Because if we do this Raymond, there can be no turning back... *ever*! We are about to unleash mysterious and powerful forces that we have absolutely no control over... and the consequences could be dire." The warning was an ominous one.

Raymond was silent for a moment, as if debating with himself whether to take this step or not; on seeing this hesitation, Brima sighed and warily continued.

"Blood has to be spilled in order to appease the gods. You know that don't you?" The question was a menacing one; the type he was afraid to answer, but knew he had to.

"Y-yes baba Brima."

"You must understand, too, that this visit cannot, under any circumstances, be revealed to anyone. You must not come back here either because I cannot undo this once it is done." For an extended moment, nothing but the sound of crows could be heard.

"I fully understand," Raymond agreed, feeling his heartbeat accelerate.

The older man nodded and said, "Good, I see you have brought the items."

In response, Raymond reached behind him and came up with a cage containing a live chicken that he had bought from a farm in Chino. Not many people living in Southern California knew that you can buy livestock ranging from chickens, pigs, sheep, goats, and even cattle at this humble farm. The place was a haven for those who knew about it, especially foreigners that prefer to slaughter their own meat for special occasions.

Brima cleared his throat and studied the cage and its contents for a brief moment. The hen was brownish-red and reminded him of the chickens that roamed freely in his mother's backyard, many years ago in Haiti.

"Now you know what to do to invoke *Nana Buluku*, the god creator, and *Mawu*, goddess of the moon, because it is to them that you will be offering the sacrifice. These are the ever-present gods who will lead you to superstardom if and when appeased"

Without another word, Raymond gave the witchdoctor a wad of cash that he had been concealing subtly in his hand. He then took the chicken out of its cage, stood up, and stepped on the chicken's wings to stop them from flapping while pinning the legs with his other foot. He grabbed the outsize knife in Brima's outstretched hand and cut the chicken's head off clean. As blood from its severed neck drained into a large dish, Brima looked up at the ceiling, his eyes seemed to be staring inward as he chanted incantations in a chilling voice that was hardly recognizable. He did not stop until life of the chicken completely ebbed; Raymond could feel the body vibrating violently as he kept a steady grip on it. And as if on cue, Brima stopped the incantations the exact moment when the chicken was fully dead.

There was perspiration on Brima's forehead, and he was breathing hard as if he was battling some invisible foe. He very well could have been, Raymond thought, because all of a sudden he felt as if there was another presence in the room. It was the kind you could not see, but some sixth sense told you there was. He felt the little hairs on the back of his neck rise, and his body shuddered involuntarily – he had reached the point of no return; he had crossed to the other side.

Brima closed his eyes again and sighed before saying, "It is done. Now the rest is up to you."

"Thank you Baba Brima," Raymond managed to say as he got up and left swiftly, leaving the witchdoctor, eyes still closed, communicating with the spirits.

He whistled along with the beat playing on his car stereo, now certain that superstardom was within his grasp. All he had to do was find a suitable sacrifice to appease the gods, as Baba Brima had instructed, before the next full moon.

He already had a viable prospect in mind. He had been watching her for the past two months, studying her movements, stalking her incessantly to a point that he knew her well. He had become able to anticipate every move she would make, even though he could never look her in the face. She was the link between him and his chosen destiny, and he knew that it was a task at which he could not fail.

CHAPTER 1

JEAN PATA, RAYMOND'S MOTHER, migrated to the United States from Haiti in the mid- 1980s, determined, like most immigrants, that she was coming to this country to make a good life for herself and her only son. She had originally left him with relatives in Port-au-Prince with the promise that she would send for him soon (in her estimation it would be in less than a year). Instead, it would be another 11 years before she would be reunited with her son, who was now 16 years old.

On her arrival in Miami, Florida, the only job she could get was that of a maid; however, she took to it diligently, saving almost every penny she earned. Within a year, she had her own cleaning business comprised entirely of undocumented workers, many of whom were compatriots and had no formal education or means to be gainfully employed any other way. As the business blossomed and profits started to soar, only then did she send for her only son.

Even at age 16, Raymond Pata knew that the United States was the land where his dreams of becoming a world-renowned superstar would be realized. After all, this was known as the land of opportunity. He had no doubt in his mind that fate, and the powers that be, had conspired on his behalf to bring him here; those '*powers that be*' were the gods that he believed controlled the destiny of every man. This was a belief that was rooted in many parts of Haiti and in him.

The fact his mother, a single woman with no formal education or even a dollar to her name, could come to this foreign land and carve out a decent living for herself over the years could only be attributed to her dutiful homage to the said deities. Her bedroom was adorned with all kinds of altars and ritualistic materials hanging from the walls, so Raymond had no doubt that she was adequately protected. Whenever he doubted the viability of the deistic power, he would recall one incident in particular when he saw this power in action. It was shortly after he arrived in the US, legally he might add, because Jean Pata was determined to see her son succeed in this country without having to encounter the same hard obstacles that she had to endure.

Jean Pata had operated her cleaning business without a license for a long time. All transactions were cash based, due to her fear of leaving a condemning paper trail. even though her workers were also paid in cash, not once did she exploit them out of even a cent of their hard earned wages. She did not believe in keeping money in a bank; they were all a bunch of thieves as far as she was concerned. Instead, she kept all her money, or rather most of it, in a safety deposit box at a local bank. The rest of it lay safely in yet another safe, this one hidden in a secret compartment somewhere under her bed.

It was not long before word got around, and legitimate business owners began noticing that her 'small' enterprise had started cutting into their profits. They were just upset that she was so successful without exploiting any of her employees, as the majority of the industry did just that.

Jean's business started growing, with a full staff of 15 and two vans fully equipped with all the latest cleaning equipment supplies. Her success caught the attention of one lady in particular, Erlinda Ramos, who owned a rival cleaning company with her husband, Fernando. Unlike Jean, they had a business license and regularly paid their taxes; so, naturally they did not take well to a 'peasant' from Haiti, semi-illiterate at that, cutting into their profits. This in spite of the fact that they had a large and lucrative account with the City of Miami that allowed them, among others privileges, to clean municipal buildings and parts of the City Hall. They also had a separate account that took care of the municipal garbage. These accounts alone could have kept them living comfortably, yet they also had small 'side jobs' with individual homes and many 'mom and pop' businesses which, excluding the city accounts, netted them profits in excess of $250,000 annually.

Even though their wealth and yearly profit surpassed Jean's, the sheer idea of someone else having a foothold in the business was enough to enrage Erlinda to the point of action. One morning she drove over to Jean Pata's house, just as Jean was getting her workforce ready to tackle that day's assignments,…and berated her in front of her workers and neighbors. She told Jean, in no uncertain terms, to shut her operation down in a week; failing to do so would result in a more permanent shut down.

Additionally, she was, as she put it, going to make sure that Jean and her 'cronies,' including the 'wetbacks,' would be deported back to their backward third world countries. She shouted these insults across the street in her brand new SUV, in a clear attempt to humiliate her in front of her workers and neighbors, thus adding insult to injury. On the other hand, Jean listened patiently, …not even remotely troubled by the abuse. However, she could not help but wonder how it was possible that a woman of Erlinda Ramos's standing who acted so stupidly could rise to head a company that was worth hundreds of thousands of dollars, or perhaps even millions! This was something to think about, because lately Jean Pata had been looking into expanding her business even further. Her son had been raving about launching his music career, which would require a lot of money, and growing her business would definitely give her the extra cash to help her son in his career. Her one condition to supporting him financially was that he finish college and earn his degree, and thereafter do whatever he pleased. He would have to have a degree to fall back onto, in case his music career did not pan out, she would always say to him. But her son had other ideas.

And if this so-called brain-of-the-business was so dumb, going legitimate and securing those lucrative accounts from the city, and even the high-rise buildings in downtown Miami might just be the thing.

In the end, Jean Pata decided to ignore the outbursts from this woman and went about her business. However, after Erlinda left, she walked across the street to the exact spot where Erlinda had parked her car and scooped the dirt where the tire marks of the SUV were still visible. She then went inside her house, clasping the dirt as if it were gold dust, and did not reappear until after an hour or so, her brow bright with perspiration and her eyes bloodshot.

A week later, at the Florida Turnpike, Erlinda had one of the tires of her SUV burst while driving to work. The vehicle zigzagged across the freeway, miraculously not hitting other cars in the process, but capsized nonetheless. The car then slid on the tarmac and burst into flames when it hit the guardrail on the side of the freeway. It was a gruesome sight. By the time the fire engines arrived, the SUV and the driver were burned beyond recognition.

Not too long thereafter, Jean Pata got her business license and took over all of Erlinda Ramos's contracts and more. Erlinda's husband Fernando later filed for bankruptcy and moved to Tampa; and, after friends and family scattered with the four winds, Fernando found solace only in the bottle. Those who knew Jean Pata, and who also knew or heard about her little skirmish with Erlinda Ramos, could not help but put two and two together; they all reached the same chilling and deadly conclusion: Jean Pata was not a woman to be trifled with.

෴ ෴ ෴

Raymond was twenty-four years old when he decided to move to Southern California to pursue his music career. Los Angeles would be his final destination. It was the 'City of Angels' where his dream of becoming a successful recording artist would be realized. He had written a few songs, and had relative success at the local clubs, but nothing to write home about. The only drawback was that he would not have the financial backing from his mother. Jean Pata had made it dreadfully clear to her son that she would only back him if he finished college and got his degree. It did not matter, as far as she was concerned, what his major was. It could be in Art History for all she cared, as long as it was a college degree.

Jean Pata, from the little that she knew and saw, was always of the opinion that the very notion of a music career was very much a gamble, much like playing the lottery. Many were called and yet very few were chosen. So when her son dropped out of the University of Florida at Miami, she was greatly displeased with him. She had worked her fingers right to the bone to see to it that her one and only son was equipped with the right tools to survive this cold, harsh, and brutal world. An education, she believed, was the only shield that could deflect any of life's blows.

As a cleaning woman, her profession exposed her to many affluent houses and neighborhoods. She saw that the common trend of success with these families was a solid education. That is why Jean Pata took her son's dropping out of school a few years earlier as a personal failure. Her own story was the classic American 'rags to riches' story, and she did that with the belief that one day her son would reach heights hitherto undreamt of even by her.

Raymond, on the other hand, saw education, or rather the drudgery of having to go through four long years to get a degree as a major hindrance to his given destiny. His dream, no matter the outcome, could not be put on hold any longer. The way he saw it, his own mother had succeeded in life with hardly an education, much less a degree. So what would stop him, her own flesh and blood, from achieving success? Besides, having grown up with her, he knew that she also sought help from the gods. He too felt he could walk the same pious path. And with that kind of power at his disposal, who was to say his dream would be forfeit?

This is something mother and son argued about constantly, though not disrespectfully on Raymond's part. In the end, the lines were drawn. Nothing could stand in the way of Raymond heading to Los Angeles, he was an adult after all, and Jean Pata would not lift a finger to help him financially. Raymond learned to be quite content with that, even though deep down the thought of not having money was a scary one. He had grown up wanting for nothing. But so strong was his dream and conviction that he was certain he would find a way to survive before he hit the big time and make his mother proud in the process, because her praise was the only thing he cherished other than his dream. Los Angeles, after all, had many such tales of people arriving penniless, and finding a way to survive before the inevitable big break that was sure to follow if he stuck with it. Having reached this decision, he began packing his bags.

The morning he was set to leave, his mother handed him an envelope. In it were crisp $100 bills that amounted to $4000. Enough to get him started, he thought.

"That is all you will ever get from me, Raymond," she said after a brief embrace from her son, a mark of a son's affection for his mother and gratitude. "That is until you realize that in order to get more from me, you must first get your degree," she continued.

"Thank you Ma, but really now is the time to chase my dream full force. I understand that you mean well. However this is a dream that I have chosen."

"Dreams are what make life tolerable, but you still need something to fall back onto in case things do not work out," she said in her affected Caribbean accent with a French twist to it.

Conversely, Raymond could not help but wonder how many times he had heard that from her. A thousand, a hundred thousand? He had heard it so often that it lost its desired effect long ago.

"I know that Ma." There was just a slight trace of agitation in his voice. "I have got to follow this."

"Okay," his mother threw her arms in a helpless gesture. "If that is what you want, but remember that part of growing up is making your own decisions and sticking to them no matter where they lead you," she added.

"I understand you want the best for me Ma, even though we do not necessarily see eye to eye on what really is best, but my mind is made up. I have *got* to do this."

His mother sighed before saying, "Okay Ray, it's your life, do as you please, but don't ever say I did not warn you."

Raymond just acknowledged that with a grunt as he continued to pack his bags. He was scheduled to catch the Greyhound Bus to Los Angeles later that afternoon.

Jean then handed him a piece of paper on which she had scribbled something down. "This is the name and number of someone who may be of some help to you, particularly in what you are trying to accomplish. He is also from Haiti, and is one of us. His name is Brima Francois Bolatelli, but you call him 'Baba Brima.' He migrated to this country over 30 years ago. He has helped many people," she said.

The phrase 'one of us' had an unsettling connotation to it, and Raymond immediately understood that the man, whoever he was, was a witchdoctor, a liaison between this world and the other one – the dark and mysterious type that he would soon get to know.

He took the piece of paper, folded it and carefully placed it in his wallet. He knew that to get to where he wanted to get to in his life, he would definitely need the help of this inexplicable man.

CHAPTER 2

LOS ANGELES, downtown Los Angeles in particular, was not like anything Raymond had imagined it would be. When the Greyhound Bus drove down Broadway in the heart of downtown, three days after leaving Miami, the street looked like a scene from some post-apocalyptic movie. There was trash everywhere, it was overcast, and newspapers were blowing around. It had somewhat of a depressing feeling to it, and he could not help but wonder if this was some sort of omen of things to come, but he discarded the thought quicker than it came.

With a little over five thousand dollars to his name, he checked into the Bonaventure Hotel on Figueroa Street. The cheapest room cost $169 per night. He ordered room service, which consisted of a big steak, a strawberry milkshake, and fries, and thereafter fell into a deep sleep; up until then, he had not realized how tired he was. He woke up refreshed the next morning, and browsed the 'classified' section of the *Los Angeles Times*. It did not take him long to realize that accommodation in Los Angeles was very expensive.

A studio apartment in downtown Los Angeles cost an arm and a leg. Other places in the surrounding area proved to be just as discouraging.

He was about to give up and maybe try looking at some hostels he heard about in Hollywood, or even try looking through *Craigslist*, when, as an afterthought, he decided to look through the *Pasadena Star News* and the *Pennysaver*. It was in the *Pennysaver* that he saw a house for rent in Altadena, an unincorporated city in the Los Angeles County, approximately 14 miles from the downtown Los Angeles Civic Center and directly north of the city of Pasadena.

To educate himself more about the area, he looked up the city on his iPhone and got to know more about it. Altadena is part of the county of Los Angeles, and is politically run by the Los Angeles county board of supervisors who have executive, legislative and judicial powers. The Altadena Town Council acts as an ombudsman group to express state and federal agencies the will and wishes of the Altadena community. However, the council has no legislative powers and makes no legal decisions for the community; it only operates to express consensus to governmental officials. In other words, Altadena was a typical all-American city. He was also quick to note that the Los Angeles County Sheriff's Department (LASD) operates the Altadena Sheriff Station in Altadena.

Located at the foothills of a breathtaking range of mountains, the city has many places of interest. One of which is 'Christmas Tree Lane,' an almost mile long stretch on Santa Rosa Avenue from Woodbury Street to Altadena Drive. This place has been a holiday attraction since 1920, and it is the oldest, large-scale outdoor Christmas lighting venue in the world. Each December, members of the Christmas Tree Lane Association festoon the 110 deodar trees that line the street with thousands of Christmas lights. 'Christmas Tree Lane' was placed on the National Register of Historic Places in 1990, and is a California historical landmark.

The one place that for some reason brought a grin on Raymond Pata's face, as he read along, was the historic Mount Lowe Railway. This was a scenic railway that once carried passengers to any of the resort hotels high in the San Gabriel Mountains above Altadena and Pasadena. Although the mountains and the remains of the railway are not strictly in Altadena, the most direct trail to the sites, the 'Sam Merrill Trail' starts in Altadena at the top of Lake Avenue, and leads to Mount Echo, about 3 miles away. Chaney Trail, just west of the intersection of Fair Oaks Avenue and Loma Alta Street, is a forestry service road leading to the old right of way. The Mount Lowe Railway site was also placed on the National Register of Historic Places in 1993.

The Cobb Estate at the top of Lake Avenue is now a free botanical garden, operated by the United

States Forest Service. It is guarded by its historic gates, which are easily passed to allow visitors and hikers to ascend its long and winding paved driveway of what was once one of Altadena's premier mansions. This site is also found alongside the same Merrill Trail; which has access to Flores Canyon on the way to Echo Mountain. He had no way of knowing this at the time, but this would prove to be a perfect place to offer sacrifices to *Nana Buluku* and *Mawu* goddess of the moon.

With the help of the hotel receptionist, he managed to rent a Toyota Camry Sedan for a week from Enterprise Rent-A-Car, and drove out to Altadena to meet the owner of the house he was interested in renting. Surprisingly, the drive from downtown Los Angeles to Altadena was a smooth one, especially at that time of the day. With the aid of directions he downloaded from MapQuest (his rental car did not have GPS trekking), he took the 110 freeway north, all the way to the end where it turned into a street named Arroyo Parkway in Pasadena. From here he was able to connect with Lake Avenue, and drove north toward the mountains. The scenery was even more stunning in person.

The property in Altadena was located on Morada Place, a small street off of Lake, and not too far from the popular 'Coffee Gallery.' The landlady was a pleasant-looking, older white woman named Katherine Barnard. She was a widow; her husband

Frank had died over 20 years ago. She met Raymond at the front of her house.

"Oh so you are the young man that called earlier this morning," she smiled after the normal introductions. He liked her instantly.

Raymond flashed his best smile and extended his arm for a handshake. He could be disarmingly charming whenever the need arose. "Yes, Raymond Pata, but my friends and everyone else call me Ray," he said, still flashing his award-winning smile.

"I am Mrs. Katherine Barnard," she said, accepting his handshake. Her arm, like the rest of her body, was pale and bony; the blue veins on her hands were quite distinct.

"Pleased to meet you, Mrs. Barnard."

"Likewise. I detect a slight accent. If you don't mind my asking, where are you from, Ray?"

If he had a dime for every time people asked him this question, he would have been able to buy 'Capitol Records' in Hollywood a long time ago.

"Haiti, but I grew up in Miami and Jacksonville, Florida for the most part. I just moved to Los Angeles."

"Oh."

"Is this the house for rent?" he asked as he looked passed her and through the window into the living room. They were standing on the porch, which had a beautiful shed covered with overgrowing vines, and other creepers that provided a nice shade.

"Yes, absolutely," Mrs. Barnard said as she reached into the front pocket of her apron and pulled out a bunch of keys. She separated one from the others, which all looked the same, and miraculously it was the one she needed to unlock the front door. "Come on in." Ray followed her into the house.

The living room was large and sparsely furnished. The whole house smelled of fresh paint.

"My late husband and I lived in this house for over 50 years. Our kids have since grown up and moved away with their own families, and all of a sudden this became too big for me," she said as she led him through first the living room and then the kitchen, with its adjoining laundry room, which was empty but still had the necessary hook-ups for a washer and dryer. "There are about two or three laundry mats not too far from here. There is one down the street on Lake, which is always crowded, and another up the street on Altadena Drive and Lincoln," she was saying as she showed him the dining area and the three bedrooms, one of which was the master. "I was renting every room out individually, and all the tenants shared the kitchen and the two bathrooms, but it was like a mad house, and I had to get rid of them."

"I see," Raymond said. He was in deep thought. The house was very nice inside and outside and spacious too.

"Are you married?" At first, he did not hear her since he was in deep thought, already picturing himself in the house.

"Huh?"

"Oh, I asked if you were married."

Marriage was something that was farthest from his mind. He imagined how he would maybe convert one of the rooms into his own mini recording studio. Completely soundproof and furnished with all the recording equipment, mixing boards, synthesizers, the like. And even a state-of-the-art microphone that would catch even the sound of the flapping wings of a hummingbird. This daydream continued until Mrs. Barnard's voice interrupted it. "Oh no, not yet," he managed to say.

"Girlfriend?"

"No."

"Kids?"

"No."

"Pets?"

"No ma'am." He felt as if she was asking too many unnecessary questions, but he quickly realized that these were typical questions asked on a rental application. He was waiting for her to ask him about his credit. He had an answer for that one too, and it was good. His mother had seen to it. Good credit goes a long way, she had told him, and he found no reason to doubt her; she had a thriving business that she had started from the ground up, and one of the first things she learned about this country was that good credit was the key to success in life.

"No kids, no pets, and no girlfriend?" she sounded a bit surprised. Raymond Pata was a good looking young man, it was hard to imagine him without a woman in his life, or so she thought.

He flashed yet another of his inviting smiles, and she could not help but smile back. "No, Mrs. Barnard. No pets, no kids, and certainly no girlfriend, but I am looking, though."

They both laughed.

"This house has three bedrooms as you can tell, but isn't that too much for a young bachelor?" Mrs. Barnard wanted to know.

"Not at all."

"Very well, let me show you the backyard."

She opened the back door, which was a glass sliding door. It led them to the backyard, and the sight made it hard for Raymond to contain his elation. Sparkling in the late morning sunlight was a well maintained midsize swimming pool; the deep end, he was able to tell, was ten feet. The listing said nothing about a swimming pool, and thus this caught him totally by surprise. He was sure the old lady deliberately withheld this information. This was her 'ace' in the hole – the clincher.

On the western side of the pool was another shed, similar to the one at the entrance. It was covered with creepers and other beautiful plants, giving it a spectacular shade complete with all the outdoor furniture: a garden table, five chairs, and a long chair that one could lie on while sunbathing or relaxing. There was also a barbecue stand on the eastern side of the pool. *This is where I will hold my parties. I will throw numerous of them, barbecues, pool parties, parties to celebrate the release of a new CD, parties to celebrate my birthday – you name it*, he thought to himself with a smile.

There was an orange wall on the north end of the yard. On it was a door that Mrs. Barnard quickly explained that it led to a two car garage. Upon inspecting it, Raymond was surprised to find it completely empty, and had not been used for years.

"I stopped driving about twenty years ago," she said. "As you can see, you can park two cars in here, and still have adequate room for storage."

Raymond's mind was racing again, as his imagination was inflamed even further. *This would be a perfect place to arrange a set of drums, guitars, amplifiers* ... in other words, an ideal place for a band to rehearse incessantly, he thought.

"This is really nice Mrs. Barnard," he said. And he really meant it.

"Thank you."

She led him back into the living room. There was a rental application form on the kitchen counter that he had not noticed earlier.

"Now the rent is thirteen seventy-five with a deposit of the same amount, and is due on the first of every month. Can you live with that?"

Raymond's mind started working quickly. That would mean twenty-seven fifty. He had forty-five hundred after renting the car for one week; after paying the first and last month's rent that was going to leave him with one thousand seven hundred and fifty dollars. And there were gas and electricity hookups, not to mention furniture, food, and other basic necessities after which he would be left with nothing. He would have to come up with a plan immediately. He would get a job or something to bring in some money before his music career started paying dividends.

"Okay, all you have to do is fill in this form here," she handed it to him, and amazingly made a pen appear from nowhere. "There is an apartment duplex at the back with four one bedroom apartments; I live in one of them. Are you honest?"

The question caught him off guard. "Yes, ma'am, or at least I would like to think so," he flashed another one of his disarming smiles that always seemed to work its magic on members of the opposite sex – regardless of age.

"Good, now something tells me to take a chance on you, Raymond. I am doing this even without doing a credit check on you," she said.

"You will not regret it, Mrs. Barnard."

"I sure hope so Raymond," she smiled.

"So when can you move in?"

"I already have all my belongings at the back of my car."

He then counted out two-thousand seven hundred and fifty dollars cash and handed it to her. The old woman was visibly impressed, and any lingering doubts she had about her brand new tenant were soon put to rest. "That should take care of this month's rent and the deposit."

"Thank you very much; I will give you your receipt later today. In the meantime I would like to welcome you as my newest tenant."

They shook hands, and she handed him the keys, one for the front, and one for the back. It was that simple.

"Thank you, Mrs. Barnard."

"Oh, it is Katherine now," she smiled as she patted him on the shoulder.

"Thank you again, Mrs. Barnard— I mean Katherine," he smiled again. He suddenly realized that he had not eaten anything since very early that morning now that he had secured a place to live. "Is there a place in the neighborhood where I can go later on for a sandwich or any other fast food?"

"Oh yes, the Coffee Gallery is just across the street on Lake Avenue. They have a great deli. Up Lake, a little further, there is a Ralphs Supermarket, and right next door is Everest Restaurant, a fast food joint with delicious burgers and hot dogs," she smiled again as she put the money in the front pocket of her apron. She was beaming, and Raymond could not help but think joyously about the power of cash in hand, and what it can do in almost *any* situation.

🌼 🌼 🌼

The Coffee Gallery, literally a stone throw away from his new residence, was an artist's haven. The patronage is often the intellectual and artistic type, as they are on their laptops taking advantage of the free *WIFI* that comes with purchasing even something as small as a cup of coffee. But most importantly, and this he could attribute to serendipity and the gods smiling on him, was that there were two stages, one in the front and the other in a mini hall in the back called 'The Backstage' where anyone could perform just by booking a Friday date in advance. This is where musicians like him, and up and coming stand-up comedians, could showcase their talents. He had already started making plans of forming a band, and this was one of the places he could launch. He could hardly contain his excitement as one of the workers gave him a breakdown of the place.

However, over the next few weeks, it became apparent to Raymond that breaking into the music business was not going to be easy. Worse still, he did not know anyone who would at least let him get his foot in. So he did what millions of other unknown artists do when desperately seeking that elusive break. He sent his demo tapes to over a hundred recording labels, from established entities like Columbia and Warner Records, to unknown indie labels he and the majority of other people had never heard of, and all of them rejected him with their insulting little notes. 'Thank you for submitting your demo CD that we are herewith returning. It does not fit our present needs.' And: 'Thank you for your submissions. Your songs are too similar to what we have already produced.' Or simply: 'We are returning the demo CD you sent us.' The most common: 'We DO NOT accept unsolicited materials.'

Before long, his funds started running low. He somehow managed to sweet talk his mother to wire him another two thousand dollars, but she made it clear that that was it – the 'Mama Bank' was closed for good, and to not even bother asking again because such a request would not be entertained nor listened to. If he needed money, he would have to earn it the old-fashioned American way – work for it. Fend for himself was more like it.

And Raymond knew that once Jean Pata's mind was made up, nothing else could make her think otherwise. It was either he found some sort of income to sustain him while he chased his dream, or return to Florida with his tail tucked between his legs, a defeated man. The second option was less than appealing.

The opportunity came from an entirely different and unexpected source. It happened when he was forced to return the rental car at the 'Enterprise Rent-A-Car' office in Pasadena, located at the corner of Orange Grove and Lincoln Avenue. It started off as being one of the worst days in Raymond Pata's life. Without a car in Southern California, one was truly limited. He learned this pretty quickly. It was not like New York, where one could simply jump onto a subway train that could take him to any chosen destination.

Southern California was vastly spread out, with its cities linked together by numerous freeways. The bus and train system, called the 'Metrolink,' though adequate, and fairly effective, took way too long. So without a car, Raymond was doomed before he even started.

Thus with a heavy heart, he returned the vehicle that Wednesday morning, two days after the promised due date; the threatening calls were already being made. And after closing out the contract, and paying the necessary fines, and for the extra mileage he was down to $175, and rent was barely three weeks away. Even more depressing, was the fact that he was no closer to realizing his initial goal of forming a band within the first six months of his stay in California.

With a band, one totally under his control, he would start showcasing his talents first at the Coffee Gallery, and then at bars in Old Town Pasadena like the 35'er, and clubs like 'The Dugout.' From there, after a little bit of exposure, they would book gigs at more established clubs around Southern California, and then later the entire state, and then neighboring states, until a tour of the whole country was in the works.

At this time he figured that they would have a following, and that would be the perfect time to record a CD that they would sell at their shows, and from the back of their trunks. After all, many artists who made it big went that route. He thought no further than Christopher Brian Bridges, who was better known by his stage name 'Ludacris.' Already a fellow by the name of Chico had promised to record their first album at his home in nearby Eagle Rock, where he had converted his garage into a state of the art recording studio. The possibilities were endless. Only money, and a steady flow of it at that, would alleviate all his problems.

He could get a job, but so far the only jobs he was qualified for, and were hiring right away, were vacuum cleaning sales jobs done door-to-door, and telemarketing work that was spread all over the classified section of any newspaper or *'Employment Guide.'* Raymond Pata hated these types of high-pressure sales jobs.

These were the thoughts going through his mind as he walked out of the 'Enterprise Rent-A-Car' premises. The bastards would not even take him home right away, because they were suddenly too busy with other customers, and he would have to wait another two hours before a 'courtesy ride' back home could be given. He told them not to bother and that he would walk back home instead. Actually, he figured that the long walk would clear his head, force him to think things through, and come up with a plan to make money and quick.

"Excuse me, bro," a voice interrupted his thoughts. He turned to see a fresh cut, well-dressed black man with a clean shave standing besides the latest Mustang GTS that was diamond black. He looked to be in his late 40's. One could say he was handsome, except for the eyes; they were deep set and penetrating, but imposing would be most accurate.

"Yes," Raymond answered with a slight sneer, and a look that told the other man that this would be the wrong day to mess with him.

"You're not from around here are you?" the man smiled as he walked up to Raymond with his hand outstretched for a handshake.

Raymond regarded him suspiciously as he carefully shook his hand. It was a cold, hard hand; the kind that had done a lot of manual labor in the past.

"Yeah, so?"

"Peace, my brother. My name is Larry Allen; I just overheard you talking to those people inside the rental car place.

Raymond was getting impatient. "I'm a busy man, Larry, what can I do for you?"

"As a matter of fact, I was wondering if you could do me a small favor. You need a ride back home, yeah? What if I asked you to help me drive my other car parked across the street? What you would do is follow me to my body shop up the street on Lincoln and Altadena Drive, and then upon delivery, I will gladly drop you off wherever you are headed."

Some gut instinct, a cold chill at the back of his neck, told him that something was definitely wrong with this picture. He was going to ask why Larry couldn't have one of his friends do it ... but something held his tongue. He was to look back at that moment over the next few years.

Larry could immediately read the uncertainty on the other man's face. "I'll pay you. Look, I am a business man, and time is money. Can you do it?"

Raymond started thinking fast. Surely a couple of bucks would not hurt, especially now that he was counting pennies instead of dollars. Besides, the stranger said his body shop was in Altadena, so there could be no harm in that.

"Sure, I can do it. And my name is Raymond Pata, but my friends call me Ray."

The two men shook hands again. Larry was still smiling, but the eyes were the same as before.

"Pleasure meeting you, Ray. Where you from?"

"Jacksonville, Florida, but originally from Haiti," he said.

"Interesting. I could tell, you have a slight accent. How long you been in the US?"

"Since I was 16."

"So you are practically American, bro. Always a pleasure to meet someone from the Motherland or the Caribbean. Can you drive a stick shift by any chance?"

"Oh yeah."

"Thought so. Here, follow me in that car," he said as he handed Raymond a set of keys and gestured at a vehicle across the street that Raymond had not noticed up until then. The sight almost took his breath away. The car was a silver-gray 2013 Porsche 911 Carrera 4S Cabriolet – one of his dream cars.

"Are you sure about that?" Raymond asked before he could stop himself.

"Yeah, why not? Just make sure you stay close to me. I will be driving this," he pointed at the Mustang that suddenly looked inferior. "It's a seven speed, so be careful with the gas pedal. The car has a lot of pull."

Raymond could not believe it as he sat behind the wheel, and drove the luxurious car along the road as he followed Larry a few minutes later. The journey lasted only seven or eight minutes, but the experience was enough to last a lifetime. This was living.

Larry's body shop was at the north end side of Lincoln and Altadena drive. There were quite a few cars in the parking lot; mostly foreign, but a few domestic. Some had 'For Sale' stickers pasted on the windshields, and looked like they had never been involved in any kind of accidents. Others were wrecks that were waiting to be fixed, and needed paint jobs.

He was directed to park the car by one of the workers, at one of the empty spots, which he did, and soon thereafter Larry summoned him to his office. The place looked busy with a lot of activities going on. Larry Allen was already seated behind his desk in his nicely kept office by the time Raymond walked in. There was a window with a one way glass on the right side of the office walking in, which gave Larry a full view of the inside of the huge garage where three men were busy working on a car that looked to be one of the newest Mercedes Benz 300 series. It seemed to Raymond that for a body shop, Larry seemed to be dealing with high end cars.

"Please sit down Raymond," Larry waved at a chair in front of his desk. "And thank you very much for helping me bring the car over here."

"Not a problem, Larry. It was a pleasure." And indeed it was in every sense of the word. Already, Raymond Pata was dreaming of how life would be like when he finally hit the big time. Driving luxury cars like the Porsche he just drove would be the norm. This man, Larry Allen, had given him a small taste of that.

"I'm a very good judge of character, Ray. That is what has kept me successful in all the years that I have been in this business," Larry said as he undid his tie, and thereafter cracked his knuckles. "Coffee, tea, juice, anything?" he offered.

"No thanks." There was a purpose to this meeting, Raymond sensed, regardless of how impromptu it was.

"Fine, anyway as I was saying, I'm a very good judge of people, and I have a feeling that you want more out of life than you already got. Am I right?"

The man was a mind reader.

"You got that right, Larry."

"I am sure a young brother like yourself, and no offense, a foreigner, knows that the white man ain't gonna do it for us; that is why we African brothers got to stick together."

Oh, one of those idealistic brothers, Raymond thought drily. How many times had he heard that before? A hundred? A thousand? Pick a number. Normally, he would have scoffed and placed his mind elsewhere as Larry rumbled on. However, this was a different kind of brother who obviously had it together. So he was content to sit and listen. He just told himself that there could be something of benefit, something at the end of the rainbow that could be worthwhile, something in it for him; particularly now that the chips were down.

"None taken, Larry, and you are right. The white man ain't gonna do jack for us unless we do it for ourselves." He felt that it was necessary to placate the man, even though all he was looking at was his own interests "Exactly," Larry said as he fished out a cigarette. He offered Raymond one, who politely declined, just like he did with the coffee. "Do you mind?" Larry asked as he got ready to light it up.

"Not at all," he said even though the smell of the nicotine had always been repulsive to him.

"Good, and if you don't mind my asking Ray, what do you do for a living?" He was fishing, and Raymond realized that quick enough, and he was ready to bite.

"I ... I'm an artist ... a musician," he added quickly, but at the same time proudly.

"I see. Starving?"

"Excuse me?"

"What I mean is that with art it can only be one of the two. Either you have made it big, or you are starving and on your way. There can never be in between."

"Starving, but definitely on my way," Raymond said.

"Good, that means you have a lot of time on your hands."

"I don't think I follow you, Larry," he said truthfully.

"I need someone to work for me, more like freelancing really, and that could mean a few extra bucks in your pocket," Larry said as he puffed a film of smoke through his nostrils and watched it dissolve somewhere up near the ceiling. He was fishing again, and Raymond knew it would not take much to get caught.

"What kind of work do you have in mind?" Raymond wanted to know. At this point, even washing cars would be a viable option to selling vacuum cleaners door to door.

"Delivering cars like you just did." There was a brief silence as both men pondered the last statement, Raymond in particular, as Larry watched him patiently without blinking.

"Just delivering cars to your shop?"

"Yep, I tell you where one is, and you pick it up and bring it over to me, and I pay you cash on the spot; the amount depends of course on the make and model of the car," Larry answered.

"That's it?"

"Pretty much," Larry said as he pulled at a drawer from underneath his desk. He retrieved a brown manila envelope, which he slid across the table at Raymond. "That's for helping me bring the car here and a little advance to top it all." The envelope was thick with money, and Raymond's heart started pumping even faster. "Go ahead, open it, it's yours – all of it," Larry invited.

Raymond took the envelope; it felt heavy, and he could only guess how much was inside. When he opened it, he almost whistled in amazement. There was a stack of crisp tens, twenties and hundred-dollar bills.

"H-how much is this Larry?" he asked, visibly shocked. His mouth was dry and his fingers were suddenly moist from nervous tension. He suddenly found it difficult to breathe and keep his hands from shaking.

"Two grand," Larry said nonchalantly, like a person who was used to handling large sums of money all the time.

"That's too much, Larry. All I did was just drive a car here and even that took less than ten minutes," Raymond protested, but rather weakly because, in his mind, that was the right thing to do. But he had already started spending the money in his head.

With the two thousand dollars, he could pay next month's rent. With the remainder, after paying the necessary bills like lighting, heat, and food, he could definitely buy the drum set he saw at almost a giveaway price on 'Craig's List.' along with two electric guitars, an amplifier, synthesizer, and mixing board. All these were worth over three thousand dollars easy, but the seller, whoever he was, was willing to part with all that for $500 or best offer. Raymond could not believe his eyes when he saw the ad. The only difference was that he had the money now, assuming, of course, the guy had not sold them already.

On the other hand was that tiny voice at the back of his mind that warned if he took the money, he would be a slave to this stranger sitting across the table from him who was watching with what looked like sinister patience. In other words, Larry would own him. However, he had to remind himself that he was first and foremost a Pata, a different kind of breed owned by no one. The Patas determined their own fate; or rather only the gods, and not men, determined their destiny. This is something his mother had instilled in him. And that was why she stressed, rather strongly, that once in California, Raymond should seek a man, who was Haitian like her named Brima. This man, Jean said, would make sure that he was protected from any man's bad intentions, and also help him in his quest to become a superstar. But his mother had forewarned him that he would only seek this man if he was willing to pay the price, because as she put it – every dream has a price.

With these thoughts in mind, Raymond accepted. It also his strongest conviction that the gods had led this man to him. There was no other logical explanation, because it was not every day that a total stranger comes up to you and offers you a small assignment, with the promise of more, which paid so much. At this rate, assuming of course that all Larry told him was accurate, there would be no need to get a 9 to 5 job; he could concentrate entirely on his music and forming a band. The gods were surely smiling at him. Mama was right; the Patas were a whole different and unique breed. He almost smiled at the thought.

"That's nothing Raymond, as you will soon see," Larry assured him. "All I ask is that you keep all this to yourself. In the unlikely event that you are stopped by the police, and I might stress, in the unlikely event, do not, I repeat, do not say anything before you speak to me."

On the other hand, Raymond had to wonder why he would be pulled over, and the question came out before he could stop himself.

"And why would they want to stop me, Larry?"

"Come on Ray, you know how it is when the cops see a young brother driving a nice car like the one you just drove, worth more than their whole year salary. What's the first thing that goes through their mind?"

"That it was stolen."

"Exactly, that and or you're deep into some shady stuff like drugs, which kill more people than all the wars we've fought put together. I tell you again man, we are up against a system that does not want to see a black man make a good life for himself. Did you know that in this great state of ours there are more prisons than there are state universities? And guess who makes up the largest inmate population ... Yeah, you guessed it right, brothers like you and me." Larry at this point decided to hammer the point much closer to home to get Raymond Pata's full and undivided attention. "You will see a lot of that in your music career; make no mistake about that Raymond. I had a cousin down in Kansas City Missouri who, just like you, came out here to make it big in the entertainment industry. He was into music just like you, but he had hopes of writing soundtracks for feature films, commercials, TV spots, and the like, but with no connections, and most importantly no money, he struck out without even getting to first base. He went back home a beaten and broken man, and why? Not because he wasn't talented, but he tried to do things by the book, the right way, but got frozen out. You need to be a fox to survive in this world."

And with that, he had driven the point across. He, Raymond Pata, was not going to be a statistic. He was not going to return to Florida with his tail tucked in between his legs. He was ready now to slay dragons for this man.

"Alright, I hear you Larry; I will do as you say." There was a slight smile on Raymond's face as he said this. Of course, any starving artist with two grand suddenly ... in his hand will do or say anything to keep the goose that lays the golden eggs alive and happy.

"That's the spirit, my brother. I will definitely be in touch."

"Great."

"I guess that's all for now. I will have one of my workers take you home. Where do you live again?"

"Right here in Altadena, on Lake and Morada."

"Is that by the Coffee Gallery?" Larry asked with a smile.

Somehow, Raymond had a feeling that the other man knew exactly where that was, and the question was not an idle one. He wanted Raymond to know that he knew the area very well, and if need be, he could find him easily.

"Yep, that's the one."

"Good," Larry said as he reached for the intercom on his desk, and pressed the button. "Jorge, come in here please," he said after the connection was made.

"Sure boss," a voice sounded through the speaker almost at once.

A little later, a young Hispanic man dressed in greasy overalls entered the office after knocking ever so slightly at the door, wiping his hands with a rag. Raymond instinctively turned around to see him, and estimated him to be in his early 20s. He smiled rather nervously as he offered his greetings, and Raymond was forced to wonder why.

"Oh Raymond, this is Jorge — or George as he prefers to be called."

"Pleased to meet you, Mr. Raymond," Jorge said politely.

"Likewise," Raymond responded with a nod directed at the younger man.

"Raymond needs a ride home as soon as possible, so stop whatever you are doing and drop him off okay?"

"Sure boss, anything else?"

"No. Oh, just pick up something for lunch along the way, preferably some *El Pollo Unico* from that chicken joint on Lake and Orange Grove. Their lunch special should do, and a Jamaica drink. Get something for Mr. Pata here."

"Already done."

Looks like the man is running a tight ship around here, Raymond thought to himself, but if he thinks I will become one of his 'yes men,' he is gravely mistaken. That I promise; I have powers beyond measure that he will soon know about. But he was grateful for the offer of lunch, because all of a sudden his stomach started growling at the mention of food.

"Okay, not a problem boss, I just need to quickly change and wash my hands," he said.

"Fine." It was a dismissal.

A little later, Jorge came to announce that the car was ready, and quickly left the office as if his presence was an annoyance. The two new friends soon after shook hands; with promises to stay in touch.

Raymond was already at the door when Larry said, very much as an afterthought, "Oh Raymond? You are a good man, I can see, so I will only tell you once: don't ever try to screw me, is that understood?" Those deep-set eyes were once again penetrating.

"Understood," Raymond answered sincerely. "I am looking at this as a great opportunity to launch my career, so there is no way in hell I can mess this up." He tried to sound as pious and as confident as possible, even though that chill at the back of his neck returned, making him wonder again what exactly he had gotten himself into. But then he was able to dismiss that thought again with his own delusions of grandeur by thinking of the magic doll he had safely tucked away in his house — a doll his mother Jean had given him, and a doll she had taught him to use as a way to invoke the power of the gods. A doll many people who knew no better referred to as a 'voodoo doll.' He smiled inwardly, and not for the first time, he believed that Larry Allen had met more than his match in Raymond Pata.

෴ ෴ ෴

The used drum set and other equipment, to his utmost and pleasant surprise, was in even better condition than he had expected and the purchase went smoothly. The seller, a kid named Jack, who lived in nearby Glendale, was anxious to part with it. He told Raymond he had once dreamed of becoming a rock star and had convinced his parents to buy him the equipment. But after a few attempts, he decided to discard that dream and go to college instead — much to the delight of his parents. Even better, he went down on his asking price to as low as $350.00, agreed to transport the gear for him, and even helped him set it up in his garage. Raymond could not believe his luck once again. He stayed in his garage for a while after Jack had left, admiring the view of his new rehearsing studio.

"This is just the beginning, but I have arrived," he kept saying to himself over and again. He was now totally convinced that superstardom was within reach. He felt the need to celebrate that very evening.

CHAPTER 3

THE COCO'S RESTAURANT in Pasadena is less than 3 miles heading down south on Lake Avenue when coming from Altadena after crossing the 210 Freeway overpass. The location is almost in the heart of Pasadena's financial district. The restaurant is not pricey but has good food and caters mostly for a family-type environment. There are many of these types of restaurants scattered all over Southern California. It was here that Raymond Pata decided would be the perfect place to celebrate.

Though not too far from where he lived, the restaurant was not exactly within walking distance. So he decided to catch the bus. The Metro Transportation Authority (MTA), the transportation system in the Los Angeles County, had a few buses running this route all the time, meaning that he did not have to wait long to catch a bus that would drop him off right in front of the establishment. Under normal circumstances, Raymond would have cringed at the thought of depending on public transportation to get to where he wanted to go, but today was different. His spirits were high, and in his inflamed imagination, it would only get better from here on out – that he was absolutely certain about.

When he got inside the restaurant, he was ushered to one of the tables next to the window by an ever smiling *maitre d.'*

"Your server will be with you shortly to take your order," she said with a dazzling smile.

"Thank you."

No sooner had he settled in his seat did the waitress appear. He was already flipping through the menu and decided almost instantly on what he was going to get. It was the 'dinner special'; sirloin steak, shrimp, broccoli, fries, and a side dish of salad dressed with Thousand Island.

The waitress was a stunning redhead, dressed in a light blue t-shirt and khaki shorts. She wore her hair in a short, pixie cut. She appeared to be no more than twenty-five, and had a ring on her right nostril, which somehow added to her radiance. The name tag on her lapel read 'Sofia.'

"Good evening sir, my name is Sofia." She instinctively tapped her pen on her nametag as she smiled. "I will be your waitress tonight; can I start you off with something to drink?"

"Most certainly." He was glad that a beautiful woman would be waiting on him. "Lemonade will do." He returned the smile.

She pulled out a miniature notepad from her side pocket and began writing. He noticed that she had a tattoo underneath her left hand; the kind that told him that she was an artist of some sort. She was a leftie too, which further confirmed his suspicions to some extent. For some reason unknown to him, the majority of artists he had come across were left-handed.

"Are you ready to order, sir?" Her soft voice was musical, and her accent suggested that she was somewhere from the Midwest; definitely not from California.

"I'm Raymond Pata," he said blurted out before he could stop himself.

"Pleased to meet you, Raymond Pata." He liked the way she rolled each syllable of his last name in her mouth.

"Likewise, Sofia. I will have tonight's special," he said with a wide grin as he quickly glanced at the menu and then at her. Their eyes met for the briefest of moments. However, in that brief instant, a lot was said without words. There was an obvious attraction between the two.

"How would you like that steak? Well done? Medium? Or bloody as hell?"

"Bloody as hell."

"Soup or salad?"

"Salad."

"And what kind of dressing?"

"Thousand Island please."

She wrote all that down as she said to herself 'bloody as hell and thousand islands.'

"Might as well get the best on a day like this," he said, opening the door for a conversation.

"On a day like this?" she asked, swallowing the bait.

"Yeah, it has been one of those special occasions when one has got to indulge himself," he said coyly.

She smiled at him, showing clean, white, healthy teeth. There was also a quality of innocence in her beautiful, knowing eyes.

"What's the special occasion, if you don't mind my asking?"

"Oh, things have fallen into place, and I'm ready to start my band."

She was impressed as she involuntarily put her left hand on her hip and stood akimbo, as if sizing him up.

"No way. You're a musician?"

"Yes, or at least I'm trying to be one," he said rather modestly.

"I am too," she said, eyes wide with amazement. "I play the drums, guitar, and can sing too."

Raymond made an 'O' with his mouth. He could not believe this coincidence.

"Really?"

"Yeah, I came out here about a year ago from Pueblo Colorado to break into the music industry."

"No way. I'm from Jacksonville Florida, on the same mission as you."

"Wow, and you're celebrating alone?"

"There is no one to celebrate with." He looked into her eyes as he said this.

"Okay, let me get your order going. I got so caught up in the moment that I almost forgot that I am on duty. Even though I am a musician, a girl's gotta pay her rent." They both smiled as she turned to head to the kitchen. "I'll be right back Raymond; I sure would like to hear more of your plans."

"Not a problem, Sofia. Go right ahead."

Her back was soon turned to him as she went to get his order ready. She had a wonderful backside, with a quick step that told him that she was an experienced runner. As soon as she left, he realized soon enough that she had a compelling presence that seemed to come at him from the moment she had been standing there beside him.

He swallowed hard as his heartbeat accelerated with excitement, but he dared not let his imagination run amok.

The rest of the evening was a blast. Whenever she had a chance, Sofia would sneak to Raymond's table and the two would talk for long periods at a time. With Sofia doing most of the chatting, they talked about a lot of things, rolling from one subject matter to another with remarkable ease. She talked about her days in college, family, friends, and relatives back in Colorado. Instead of talking about his family, Raymond found safe ground by talking about the music industry and here they found common ground and talked for even longer periods. In the end, they realized that they shared one thing in common: the dream of making it big in the music business – cutthroat as it was.

When it was time to leave at last, Raymond was surprised to realize how quickly time had flown by, and how late it was, it was almost 1:30 am. He paid his bill and left Sofia a more than generous tip. When she came back with the receipt, she left it on a little platter in front of him; there was also a little note from her accompanying the receipt.

'It was nice meeting you Raymond. I would like to see your band set up. Call me when you get a moment,' was the message. Underneath it was a phone number.

In bed alone that night, he relived the events of the day, particularly his meeting with Larry and later Sofia. Larry did not have to spell it out to him. He was involved in a shady syndicate that involved stealing cars, and he, Raymond Pata, had been sucked into it. But as long as it paid the bills and kept a roof over his head before the big break came, he did not care who he hurt in the process, or if this latest venture deprived some unlucky son-of-a-bitch of his most prized possession. Danger would always be lurking, that he knew, but he was not afraid; in his mind he knew that he was well-protected.

And as if to validate that fact, that night before going to bed he stepped into his walk-in closet, which he had converted into a shrine. In it was an altar he had made from plywood and covered with a white cloth. On it were items like cowries, sea shells, dried chicken bones, and the like. Hanging on the walls were demonic-looking wooden masks; but most significant of all, at the center of the altar was a rag doll, strange in sight and scary even though it was no more than two feet long. There was a strand of hair around its neck, and the eyes seemed alive. It was around this doll and the altar where he kept candles alight and incense burning at all times. There was also a bowl full of fruits that had to be kept fresh and replenished constantly. That way the gods would not be offended, his mother had warned him time and again, when she flew in briefly for that one day to help him erect the shrine. It was almost an exact replica of the big one Jean Pata had in a room in Jacksonville.

This room was definitely out of bounds to anyone other than Raymond after it had been erected; this had been another one of his mother's stern warnings. It was here that Raymond felt at peace and sensed a power that could not be described with words. Before he went to bed that night, and every night thereafter, he took the doll in both hands, and looked up to the ceiling before uttering the words: "*Nana Buluku* the god creator, and *Mawu* goddess of the moon, nothing happens by chance, *nothing* happens without your making. I know meeting that man, Larry Allen, and the opportunity he gave me was your doing. Also meeting this woman Sofia was your will. For that I thank you, and ask for your continued protection in my quest of being the biggest superstar – bigger than even Wycleaf Jean."

His mother had told him stories of his heritage dating back to the days of slavery and how Haiti became the only nation where slaves successfully revolted against their oppressors and won their liberation. This feat, Jean Pata told her son, was because the slaves from the motherland, Africa, came together and among them were many who possessed powers, mystic powers. These powers. Which defied logic, were used to aid their cause. Black magic was a potent and secret weapon not understood by the westerners, hence why it was so powerful, and it was a secret that was passed successfully from one generation to another. The gods they worshipped were the guardians of his people for over 400 years, dating back to his ancestors, who could be traced all the way back to the 'dark continent.' In short, he was adequately protected.

ᬽᬽ ᬽᬽ ᬽᬽ

Over the coming weeks, Raymond and Sofia saw a lot of each other. She was awed with his garage setup, which now, thanks to his new contacts with Larry, he was able to soundproof. In the midst of all this excitement, Sofia was quick to mention that the garage has always been the cornerstone of the American innovator. Many dreams started in garages: Mark Zuckerberg, the Facebook mogul, started his business in a garage; Walt Disney, Bill Gates, the list was endless. All this knowledge brought nothing but sheer joy to Raymond. He just knew that his moment had come, and it was in this very garage that his dream would be launched and realized. He just *knew* it.

Next, with the help of Sofia, whose energy and stamina proved to be compelling and with whom a sexual relationship was starting to blossom, he put an ad in *Craigslist* looking for three more band members. The response was overwhelming; within days, the mail had to be delivered in boxes right at his doorstep. For days on end, he and Sofia had to sort through headshots, demo tapes, and all other submissions, including electronics, to cut them down to a manageable number.

With that achieved, Raymond conducted auditions at the Fawnsworth Park recreation hall in Altadena, where Lake Avenue ends and meets with Loma Alta Street. It was a long and tedious process that took the whole weekend, but thanks to Sofia's input, he settled on three musicians, two women and a man.

They were Danielle Jacobs, a beautiful petite guitarist from San Diego California but who lived in nearby Monrovia with her aunty who was a dentist – very easy going. She was, like Sofia, 25. Jeremy Yee was a fifth-generation American Chinese who lived in Alhambra, but was originally from Seattle Washington. He was age 26, a bass guitarist and could also sing very well. Then there was Laura Jaeger, tall, slim and with long, blond hair, originally from Mesa Arizona, but living in Pasadena.

The trio, just like Raymond and Sofia, shared one thing in common. They were all driven by a burning desire to succeed. They were hungry and were willing to do whatever it took to get to the top. They also shared one other common trait: even though they were college educated (and had even suggested naming their group *'The Collegiates'* but for Raymond's vehement opposition), they all worked odd jobs to keep the wolf away from the door while they chased their dream with single minded fortitude.

The name for the group, which Raymond gave, was '*The Rhythm Makers*.' With typical vanity, he had wanted the group to be named '*Raymond Pata and The Rhythm Makers,*' but that suggestion was unanimously shot down by the rest of the group – the first of many disagreements that would soon take center stage with this band for months to come, and one of the reasons that led to his breakup with Sofia

For instance, when he left Jacksonville and headed for Los Angeles, he had a lot of songs written of the 'Afro-Fusion' type, with one favorite '*Caribbean Rose*;' and when he tried to suggest that most, if not all, of his songs, be in their first album, he was instantly opposed. The band, the rest of the members agreed, did not have an identity yet. They had to explore all other avenues, find a beat that resonated with their audience, and build from there. In the end, Raymond had to agree with them, but he secretly vowed that this band was just a stepping stone, an introduction of Raymond Pata to the rest of the world.

In spite of all this, the band rehearsed at least three nights a week, sometimes even more. It was hard at first, and the fights over creative liberties were constant; but gradually, everything began to gel, and once in a while they would book a gig at a party or at a bar in Old Town Pasadena, Monrovia, and Culver City. "Start small and build from there," so went the axiom. The results were lukewarm at best, and the little money they made barely covered the overhead; they were kept afloat mostly by the deal Raymond had going with Larry. They soldiered on nonetheless, dreaming of that one big, elusive break.

What Larry would do was give him a call, mostly at odd hours of the night, and let him know where a car was supposed to be picked up, be it at a shopping mall underground parking lot or someone's garage. It was always easy. So easy, in fact, that after a while Raymond began thinking that he could deliver the stolen vehicles to other prospective buyers who would most likely give him a better deal than what Larry would give at times. These were competitors that he soon grew to know about, like one Buford Green who set up shop in Marina Del Rey. But at the same time, Raymond did not want to offend his benefactor, even though he was starting to believe that Larry was not really paying him what he deserved.

What concerned Raymond more than anything was the pace at which his music career was heading. It was too slow. The Larry pool, he knew, was not going to last forever. The risks that came with it were not even worth contemplating, added to the fact that quality cars were becoming harder and harder to steal thanks to the latest technologies that came with them. At times, he was forced to go to far off places like Pacific

Palisades, Santa Barbara, and San Francisco where the police presence was at times overwhelming. But superstardom was a drug that kept calling him – he had to reach the top, whatever it took.

It was after he addressed these concerns to his mother, not mentioning his latest venture with Larry of course, that she advised him to visit the witchdoctor they called 'Baba' Brima. By this time he had his own car, which he got after he mustered the courage to ask Larry if he could loan him a car that he could use whenever he wanted. Larry brusquely informed him that with the job he was doing for him, he did not have to ask. It was his right. So Raymond found himself owning a clean and well-running 2008 Toyota Camry courtesy of Larry, and validating his status – at least for now – of a starving artist.

CHAPTER 4

IT WAS A FEW WEEKS after visiting the witchdoctor when the first major cracks started to show, and Raymond knew that it was time to take the step he was a bit hesitant to take. In doing so, he knew that his life would never be the same again.

It started off first with his connection with Larry. All of a sudden business slowed down considerably. It was a month and a half since he made his last delivery. The bills were starting to pile up once again, and more pressing was the fact that he was one month behind on his rent again. To top it all, the band was getting impatient, anxious to record their demo CD. He, on the other hand, was waiting for the new moon to rise in a week, at which time he could make his move. But somehow fate forced his hand, and he was compelled to act a little earlier than he had planned.

It happened one Sunday early evening, when the band was in the garage taking a short recess from a rehearsal that had taken almost that entire afternoon. It was a hot day and everyone was exhausted, hungry, and stressed, so tempers were short. While everyone was taking a break, Raymond was busy, still engrossed with his bass guitar, trying out a new tune that he had been playing in his head for the past week. He alone, out of all the band members, showed no signs of distress.

Over the past seven months together, they had come to know that everything with Raymond was full throttle. Work, play, food, and those extremely rare moments when he drank after a successful gig; he would go from martinis to wine with ease, he would leave the restaurant long after the rest of the band had retired, and he would be up at four in the morning fiddling with his laptop, working on beats in his beloved garage-turned-studio, shaking off the king-size hangover as just another part of the day. That he was blessed with incredible stamina was beyond question, but they could only speculate what drove him to such extremes.

The four walked back into the garage following a brief huddle outside, while Raymond was lost in his guitar, unaware of their presence. They were a little tense, one could tell because Laura was smoking a cigarette – something she very rarely did, except of course when she was troubled.

It was Sofia, the apparent leader of the pack, who called out at him first.

"Excuse me, Raymond … Raymond!!!"

His back was turned to them when they walked into the garage. He had been aware of their secret bonding over the past few months, and knew that sooner or later the moment would come when they would gang up on him, but as far as he was concerned, they had no idea who they were dealing with. He was Raymond Pata, a man who possessed powers they could never fathom, let alone imagine. He also knew that it was in fact Sofia who had instigated this possible mutiny. He continued fiddling with the guitar as if he had not heard her.

Sofia then raised her voice, "Raymond!"

"What?" he hissed as he turned around to face them.

"We need to talk," Sofia said.

Here it comes. "Yeah, what about?" He knew exactly what they wanted to talk about. The truth could not be hidden any longer. But the look in Raymond's eyes made them flinch, and they hesitated as they looked at one another. And the general consensus, it seemed, was that they needed someone with the guts to break the brief but uncomfortable ice. Laura took a long drag at her cigarette, almost choking on the smoke.

"We spoke to Chico," Danielle said at last.

The words fell heavily on the band equipment in the garage turned studio. There had been many more additions to the equipment ever since Raymond had purchased the drums, guitars, synthesizer, and other odds on end from that kid in Glendale. The statement got Raymond's full attention as he let go off the guitar and gently placed it against the keyboard stand.

"You what?!"

"Spoke to Chico." It was Sofia who spoke this time.

Chico Valenzuela was his contact. No one spoke to him but Raymond. He could only guess that Sofia, during their numerous sexual liaisons, had gone through his stuff, like his very personal address book. *The sneaky bitch*, he thought.

"What the hell you talk to Chico for?"

"We just wanted to find out when we're going to record that demo CD," Laura said.

"By going behind my back? Why the hell you got to do that for?" Raymond was furious, but he tried his best to keep calm. He knew that to stay in charge and control, he had to maintain his cool.

Sofia took a step forward, and looked Raymond straight in the eye. She, of all his band members, was the only one who could do that, because they had shared many intimate nights together where any person was venerable, including the great Raymond Pata.

"Ray," she said softly, but the words were icy and piercing. "We all busted our butts to come up with a thousand dollars each to give to you to pay Chico for studio time, the CD label, and two thousand plus copies to distribute ..."

"Don't forget my two grand," Raymond, not to be outdone, interrupted. "It did not just fall from the trees you know."

Jeremy Yee, who had been silent all along, and normally a wimp as far as Raymond was concerned, finally cleared his throat and, as if prodded to say something, announced, "See, thing is, Chico says he never saw any of that money. Our guess is that it went straight into your pocket."

For the first time Raymond felt blood drain from his face, but he did a very good job of not showing it. The allegations were true.

"I cannot believe this," he said with a straight face, and not betraying what he was feeling because if they had really spoken to Chico ...

"It's true though isn't it?"

It certainly was, and he had been hoping that his little scheme would not have been found out before he had time to fix it. But Raymond was not about ready to admit it now; that would definitely be the end of him, and he knew it.

"I put you guys together," he said softly, totally ducking the question. "I wrote over 20 songs, and all you could do was just put one song of mine on the upcoming CD. I had to live with that, and now you guys got the nerve to go behind my back and talk to Chico—my contact, mind you—and then on top of that you accuse me of embezzling money?"

Laura said, "Oh, so what you are saying, Ray, is that Chico is lying, and that you did indeed give him the money? Is that what you are telling us?"

"I'm not going to dignify that with an answer."

He noticed that Laura, the supposed weak link of the quartet, was trying to act tough, but her eyes told him otherwise. But before Laura could open her mouth to say something in response, Sofia's bitchy voice cut in.

"Ray, do you have any idea how long it took me to save that money I gave you? Bussing tables, working overtime, being nice to customers who treat you like shit, and you still have to smile at them hoping that they leave a tip worth something even though you wanna kick the snot out of them – do you?"

"Yeah dude," Jeremy agreed. "A thousand bucks is a thousand bucks, I'm with Sofia on that one." And Jeremy was the one guy he was hoping would at least have his back.

"Oh you are now, are you? What the hell is this, some kind of sedition?" Raymond was exasperated now, incensed mainly at being caught than by Jeremy's supposed betrayal.

The anger, simulated as it was, managed to thaw the room temperature a few degrees, and for the first time, Raymond sensed a bit of uncertainty among them. He saw a chink in their armor. He paced himself, and like a mamba, he would know when to strike.

"We just want to be in a studio Ray, and record our very first CD, that's all. Is that too much to ask?" Jeremy asked, but really his voice was somewhat placating.

"And I say we will," Raymond said. "Maybe we are ready as a band, but our repertoire is still weak. We got to get it right before we step into a studio."

Laura then said, "Well, we all feel we are. For months we've been rehearsing nonstop, putting in incredible hours. We have even performed most of our songs before live audiences, and many people are already asking if we have a CD out and where they could buy it."

"That's true," Jeremy concurred yet again.

"And we've been together for almost a year," Sofia added, the iciness in her voice still apparent.

"Nine months, three weeks, and 4 days to be exact," Raymond Pata said rather absent mindedly, but that froze them up a bit, just as he intended, and he loved seeing them squirm. He was more in touch with the band's pulse than they thought.

And then Danielle, who had been quiet all along, as this was a natural trait of her, said, "And now it looks as if we have each parted with a grand of our hard earned money, and for what?" at this point she looked Raymond in the eye before concluding with an emphatic "NOTHING!"

"But I'm telling you …"

"Ray!" Sofia interrupted.

"I'm telling you that …"

"Raymond!!!" she screamed, almost startling the others as this was unexpected.

"What?!" Raymond looked at her, still very much in control of himself.

"What happened to the $4,000.00 we painstakingly saved to pay for studio time, huh?"

At that moment Laura pulled out her cell phone from her pocket, ready to dial a number.

"I think we should get Chico on the phone right now to straighten this mess out."

Raymond knew that he was in deep trouble. A phone call to Chico would kill him. Hi, this is Laura, a friend of Raymond Pata…actually we are band members. It is our understanding that Ray gave you $4,000 to pay for studio time to record our CD. Did you receive the said money? Has there been any discussion of money changing hands? And lastly, is your fee really four grand to record a 9 track album including studio time. "No" to all your questions. Next for Raymond Pata? Small claims court, and God knows what else Sofia would think of, to an extent he did not care to imagine. He had to do something, quickly.

Without another word, he walked over to a desk at the other end of the garage. In it, he kept meticulous files, and every piece of paperwork even remotely related to the band, neatly put together. It was also in here, in one of the drawers, where he kept a checkbook for an almost dormant checking account that probably had a balance of $10 at best. The account was at a local Chase Manhattan Bank.

He pulled it out, after making himself comfortable on the swiveling leather chair he was lucky to get his hands on, at a local flea market on Los Robles and Woodbury Avenue, and started writing on the first leaf.

"You know what," he said almost under his breath, "Enough of this nonsense." The rest, including Sofia, looked at him in total perplexity.

He finished writing the first check, calmly ripped it out of the book, and practically tossed it at Sofia. "Here, take your measly little one grand that you keep bitching about, and get the hell out of here, and find someone with a garage who will put up with all this crap."

He then started writing another, and another, a total of four, one for each of them, and all for the same amount—$1,000. They looked first with curiosity, surprise, shock, and then fear.

Danielle was the first to recover. "Ray, w-what are you doing?" Her face was flushed and there was obvious panic in her voice. And right there and then Raymond Pata knew he had them where he wanted.

"What the hell does it look like? I am giving all of you your money back. I can always put another ad on *Craigslist*; and believe me, I will have my phone ringing off the hook by morning. This is LA babe; there are too many starving acts out there."

Danielle was the first to crack.

"Hey, hey, y-you don't have to do that Ray." She was almost beside herself with panic.

"You think?!" Raymond retorted. There was a frown on his face as he stared at each one of them, but they were unable to maintain eye contact this time. Jeremy was pinching the bridge of his nose, and suddenly had perspiration on his forehead.

Danielle was suddenly picking her cuticles, the color drained from Laura's face, and Sofia appeared to be on the brink of an attack of some variety.

"Yeah, come on Ray, you don't mean that," Laura said.

Sofia smiled nervously as she said, "Yeah, listen Ray...we were just kidding."

This somewhat stopped Raymond in his tracks. "What do you mean, 'you were just kidding'?"

Jeremy Yee took a look sigh and said, "We did not talk to Chico at all dude; it was a bluff. To be quite honest we are just anxious to drop this CD man, and we thought this would get your attention Ray. Let's face it, you've been dilly dallying man, and we don't understand why. I know it was wrong the way we tried to play, but hopefully you can see it from our perspective."

Raymond paused for a while, and took a long sigh of relief. He then wiped his brow, which was suddenly perspiring, with the back of his hand. Laura came up from behind and rubbed his shoulders gently, placating him even further; she was always the sweetest one among the group—that is, if she chose not to be duly swayed by the rest as was clearly the case in this instance. This softened him up much more than he wanted it to show.

"They were just joking Ray, okay babe?" she smiled at him. "You don't need to turn this into a big deal, doll."

Raymond sighed again. It had been a close call, and he knew next time he would not be so lucky. Sooner or later they were going to find out that their intuitions had been spot on—he did in fact spend their hard earned money just as they had suspected. He would have to come up with the cash quickly; he had stalled long enough, and now was the time to carry out his plan, drastic and dangerous as it was.

"Guys, let this be the last time, and I mean it. Don't play with me like that," he said.

"Sure thing, Ray," Sofia managed to force a smile.

"I'm serious, Sofia," a very relieved Raymond said as he wiped his brow again. And once overcome with relief, he said, "And when I say we will record this damn CD, I mean it, okay? We can even do it tomorrow night since you guys are so anxious." Now he knew there was no turning back. He would have to perform the sacrifice to the gods tonight, and if this plan failed, he was looking at the very least 25 years behind bars or worse, and kissing superstardom goodbye.

The rest looked at each other in disbelief. They were completely dumbfounded and surprised, not knowing what to say next or wondering if they had, in fact, heard him correctly.

"Are you serious?! Oh man!!" Jeremy was the first to recover.

"Of course I am, but you guys got to put four of my songs back in."

So there it was. There was always a catch when it came to dealing with this man—that was the thought that crossed in everyone's mind at that moment. They once again exchanged an uncomfortable look with one another. It was a discussion they had before, a discussion they had hoped not to entertain anymore because it was clearly obvious that none of them liked Raymond's songs.

It was Jeremy, as if by general consensus, who spoke again, almost whispering, "Ray, I thought we agreed that those are for the next CD."

There was not going to be another CD—at least not with them, as far as he was concerned—Raymond wanted to say; instead, he decided to play it safe by staying mum.

"So you guys are still adamant about that? Because all of a sudden I don't feel like I'm a part of this group."

"The next CD, Ray, the next one. Right guys?" Sofia said.

The rest nodded rather nervously, because they were not sure how Raymond was going to react, especially after what they saw when he threatened to disband the entire crew.

Then Raymond said, rather somberly, and mostly to himself, "Well, I suppose majority rules, but I must insist that *Caribbean Rose* be among the nine tracks we intend to record. At least give me something I can live with."

"Let's say we will discuss that further once we're at the studio Ray," Jeremy said as he patted him on the shoulder, in essence saying that was not going to happen, and forestalling any further discussion on the matter.

At last they started wrapping things up, even though it was pretty much obvious to everyone that Raymond was not too pleased; but he knew that there was nothing else he could do, at least for now, but just play along until the right moment came. When it did, they would *never* know what hit them.

"Hey anybody got a joint?" Danielle asked no one in particular, but Sofia gave her a knowing look. A little while later the four went outside again, this time out of sight, leaving Raymond alone in the garage as they went to smoke some pot.

A little while later, after agreeing on the time and place to meet, it was time to leave. Jeremy always gave the rest of the members a ride whenever he could, because his car, an SUV, could accommodate all of them. On those rare nights when they had a performance, Raymond would borrow a van from Larry, and in it pack the equipment and then drive it while the rest rode with Jeremy.

On this particular night, as they were getting ready to leave, Sofia was the last to get into the SUV while Raymond stood at the driveway of his house and watched them. She glanced at him again, hesitated, and then said something to the rest before she went back to Raymond. It was obvious that he had something on his mind that he did not want the others to hear.

"What is it?" she demanded when she got to him.

"You tried to make me look like a loser, a cheat, and why? Is it because things never worked out between us?" he wanted to know. The truth really was that the both of them realized that the band life was taxing, far more than they could have ever imagined. And to succeed they could not mix business with pleasure; that much was clear, but somehow Raymond wanted to get back at her.

On hearing this, Sofia let out a soft chuckle. She was high and her breath reeked of marijuana. "This has nothing to do with what happened, because there is no 'us' anymore. Studio time Ray; that's all we're concerned about." Her voice, throaty, even more so when she was high like this, always succeeded in turning him on.

"No Sofia, we both know that is not true. It has a lot to do with the fact that I refused to commit to you."

"There was nothing to commit to Ray! All I wanted was to move in with you; how complicated was that?"

And really that was where the trouble started; Sofia wanted a serious long-term relationship, but Raymond was not ready for that, or so he claimed. The truth really was that he had very dark secrets, like the shrine for instance, and that he communicated with spirits that he strongly believed would guide him to superstardom. Living with someone, especially if that someone was Sofia, would most certainly expose all this, and thus put his musical career in jeopardy.

He then forced a smile as he looked her in the eye again. "Aren't you going to spend a night just for old time sake?"

She was a wild mustang in bed whenever she was stoned, and suddenly Raymond felt his body twitch with excitement.

"What?! You're kidding, right?"

"Just sex … nothing more."

"If only it were that simple." She turned to leave. Raymond on the other hand was left with a sexual frustration that suddenly filled him with rage. He had to admit that it was over between them – even

the casual one-night stands; but he would, he
believed, recover very soon.

CHAPTER 5

A LITTLE WHILE LATER, Raymond was alone in his bedroom. It was already dusk and the summer sunset was still a couple of hours away, even though it was almost 7:45pm. He knew the moment of truth had come. He sat on his bed for a while, staring at his dresser; on it was a stack of unpaid bills. It was a while since he made a delivery for Larry, and he needed to make one soon or he was going to drown. There was a viable prospect, and now was the time to pounce. This time it would be different; he would use magic, the powers bestowed on him by the gods. It was time to put those powers to test, and find out exactly how efficient they were. The notion filled him with dread. What if they did not work? What if things went drastically wrong and he got caught? With much difficulty, he managed to push those troubling thoughts out of his mind.

He stood up and entered the walk-in closet after turning off all the lights, and was inside the site of his shrine, which looked ghastly with the candles being the only source of light. There was a small leather pouch that Baba Brima had given him set on the altar. In it was a strange looking white powder. He had been instructed, once ready, to take a pinch of it and scatter it in the air before he began, which he did, and immediately the room seemed filled with it. The resultant smell was pungent and seemed to be everywhere. He choked on it, his eyes were teary; and then all of a sudden he felt as if he was falling into an abyss. When he came to, he felt a sensation that he could not readily explain, except that it had a very powerful effect on him.

For a minute or so, his vision was blurry. As soon as it cleared, he again was overwhelmed with that eerie sensation like his body was possessed by some type of supernatural force. He was not high, but focused. He picked up the voodoo doll from the altar and raised it above his head. The words came as if by impulse.

"Let the blood spill and with it bring success."

Suddenly, he felt a presence in the room, he smiled. It was a sardonic smile. The gods would grant him his wish if he made this one sacrifice.

෴ ෴ ෴

Boston Street, at the east side of Altadena near the golf course, is a very quiet neighborhood, and is located at one of the plushiest and beautiful parts of this all American city. The palm trees lining the streets are a sight to behold, as in any neighborhood in southern California.

In front of one of the nicest houses and parked next to one of the palm trees, was one of the newest Jaguar F-Series Convertible. It was brownish-gold and a sight to feast the eyes on for any car lover who appreciated speed and quality. The luxurious car, like many others, belonged in that neighborhood; and, because of the fierce reputation of the Altadena Sheriff, neighbors could leave their cars and front doors unlocked at any time of the day. Raymond had been keeping an eye on this particular vehicle for the past night.

On this early evening, the street was virtually deserted, as a young lady who appeared to be in her early 20's came out of the house where the Jaguar was parked in the front, and walked briskly toward it, seemingly in a hurry. She reached into her purse and as she pulled out the keys, she did not see a dark figure peel away from behind the palm tree. In an instant, the figure was on her. Her back was turned to him, just as he had planned, for he did not want to see her face – not now, not ever. That is why with incredible deftness, he covered her head with a homemade hood that exposed only her eyes and mouth, and grabbed her by the shoulders and put a knife to her throat after smacking her on the head to confuse her further. All this had taken less than 10 seconds.

"Make a sound and you die. Understand?" Raymond Pata's voice was menacing and demon possessed. It had the chilling effect similar to that of fingernails scratching on a chalkboard, and the victim knew right there and then that if she did not do what she was told, she was dead meat.

"Y-yes," she said fearfully. "Take whatever you want ... even the car." She was hoping against all odds that someone, anybody, would notice the fracas, brief as it was, and come to her aid. There would be no such luck; she quickly came to that realization.

"Shut up, get inside and drive," Raymond said between clenched teeth.

The victim did as she was told, and he quickly placed himself behind her and ducked out of sight, making certain all throughout that she could feel the cold blade at the back of her neck.

"If you even look sideways or even eyeball me once, you die. Understand?"

She believed him because she nodded vigorously, anxious to get this nightmare over and done with. All the weeks that he had been stalking her, he tried, whenever he could, not to look at her face; it was too pretty a face to have embedded in his mind and develop a conscience, which is why he vowed never to look at her directly if he could help it. All he knew was that she was ripe for the sacrifice.

"Please j-just don't hurt me. I will do whatever you say," she pleaded, again hoping that a patrolling sheriff would notice what was going on and intervene.

"Good," Raymond said in a fierce whisper. "You can start by shutting up." As he said this, he, with his other hand, violently pulled a strand of her hair from her head. She was a brunette, and he took that strand and tied it around the neck of the doll, which he had made certain to bring along.

"Ow!!! That hurt." Her voice was slightly muffled behind the hood that he had placed over her head.

With affected unconcern he said, "Keep driving toward the mountains, and don't let a car pull up beside you – understand?"

They were heading north on Lake Avenue. She mumbled something incoherent, and Raymond viciously slapped her upside the head again. "I said, do you understand?"

If she had been able to look in his eyes, she would have seen that he was possessed, as his eyes shined brightly like jewels from the pit of hell.

"Yesss," she said. She was sobbing now, albeit softly.

By this time, Lake Avenue was surprisingly deserted with a few cars passing by. He directed her all the way to the end of the street, and made her turn left on Loma Alta Street, which ran parallel to the Foothill Mountains, and there after directed her to make a right turn down a seldom used road that went further and further into the mountains. It was here that he ordered her to stop; at a place where he knew the chances of being seen were almost none.

He then quickly dragged her out of the car; the hood was still on her face, and ordered her, at knife point, to follow a narrow winding path. The young woman was almost paralyzed with dread as she wondered what was going to become of her. God only knew what was in store for her. It was just a nightmare, she said to herself, a terrible, terrible, nightmare from which she would soon awaken. But the prodding of the sharp knife on her ribs, the caressing of the bushes and shrubs on her legs, and the sounds of the Angeles National Forest at night were all too real.

"Now mister, you can let me go, and I will just run down the road without even looking back, and I will not tell anyone about the car," she pleaded. Somehow she imagined that she would soon awake from this horrible dream that seemed all too real.

Raymond gave a mirthless chuckle, totally at ease and in control. "I *know* you won't tell anybody."

Something about her assailant's voice told her that her worst nightmare was about to be revealed.

"Mister please, just take the car, there's about $300.00 in my purse, but please don't rape …" she caught herself, and continued by saying "… I mean don't take advantage of me. Or if you are going to, you can at least use a rubber. I have some in my glove compartment."

On hearing this Raymond was furious in spite of himself. For her to think that he had gone through all this trouble, risking his life and liberty over what he was doing because he needed her body for sex. It was insulting. "And just what makes you think that I am lacking for some ass? Now keep walking and let me not hear another word from you. The more you talk the harder it will be for you," he warned.

They came to a tree where he ordered her to stop; nearby was a ditch created by water whenever it rained hard.

"Now kneel down and face the other way," he ordered. She did as she was told. "I will tell you again, don't for one second look at me or I'll snap your neck like a dry twig."

"Y-yess, I don't even know what you look like. So can you please let me go?"

As he ordered her to kneel in the exact position that he wanted her to, he then raised the doll above his head. Streaks of light from the moon penetrated through the leaves of the branches above. As he tugged at the strand of hair from the young woman that he had tied around the neck of the doll, he was suddenly seized by yet another sensation that was hard to describe, and at the same time he opened his mouth and started chanting incantations that even he did not understand. He was gripped by a power that could only be paranormal. As he tugged at the strand of hair again and again, the victim started to choke, gasping for air. She tried to reach for her throat with both hands, but suddenly her hands were heavy as lead.

She slowly fell to the ground and to her side as she continued choking. Her body suddenly went into painful convulsions. And instantaneously, the hood covering her face was stained with blood from her mouth, ears, and nose as she slowly but surely drowned in her own blood. It was a slow, painful, and gruesome death.

"*Nana Buluku*, the god creator and *Mawu* goddess of the moon this offering is for you, and let her blood spill and with it come success, wealth, and power that you will bestow upon me."

Upon uttering those chilling words, a flash appeared before his eyes, and for a moment he felt as if he had just woken from a trance; and the sight of the body at his feet suddenly made him sick to the point that he was compelled to bend over and throw up. Thereafter, he clasped the doll even harder and fled the scene in a daze.

The Jaguar was exactly where he left it. He looked around to make sure that there was no one around, and then quickly jumped in and drove away. He had broken into a cold sweat. He was overwhelmed by the fact that he had just taken a life, and the signifying power with which he had done it. He now believed wholeheartedly in the power of the gods, the power of the supernatural; up until then he was not certain of the veracity of this power but now he had experienced it and seen it with his own eyes. He was totally intoxicated by it. It was similar to the very first high of a crack addict, and he wanted more of it, oh yes he did! He now knew that superstardom was within reach. He was strangely excited to a point that it was a task just to keep his hands from shaking.

These were the feelings and thoughts that were running through his mind as he drove along the 110 freeway toward downtown Los Angeles. He was headed to one of Larry's outfits off La Brea Avenue. He needed to get rid of the car as soon as possible, and he was certain that he was going to fetch a very good price for this latest score; this in spite of the near miss that happened a month and a half earlier which had kind of put him a bit on Larry's bad side. This ride was certainly going to put a smile on that man's face, and some hard cash in his pocket. He had made it a point to call him earlier so he was expected.

It was after 11pm when he pulled into the gated premises of Larry's other lot. This one was much larger than the yard in Altadena, and certainly the busier of the two. By this time all the workers had gone home for the day, so Larry was alone in his office when Raymond knocked at the door. He did this after parking the Jaguar in a shed right in front of the office. On the premises, it was well hidden from any prying eyes if need be. The large window in his office gave Larry a view of the entire area. It was also a one-way window, very much like the one at his other shop in Altadena. The lot itself was surrounded by a fifteen-foot wall with barbed wires at the very top, and for good reason, too. There were all kinds of cars within and many different levels in appearance, because aside from being a car restoration and body shop, the place was a chop shop for stolen cars. The stripping of these cars happened in the back garage which only authorized personnel were allowed access.

"Come on in, it's open," Larry said as he looked up from a newspaper he was reading. There was a flat screen TV at the other end of the office. A Lakers game was on even though the volume was muted.

"This better be good Ray. I don't know what you are up to, but you got some nerve showing your face so soon after I told you to lay low for a while after what happened." As he said this, he stood up to get a better view through the one-way glass to take a closer look at the car that Raymond just drove in.

Raymond was unfazed by this slight rebuke from the other man. "Man, will you get off that? No one got caught; we all got away clean. How the hell was I supposed to know that an APB had already been put on that car?"

A month and a half earlier, Larry had got what was supposed to have been a hot lead regarding a 2006 Porsche Carrera in San Bernardino. This was a vehicle his buyers had specifically asked for, right down to the make, model, and color. So he sent Raymond and two of his fellows to get it. One of them, Ramon Alvarez, was an expert at hot wiring cars like these, and the other, Jose Garcia, was to be the lookout. In any case the job was supposed to be routine, but things went wrong very quickly. Very wrong in fact, because it turned out that the San Bernardino Police had their eyes on the car, using it as bait, so as to finally crack down on a series of luxury car thefts that had risen to an alarming rate lately. To make a long story short, Raymond and company barely got away, but Larry was not certain if they indeed did. There was a strong possibility that the cops had decided to perhaps tail them, and in the process lead them to the real mastermind of this criminal enterprise – in other words, him. That was why he had instructed Raymond to lay low for a while until the heat died down.

Another very likely scenario was that his many rivals could have probably set him up for the fall. Such a thing did happen from time to time. That is why, for now at least, he wanted his confederates to generate their own leads, meaning that they would have to look for cars to steal on their own and deliver them to him; that way he could have plausible deniability if the need arose.

This was less risky than getting word out to the petty street corner drug dealers, pimps, and other low lives whose credibility was always suspect, to say the least. Via this medium, his intentions were always exposed and he ran the risk of this information reaching the wrong ears—possibly competitors who would want to seek a favor with the local authorities, or even divert the heat from themselves.

So when Larry issued the order that from now henceforth, until further notice, he would have to find the cars himself and deliver them, Ray decided to pay the old witchdoctor Baba Brima a visit so that he would be empowered and protected at all times.

"Something like that can never happen again, Ray," Larry said as if Raymond needed reminding. "Because it almost brought down the whole operation, and it took a while to get some nosy detective off my back."

Raymond simply scoffed and said, "That's ancient history man. You ain't got to worry about a damn thing. I'm empowered."

"What?"

"Trust me. And all I can guarantee you is that you will never have any problems coming from me."

The conviction in his voice surprised and impressed Larry. This was a bold statement, because as far as he knew, and what experience had taught him was that there are no guarantees in life.

"Oh yeah, and how so?"

"Like I said, I am empowered, and that is all that you need to know."

"And what about that nosy detective?"

Raymond did not answer, and this was followed by an uncomfortable silence before Larry continued by saying, "I'm telling you Ray, something's not quite right about her, man."

"Her?"

"Yeah, young, hot as hell and she kept asking all kinds of questions, but you know she got nothing from me." This suddenly got Raymond Pata's full attention, even if just for a moment.

"Like what kind of questions?" It was impossible that anyone would have connected him to the murder, at least so soon; otherwise he would have been in custody. Plus – he was empowered by the gods, no one could touch him.

"Questions like if I knew you, and what kind of business we were into."

"And you are sure this woman was a cop?"

"Most likely, but she looked too young and too hot to be a cop, plus I did not think to pry any further because my brain just melted at the sight of her legs; as a matter of fact, you just missed her. Come to think of it, I'm not sure if I even saw her leave, I got distracted by your car pulling in. But like I said Ray, be on the lookout. Something about her was off, now that I think of it."

Raymond again was forced to pause and wonder who it could be, but again drew a blank. He just figured that he would deal with her, whoever she was, when the time was right. He was untouchable.

"Okay enough of that Larry," he said as he slapped him on the back. "You worry too much. Come outside and let's have a look at this baby I got for you."

Without another word, they stepped out of the office, just as Larry turned on the florescent lights in the shed so as to have an even better look at the vehicle. He was floored, and he did a very poor job of concealing it. When he noticed Raymond looking at him intently, he tried to be modest and play it cool but it was already too late; he knew he was in for a long night in as far as bargaining for a good price from the Haitian. He had shown his hand too soon.

"Well, well, well, Raymond, I must say that you were right... she is a beauty."

"That's right. So that means there will be no haggling over the price right?"

"Come on Ray, this is me you're talking to." Larry smiled patronizingly, but his eyes were not smiling.

"And that's what I'm worried about," Raymond retorted.

Larry raised his arms as if surrendering. "Okay, okay … I will give you five grand." He lifted all five fingers as he said this.

Raymond looked at him in genuine shock and amazement. "I can get at least ten grand from Buford."

"Why didn't you go to Buford's then?"

"Look at the time man, Buford's way out in Marina Del Rey. But if need be, I can hold off until the morning and then see what Buford has to offer."

The truth of the matter is that he wanted to get the car off his hands right this instant. He would not risk driving the car all the way to Marina Del Rey; there was no telling what would happen along the way. The car could very well have been reported stolen by now for all he knew, and there were not so many Jaguars like this one out there so this one would be easy to spot. And not even his new found powers could protect him from a California Highway Patrol Officer who could arbitrarily decide to pull him over. No, he could not afford to run that risk; but then of course he would have to stand firm with his one-time benefactor. He could not afford to have his plans with the band unravel before they were in full swing.

"You're going to leave the car here until morning if you're planning on seeing Buford, right?"

"Haha, who ever heard of such an arrangement? I'll save you the trouble, Larry."

Larry shook his head as he raised his hands to stop Raymond from leaving, not for a moment thinking of calling him on his bluff. "Okay, okay Ray, six and a half," he said.

"Eight." Raymond was not ready to yield an inch. He needed every penny he could squeeze out of this deal.

"Six and three quarters."

There was suddenly a smirk on Raymond's face as if he was about to cave.

"Eight," he said instead, savoring every minute of this battle of wills.

Larry sighed, and looked at Raymond again, those unsmiling eyes for once not blinking. "Gee, you're really being a hard ass on this aren't you?"

Raymond said, "You taught me well. Besides Larry, this is an F-Series, top of the line, very rare. Pay me what's right and I know we will both be happy. Most likely you will benefit more than me, because after you are done stripping it apart and shipping the parts to your clientele all across the US, you will more than triple what you pay me."

"Seven and a half, and that's it, Ray. Come on man, meet me halfway at least. I know this is business, and you learned that from me, but come on man, just for old time sake," Larry pleaded.

"Eight," Raymond said mercilessly. "And really I went more than halfway man. Like I said Larry, if you can't do eight, let me at least hear what Buford is willing to give for this baby. Look, it is clean, has genuine leather interior, and that there tells me that you will make at least two grand on the seats alone, stereo …"

"Okay, okay, you got a deal" Larry interrupted, his hands raised in mock capitulation.

They both laughed. Raymond knew that $8,000 was chump change, peanuts to Larry, and they were both happy with the deal.

"It's just that I know you're going to make a fortune out of this, Larry." As if Larry did not already know that. "And I have got to make amends with my band by getting them in a studio tomorrow."

"Oho, now I see the urgency, but weren't you supposed to have done that about six months ago?" Larry wanted to know.

"Yeah, but let's just say I was forced to delegate the funds elsewhere, and now they are leaning hard."

"You can't really blame them Ray," Larry said as he pulled out a wad of crisp one hundred dollar bills from his pocket, and started counting. Raymond guessed that the cash totaled at least ten grand.

"I know man."

"And how's that coming along by the way?"

"What?"

"The band, asshole." He was engrossed in counting the money as he said this. "Sorry, I know I have been promising to attend one of your gigs, but never got around to doing it." The fact really is that Larry did not think too highly of their music. He thought the band was mediocre at best.

"Things would be much better if that Sofia broad was not in the mix."

"Who?"

"Sofia, my ex, remember her? Redhead with short hair? She is a great bassist and all, plus she's got one hell of a voice. But now I have a feeling that she is turning everyone against me," Raymond said.

"Yeah, I hear you. It comes with the territory, especially if you are a starving group." A term every aspiring artist hated to hear.

"Not for long," Raymond said quickly and confidently that it momentarily diverted Larry from what he was doing and looked up at him.

"Oh really, and how so? You guys found a Label?"

"Well, not quite. The group feels that the time is right to drop a CD."

"And what do you think?" Larry asked as he once again turned his attention to the cash. By this time, they were in his office though both standing by his massive desk.

"Doesn't really matter what I think Larry ... they just feel we are ready and you can already guess who the instigator to all this is."

"Sofia," he deduced correctly

"Yep, that's right," Raymond agreed. "Man, that bitch," he added softly.

"Now I see why you refused to let her move in with you. You two would have killed each other by now."

"You got that right," Raymond smiled.

"Well, Ray, if the general consensus is that you are ready, then perhaps you are. There will never be a perfect time, if that's what you are waiting for. You just have to go for it, and trust yourself in that regard."

"Wow!" Raymond exclaimed in mock amazement. "Here I am thinking that you are nothing but a car thief; I did not know that you're a motivational speaker in your spare time. I'm shocked." He was smiling from ear-to-ear.

"Just giving you some advice partner, the same recommendation I made to my cousin, Andy, years ago, before he hauled on his behind back to Missouri. And that's free counsel, by the way."

"Thanks dad." His eyes were on the cash Larry was getting ready to hand to him.

"Here we go, count it."

"No, I trust you," Raymond said. He was finding it hard to contain his excitement.

Larry then patted him on the shoulder and said, "I insist."

With that said Raymond counted the cash and placed it in his front pocket. It was way too much money to put in his wallet, and the feeling sent an electric sensation throughout his body. Though the feeling was enthralling, it was nowhere near the feeling he felt when he kidnapped that girl and watched the life being snuffed out of her. This was living, and he wanted more of it.

"Have a good one Larry," he said at last as he turned to leave.

"Yeah, yeah, but aren't you forgetting something?"

"What?"

"How are you getting home?"

They both laughed as Raymond realized his mistake. He had come in the Jaguar and he was leaving it right there.

CHAPTER 6

THE ANGELES NATIONAL FOREST around Loma Alta Canyon was swarming with members of the Altadena Sheriff and the Pasadena Police Department. All of a sudden, the popular hiking trail was declared a crime scene that early Saturday morning. This was because two early morning hikers stumbled upon a gruesome scene. Right under a tree by the trail, almost hidden by a mini gorge, was the body of a young woman who looked to be in her early-to-mid-20's judging by her physique; her face was covered with some kind of mask that made the hikers' skin crawl.

It was extremely rare to find a body in these parts of the forest close to Altadena. As a matter of fact, no one remembered a body ever being discovered before there. On seeing this, one of the two young hikers used her cell phone to dial 911, and before long the first of many of the Sheriff's squad cars descended on the scene like a wake of hungry vultures. After securing the scene, two detectives from the Pasadena Police were summoned. These were detectives Douglas 'Doug' Willoughby, a veteran with twenty-two years' experience under his belt, and a beautiful, black, female partner, twenty plus years his junior, named Jennifer 'Jen' Russo.

The body, with the hood still in place, had already been covered with a white sheet. Members of the elite Crime Scene Unit (CSU) were already taking pictures from all angles, and another was gathering any piece of evidence she could find and putting it into a glassine envelope.

"What have we got here?" Doug Willoughby asked the young CSU officer who was carefully collecting as much evidence she could find, while another was covering footprints left behind by the assailant most presumably and any other facts, no matter how minute or seemingly inconsequential, that could be obliterated by such things as the weather. Her name was Rosaline Chavez, a young, bright, and intelligent Hispanic woman. Willoughby had worked with her before and liked her due diligence and professionalism. Her attention to detail was almost second nature. Many a case had been solved on her watch, no matter how strange or twisted they seemed, and this one promised to be one of those.

Willoughby was the first to crouch beside the body, and after putting on a pair of latex gloves, he very carefully removed the hood from the victim's head. In spite of all his years of being a homicide detective, nothing prepared him for what he saw. The sight gave his heart a painful lurch, as he quickly stood up and walked away. He stopped at a place not too far from the body, his back to the scene, and gazed at the breathtaking early morning scenery below. From here he could see the magnificent city that was Pasadena, and the view went beyond. On a smog free day, one could catch a glimpse of the ocean in Long Beach, some 31 miles away, give or take a few miles.

Jen Russo was instantly aware of this sudden change of mood from her partner. Without a word, and latex gloves on, she turned her attention to the body, and some 20 minutes later, she was standing beside her partner, who was still gawking at the scenery below in deep thought. They were both dressed in suits, and at a slender five feet nine inches, detective Russo had a face that had won many local beauty pageants in her home town when she was younger. Three years after making detective, she had yet to crack the big one on her own or with as little help from her partner as possible, and she was determined that this would be the one. Her relationship with Willoughby was cordial, and at times icy, but they made a great team – thoroughly professional.

"What have we got?" Willoughby wanted to know; his eyes were still fixated by the scene below it seemed.

"No sign of sexual assault, but I will have to have the coroner conduct a rape kit just in case. No physical trauma other than the fact that she drowned in her own blood. The rest of course I will leave again to the coroner," she said.

"How about time of death?"

"CSU puts it at about 10 to 12 hours. Coyotes did a number on her; they chewed off parts of her calves, thighs, and breasts. Amazingly her face is still intact, I would have to guess it is because of the hood, and it looks like the perp threw up after the killing, but again we will have the lab verify that, and hopefully we will get a match on the DNA."

Willoughby, his back still turned, almost grimaced at the details, but quickly contained himself.

"We're still in the process of trying to ID her. I guess once ..."

"No need for that," Willoughby interrupted rather gruffly.

Jen Russo was stunned by this response, but her training helped her mask her emotions pretty well. Like any good detective she was indoctrinated in the code of expecting the unexpected.

"And why the hell not?"

"I know who she is."

This time the astonishment on Russo's pretty face was apparent.

"Her parents live in this community and she is their only child. Her name eludes me, but I know her parents adopted her when she was a baby because the mother had her ovaries removed years ago thanks to ovarian cancer."

"My goodness Doug, how do you know all this?"

Willoughby sighed and said, "The parents are regular contributors at our annual fundraisers."

Detective Jen Russo thought about this for a moment. "Maybe we should ask the captain to assign someone else... you're too close," she said.

Willoughby was already shaking his head 'no' before she even finished her sentence. "No, I have the burden of breaking the terrible news to them Jen, and I will owe it to them to catch the son of a bitch. So, please, not a word to the captain. Is that understood?"

Jen looked again at the crime scene, and then at her partner, as if she was struggling to give an answer. "Yes," she agreed at last.

And for added emphasis, Willoughby said, "I mean it Jen, not a single word. This is my case."

"*Our* case," Jen Russo corrected him. Sometimes Willoughby needed to be reminded.

"Yeah," he agreed, and changing the subject he asked, "Any news from Professor Duncan at UCLA?"

Professor Duncan was a forensic expert, who also specialized in the behavioral tendencies of criminals, and the two detectives had worked with him in the past; his analyses were seldom off point. Even the local FBI's CSU Behavioral team sought his advice from time to time. Earlier on after arriving at the crime scene, Detective Russo had called the professor, describing the scene in great detail, and thereafter took pictures with her smartphone and sent them to him. Over the years the two detectives had learned to trust him with such sensitive information, particularly on an ongoing investigation since he was a civilian. He had called back some twenty minutes later with his findings.

"From the way I described it, and after seeing the pictures taken from all angles, he said it looked very much like a ritual killing," she said.

On hearing this, detective Willoughby turned to face her. This certainly was out of the ordinary as far as he was concerned.

"What?"

"He said this type of thing is common in Haiti."

"Are we talking voodoo mumbo jumbo here? Is that what the professor is suggesting?" If it had been anyone else, detective Willoughby would have scoffed at the thought as mere hogwash, but his training and past encounters with the professor would not let him. In his line of work, anything was possible. Aliens from outer space could have done it for all he knew and he would still have to investigate.

"I would think so. He also said to brace ourselves, because this may very well be the beginning of a series, unless of course we catch the perp before he strikes again."

The news from the professor had a chilling effect, not just on Russo, but on her partner as well. "So what does this mean?" Willoughby looked into his partner's eyes, with a gaze that suggested that calamity was about to dawn on them.

"Means we should be looking for a Haitian. If we are lucky, our guy may be local."

"Talk about looking for a needle in a haystack and not knowing where the haystack is," Willoughby said thoughtfully.

Southern California was known as the melting pot of the state. Nationalities from all over the globe migrated to this area, which made California such a diverse state. That is why detective Willoughby was right in suggesting that finding a suspect who they thought was Haitian would not be easy, but it was a start nonetheless. They would need to gather as much evidence as possible in order to track down the killer, but with the scenario presented, and the way it was done, this was going to be a challenge. Both detectives knew that, but both were willing to reach the ends of the earth to crack this one wide open. They then turned around and walked back to the body. By this time the Los Angeles County Coroner had arrived and were waiting patiently for the detectives to finish their preliminary work before they placed the body in a body bag and took it to the morgue.

All the while, Detective Willoughby was wondering when and how he was going to break the news to the victim's parents. This was the part of the job he was ill equipped for. No matter how many times he had done it, he could never get over the fact that he was going to tell someone, or in this case the parents, that they will *never* see their only child alive ever again and, worse still, that her life had been snuffed away so violently by some sick bastard who then left her body to the mercy of wild animals that descended on it like it was some carcass.

CHAPTER 7

EAGLE ROCK IS A CITY just west of Pasadena off the 134 freeway. It is widely believed that the city got its name from a huge boulder visible from the freeway that is close to a mountain range that was said to have once resembled an eagle, but over the years it had lost that eagle-like look due to weathering. Mostly a residential area for the upper and lower middle class, it is where Chico Valenzuela, the music producer, lived.

His house was located at Colorado and 5th Street. Eagle Rock had been his home from birth. An aspiring musician when he was younger but finding his true calling as a producer, he worked nights at a hamburger joint not too far from his home until an accident unloading a truck full of pallets left him with a herniated disc, resulting in a $12,000 settlement. Chico and his wife Maria would stay up late at night, watching 'egg and hammers' on late night TV giving tips on investment opportunities, like vending machines with dedicated and profitable routes to cleaning building franchises, none of which appealed to him them.

It was then that, with the help of Maria, he came up with the idea of converting his back car garage into a small studio, where he could record demo tapes for up and coming musicians. From talented performers to wannabes, the idea of recording people professionally and packaging their demos in casings that looked like the real thing was more than appealing; and the idea proved to be a stroke of marketing genius, because in no time business began to flourish. And to further enhance his knowledge, he took business classes at nearby Glendale Community College, and soon learned that with advertising and creating demand, he could not fail.

That was five years ago, and even though he was not big time like, say, Quincy Jones, Jermaine Dupri and other recording producer moguls, he was getting more work than he could handle in the independent music arena. In no time, that small studio grew into one equipped with all the state-of-the-art facilities, which rivaled many that were owned by the more established record labels.

It was at this studio facility where Raymond's band, 'The Rhythm Makers,' found themselves the following night, as promised by Raymond soon after he sold the Jaguar to Larry. After getting rid of the Jaguar's owner, that feeling of total domination and power over another human being left him with a thirst of wanting more of the thrill that had gripped him when he witnessed firsthand the power of the gods and black magic. Nothing, not even the band, was going to stand in his path to superstardom. Not just mere superstardom for the sake of it, but superstardom larger than that of his compatriot Wycleaf Jean, who was now also being offered juicy roles to star in such blockbuster movies like the 'X-MEN' franchise. He, Raymond Pata, would not be far behind, as far as he was concerned.

With the eight grand he got from Larry, he was quick, first of all, to pay Chico the $2,000 that he was supposed to have paid to him some six months earlier; Ray made him promise to claim that the money had been paid all along in case some nosy band member, Sofia in particular, found it necessary to probe. Chico understood, after all, he was a businessman first and music producer second. Plus, a man with two grand in his hand, something Chico considered easy money, would do or say anything to please the hand that gave it.

The rest of the money Raymond used for paying his rent and staying current by paying at least two months in advance. He did not want to have to worry about this aspect of his life again. Thus he had a plan for his landlady, Mrs. Barnard, in the near future. He would make her an offer so good that she would be foolish not to accept; in other words, he planned to buy the house from her. If she, however, refused, like old people tend to do due to their personal attachment to something of sentimental value, he would dispose of her quickly and easily. These were plans to be executed much later if the need came.

When he finally called the band to let them know that Chico would be ready for them to record their first CD that night, they were beyond euphoric. Finally the dream, and the realization of the fruits of all that hard work, was becoming a reality. Even Sofia dared to call Raymond 'a darling,' and was willing to make it up to him after the recording session.

The recording lasted into the wee hours of the night, and later when they started listening to the playbacks they were in raptures – they sounded much better than they could have hoped for. The man Chico was a genius. To mark this historic occasion, Chico took out two bottles of champagne from a fridge at the other end of the studio, which was always stocked to capacity with beer, sodas, and other alcoholic beverages. The band popped the bottles and merrymaking took its course. Raymond, on the other hand, did not join in on the celebrating, hardly taking a sip from the glass offered to him. He seemed preoccupied as he was content to watch, smile on occasion, and at times share in their banter, so no one noticed that he was slightly aloof. They were all caught up in a joyous moment of epic proportion.

As the champagne kept flowing, and the pizza did its rounds, the mood became all the more joyous as the night progressed.

"Guys, we did it finally! Aooo!!" Sofia became sentimental, wringing everyone's hand, and each time clashed her glass as toast at every excuse.

"Yeah," Jeremy said as he stood up and raised his glass and did a jig.

"Everything was so smooth," Laura said. "I can't believe we're in a studio listening to the playbacks of our own songs. Aooo!" The buzz was beginning to get a grip on them.

Danielle then stood up and slapped Raymond on the back so hard and yet surprisingly affectionate. "And you said we weren't ready," she said, her eyes glowing.

"What sayeth now, Mister Pata?" Jeremy grinned.

"Yeah, Mister Pata," Danielle grinned. Raymond's last name had a nice connotation, and they liked the way it rolled on the tongue; they would say it at any given excuse when the mood was right, like it sure was right now.

"Pata as in party, as in a good time," Sofia said.

Raymond merely grinned and focused his attention on the briefcase he had brought along; he was waiting for the right moment to pounce like a Cheetah on a Gazelle.

Danielle then mimicked Raymond's slight Caribbean accent "Don't worry *mon*, be happy, we're just messing with you. Come on, you gotta smile a little."

"Yeah man, we did it, our first CD among many ... we're gonna be huge," Sofia said. Her words were starting to slur a bit, but her vivaciousness was in full swing nonetheless.

"And you, Mister Pata," Jeremy said, "are going to be the most famous Haitian, more famous than what's his face? Jean something ..."

"Wycleaf Jean," Danielle corrected him.

"Yeah ... yeah ... bigger even than Wycleaf Jean; I kid you not." This got a bright smile from Raymond at last.

Danielle went behind Raymond and caressed his shoulders. Of all the band members, she was the one who showed the most affection toward him, her innocence and her sense of always wanting to please was touching; and it almost pained Raymond to know that her fate, along with that of the rest of them, had been sealed. They were the last stumbling block on that path to superstardom, and their fates were a small price to pay as far as he was concerned.

"Yeah man ... smile," Danielle said as she pecked him on the cheek and patted him lightly on the shoulders.

Raymond had suddenly become distant again and his stare was blank. On noticing this sudden change; Laura snapped her fingers at him. "Hey Raymond, where are you honey? You seem lost. What's on your mind?"

"Ahhh … sorry guys, just a bit tired that's all, and really thinking of what our next move should be."

Sofia then said excitedly, "Oooolala, yeah we should start thinking of booking as many good-paying gigs as possible."

"You are absolutely right Sofia," Danielle agreed. She, like the rest of them, was also getting plastered. "And I think that we should be on the move right away, that way we can sell our CD's at places we perform."

Jeremy reached for a slice of pizza that had been delivered earlier, and thrust it into his mouth before saying, "How about a music video of one of our tracks?"

"That sounds like an idea worth looking into," Sofia said.

"Yeah, a music video," Jeremy insisted as he attacked the pizza again.

Raymond flashed one of his award winning and reassuring smiles, one they rarely saw. The same smile that had all charmed them at the beginning, and had made the ladies' knees weak.

"One thing at a time guys, all these things like music videos cost money, money that we don't have yet. But, I got a plan."

"Okay let's hear it Mister Pata," Laura said as she sat on a table in front of Raymond and spread her legs. There was nothing to see because she was wearing a pair of faded jeans, but for the briefest of moments, Raymond's view was focused on the area right between the thighs instinctively, before forcing himself to look at her face instead.

"Please stop calling me that. I don't need to keep turning my head to see if my dad is standing behind me," he protested.

"Okay Mister Pata," Sofia teased.

Raymond then picked up his briefcase, opened it and pulled out a form he had made, handing one to each of them. The man had been busy, and seemed to have been on a mission. The four peered into the paper. For a moment, the playbacks, which were still on, were ignored. Sofia was the first to break the brief ice.

"What's this Ray?" Her speech was a bit more slurry than before.

"It takes a lot, actually more than a lot, to break a band. The competition is ruthless; I know you don't need me to tell you that."

"That's just it Ray, marketing. We need to market ourselves aggressively, leave no stone unturned. I know that sounds so cliché, but it's true," Danielle said. She had switched from champagne now to Heineken.

Sofia looked first at Danielle and indicated that she needed a beer, too. Danielle went up to the fridge pulled out another, opened it, and before she handed it to Sofia she asked "Anyone else? Laura? Jeremy? Ray?"

They all declined.

"Later most likely," Jeremy said. His slanted eyes were now beady and bloodshot.

"Anyway, like I was saying Sofia," Raymond continued. "Hiring a publicist to get word out to the world and radio time, and by that I mean serious radio play, costs at least ten grand, and then there are press releases, demos, copies for our CD's, distribution, and all that good stuff." He gesticulated with both hands to drive his point home.

"Surely we can't let something like that stop us now, can we?" Laura asked rhetorically.

"So what have we been doing all this time if we don't believe that we can catch a break like everyone else?" Sofia inquired before Raymond could give an answer.

"There has got to be another way to get our name out there," said Laura.

The bait was ready and Raymond tugged the line.

"Right Laura; that is why I need you guys to sign the forms I gave you so that I can find a way to get the money we need to cover all the publicity expenses." He swiftly diverted their attention to the paper he had handed each one of them, because of their condition they all barely glanced at the paper, let alone the fine print.

Danielle was the first to pose the all-important question, and Raymond was ready with an answer, one that he had practiced all too often in front of his bathroom mirror.

"And what exactly are we signing Ray?"

"That you are giving me permission to speak on everyone's behalf when I meet with the people with the money ready to invest in our success."

The thought that someone else could be footing the bill instead of them had the desired effect, just as Raymond had hoped. And maybe because she was buzzed or excited, but Sofia was the first to respond with an enthusiasm that even surprised him.

"Hey, I got no problem with that."

Raymond was already stretching a pen toward her.

"Yeah, gimme a pen too, and while you're at it, Danielle, would you be a doll and give me one of those Heinekens please," Jeremy said; he was totally buzzed now.

Raymond was ready, pen in hand, as he walked over to Jeremy, and had him and the rest sign before any of them had a chance to read everything through and change their minds upon realizing exactly what they were signing.

"This also lets me book gigs at places we all agree on," he prattled on to further divert their attention from the paper.

"Yeah, places like Tucson Arizona, Seattle Washington ..." Laura said.

"Jacksonville, Florida," Raymond added quickly with a grin that spread from ear-to-ear. The ducks were now in a row.

Sofia winked at Raymond and said, "Port-Au-Prince Haiti."

"And what's great about these places," Laura said, "is that we know people out there who can get us gigs at local clubs."

"That would mean travelling money plus room and board, right? And that's where I come in, see?" Raymond spread his arms once more as he looked at everyone, in a sense willing them to agree with him.

Jeremy said, "Travelling money yes, but room and board can be arranged, like in Seattle for instance

– my parents have a big house, separate rooms for the girls and we can crash in the basement; all we got to do is just chip in for food and gas."

"Remember too, Jeremy," Raymond said as he almost practically snatched the signed papers from their hands, and put them in his brief case as if they were bars of gold, "is that we will also be performing in places where we don't know anybody. So that is why I need to raise the money."

"True that," Danielle agreed

"Yeah, now this is the Ray Pata we know … the man with the big dreams," Laura said.

Jeremy raised his bottle of Heineken as if giving a toast. "I'll drink to that."

"So will I," Sofia said.

Jeremy then looked at Raymond for a while before saying, "Ray, I'm curious, why you almost never take a drink?"

Sofia answered for Raymond instead, "He is a Rasta man."

They all smiled. All of them felt the euphoria of realizing what at first looked like an intangible dream. Almost a year ago they had started this band, each of them intoxicated with dreams of stardom, like many other bands before and after them. Then came the interminable rehearsals, the realization that making music, great music for that matter, required a work ethic that would break a plow horse; they labored through that, and then came the suspicion that their leader, Raymond Pata, had stolen their hard earned money that was needed for studio time. Now that was a thing of the past, and they all had reason to believe that their moment had finally arrived. It all sounded too good to be true, but it was not. They were listening to their 9-track album, which they all agreed was far better than they had expected.

Soon after making certain that the documents were secure in his briefcase, Raymond got up and was ready to leave.

"Alright, we will meet at my place tomorrow depending on how soon you recover from the hangovers. There are a few things I have got to do. Good night, guys," he said.

"Ray, the celebration hasn't ended yet; can't you stay a little longer?" Laura wanted to know, seemingly puzzled by Raymond's imminent and seemingly sudden departure.

"I could, but there are business matters I have to attend to. The big celebration will come once our album goes platinum."

"Yeahhhh!!!" Everyone shouted their approval.

A platinum record sale meant that an album sold at least 1 million copies – every musician's dream.

In the independent realm, which Raymond and his band happened to be in, that was almost unheard of, but if a group or solo artist somehow managed to achieve this feat, that meant instant stardom! The big labels would be tripping over themselves scrambling for their signature, with promises of the moon, the sun, and the stars to follow thereafter. It was highly unlikely that it would ever happen, but the fact that there was always a chance, no matter how infinitesimal, is what made them push themselves and each other to a point somewhere beyond exhaustion.

CHAPTER 8

ONCE OUTSIDE, Raymond quickened his pace to the car, constantly glancing over the shoulder as if suspecting that he might be stopped. If someone had seen him, he would have suspected that he was up to something by the way he was behaving. He was a man on a mission it seemed. He got in the car and drove off. Once he got to the 134 on ramp at Figueroa Street, he headed west instead of east, the eastbound freeway would have taken him to Pasadena, and eventually home to Altadena; instead he headed toward Antelope Valley via the 14 freeway. Traffic was light this evening.

Some forty-five minutes later, he was driving along the driveway that led to Baba Brima's back house. The night was pitch-black when he stepped out of his car. Everything was quiet except for the thumping of his heart. He knew he was taking a huge risk coming back here, but he could not help it. He looked around. The main house was dark, but the back house, the place where the strange man cast his spells, was lit. He paused for a while, as if debating with himself whether to keep going or not; after carefully listening to the silence of the night, he thought he could hear the sound of some sort of percussion instrument being played.

He headed to the back house slowly, walking as if he was stepping on eggshells, and he was just about to knock gently at the door when Baba Brima's voice froze him dead in his tracks.

"I thought I told you *never* to come back Raymond Pata!" The voice sounded sharp as a whip, and Raymond felt his scrotum shrink with terror. For a moment he was at a loss for words. How did Baba Brima know it was him? He had virtually tiptoed to the back house, making as less noise as possible or so he thought.

"Y-yes … I am aware of that Baba Brima," Raymond managed to say at last. He looked around again, as if expecting some invisible force to strike him down. Instead, there was a gentle breeze that shook the branches of a nearby tree. In the distance a dog was barking, and once in a while a car drove by the main street. "And yes, I know what has cannot be undone, but I need more of that power," he continued.

The door opened, but Baba Brima was seated at the other end of the room. Raymond's heart gave a painful lurch, and for a minute wondered if coming back here had been a bright idea after all. There was absolutely no possible way Baba Brima could have opened the door from where he was; someone or *something* had done it for him, and yet he was alone in the dimly lit room. The room appeared to be even more frightening than it was since his last visit.

The witchdoctor was seated on the same stool like before, but this time he had a long pipe in his hand, and had since lowered the percussion instrument he was playing. His eyes were bloodshot, and the room was filled with smoke. Raymond looked around, and only sat when Brima used his pipe to point at the mat he had sat on before. There was no one else in the room, yet again, like before, he felt a strong presence—the type that made the little hairs at the back of his neck stand.

"I'm listening," Baba Brima invited.

"Talent can only take me so far," Raymond admitted. "It's a snake pit out there, Baba Brima, and to get to the very top, I will need more than what I got," he said as sincerely and as truthfully as he could.

Brima considered this for a moment, and then gazed at the dark ceiling before closing his eyes. It seemed as if he was again in communication with a being that was invisible. "But then your soul will not belong to you anymore Raymond. Are you sure about this?" Brima wanted to know. His eyes were still shut.

It was Raymond's turn to ponder before giving an answer. And again, as in such moments, he thought of the great Wycleaf Jean and knew there was no turning back, not after he had already spilled blood.

"I just got to do what I have to do, Baba Brima; a publicist is asking for fifty grand just to put me on the airwaves. I know with much more power, I can overcome that obstacle."

Brima nodded softly, as he slowly opened his eyes again. He then turned his long pipe and offered it to his client, who took a long puff. When he exhaled the smoke, it made him choke and cough, and he felt giddy for a moment. However, he felt yet again another strange sensation take over his entire body. This newest feeling made him shudder; he knew right then and there that he was in the grip of a power so mysterious, and yet so potent that words alone could not describe it. It took a while to come out of this brief trance, and when his eyes finally refocused and readjusted to the gloom, Brima was watching him intently.

"You have now embarked on a path that many before you have been afraid to take," he said.

He then spread out his arms and again closed his eyes, and began chanting again in a strange voice. After which, he opened his bloodshot eyes once more and clasped his hands.

"Alright, more blood will have to be spilled, and one of them will have to be pure at heart," he announced after communicating with the spirits.

"Pure at heart?" Raymond wanted to know.

Brima nodded and said, "Yes, a virgin, and with her the ritual will have to be performed differently. I will give you what you need, but you will have to locate her yourself."

"Yes, Baba Brima, and thank you." The witchdoctor sighed heavily as if he was conflicted in thought.

"Raymond, are you absolutely certain about this?" Brima asked again for the umpteenth time. He wanted to be totally convinced that Raymond knew exactly what he was getting himself into.

"Yes, Baba Brima," Raymond replied as confidently as he could.

"And are you willing to pay the price?"

"The price?"

"Yes, Raymond Pata, the price. Every dream has a price, and the one you have chosen may come with a very big price tag. So my question to you is that, when the time comes, will you be ready and willing?"

The warning was portentous, but Raymond's mind was made up, although the question made him feel uneasy. Somewhere in the basin of his stomach, he felt a wave of misgiving rising, but he was able to fight it off.

"Why are you asking me that, Baba Brima, when you know the true desires of my heart and what I am willing to do to achieve my goal?" Raymond asked.

Brima sighed again before giving an answer. "To do this, we're embarking on the dark side of nature. We are appealing to spirits so powerful and malevolent that with *any* slight misstep those very spirits we are trying to invoke can turn on you, and they could be your nemesis. And that nemesis can come in any form, a form that you least likely expect; so if and when that time comes, and for your sake I sincerely hope it does not, you must be ready. In other words, be forever vigilant, my son."

The last sentence struck Raymond as odd, and at the same time sympathetic. Brima had never addressed him as 'my son.' The thought made him feel much happier and secure; it was also obvious that the older man knew all too well the danger Raymond Pata had stepped into, in spite of all the powers that had been bestowed onto him.

"I will, Baba Brima," Raymond smiled at last, convinced now that superstardom was finally within his grasp.

"I know that you have work to do tonight before the sun rises," Brima said.

Raymond conversely was awestruck and yet impressed at the older man's proverbial accuracy

– he already knew, clearly, every step Raymond was about to take.

"Thank you and good night Baba Brima," Raymond said as he got up to leave, a thing he was suddenly very glad to do.

After he left, Brima continued smoking the long pipe, an imperceptible and yet mirthless smile on his face. He had seen it all before, young and ambitious men like Raymond Pata, willing to stack everything on a whim just to realize their dreams, however outrageous at times; but when it came time when they have to pay their dues, that was when the trouble really began. He hoped Raymond was different for his own sake.

CHAPTER 9

A LITTLE AFTER 3 AM, in Eagle Rock, the rest of the band was getting ready to leave Chico's studio. The celebration was over and they were all set to call it a night and wait eagerly for the initial copies of the CD they had recorded. Chico had already worked on the cover graphics, and when he showed it to them, they were floored.

As they were filing out, Chico was still working on his gigantic mixing board, fine tuning the songs and rearranging them to his utmost satisfaction. "Are you guys sure you are okay to drive?" he asked as they reached the door.

"Of course man," Jeremy said with a smile. "Ask them, we have done it a million times, and I'm always the designated driver." For someone who had had more than his fair share to drink, he seemed to be handling himself well under the circumstances, which is perhaps why Chico nodded and smiled and continued working.

"Is Raymond your manager, too?" Chico wanted to know.

"You could say that," Sofia said in a drunken stupor. "Self-appointed, if you ask me. His music sucks even though he thinks it's the bomb, the next big thing; but he is a good manager though, if and when he puts his mind to it, and stops being so damned secretive and guarded all the time. Just wish he could stick to the managing stuff, and leave the singing to us." A little alcohol can really loosen some people's tongues.

"I agree," Danielle said with a chuckle.

"Me too," Laura said "But please don't tell him that Chico."

Chico smiled and said, "My lips are sealed."

Every group he had come across had its own disagreements and politics. He had seen and heard it all. All that mattered to him was just doing the best job possible in recording artists and their music – that's what paid the bills.

"Well, I suppose we will hear from you once the tracks are finally laid, right?" Jeremy asked, instantly changing the topic.

"Yep," Chico agreed as he watched them file out of the studio and into the quiet, early morning light.

Once outside, they all got into Jeremy's SUV, which had more than enough room to accommodate all four of them and more. They were all exceptionally jazzed at the thought of finally having recorded their first album. The excitement had barely worn off; if anything, it seemed to be gaining steam as they drove through the streets of Eagle Rock heading to the 134 eastbound freeway.

"I for one thought this was never gonna happen," Sofia said in a slurred voice. She was seated in front with Jeremy.

"Yeah, I thought the studio money had ended up in Raymond's pocket," Laura said.

"I think it did," Sofia said. "Did you see how our ploy almost worked when we said we had spoken to Chico?"

"Guys," Danielle interjected. "It really does not matter. Fact is, we accomplished what we set out to do; we recorded the CD."

There was silence for a while after Danielle said what she said; only the soft humming of the engine, as it drove along the dark 134 freeway heading to the 210 east, could be heard. They were all forced to reflect on Danielle's last statement because it was true, and at times the truth could be painful to admit.

"Question is, can we still trust the Haitian though?" Jeremy broke the silence. There was always some racial nuance and prejudice whenever Jeremy referred to Raymond as 'The

Haitian;' something he did behind his back of course.

"Well, he did come through though didn't he?" Danielle said matter of factually.

"After much prying though," Sofia said. "This should have been a simple matter of just paying Chico, showing up, and recording. It should never have escalated to a point where he had to threaten to break up the band," Sofia said, hardly less correctly.

It was also at the moment when Laura brought up something profound; something all of them had missed. "I'm curious; did any of you guys read the form he made us sign?"

This was followed by yet another one of those loud and uncomfortable silences; even Danielle, who had thus far been playing devil's advocate, was suddenly assailed by a wave of misgivings.

At that moment, the vehicle tugged to the left lane. They were now on the 210 freeway headed east, as Jeremy suddenly let go of the wheel, and clutched his neck with both hands in obvious pain it seemed. His passengers were instantly horrified.

"Jeremy …w-what's the matter?" Sofia screamed.

With one hand, Jeremy tried to grab the wheel, but this suddenly was no easy task for he could not move his hands.

"H-help … I … c-can't … breathe." His voice was barely audible.

And at that instant, the SUV spun uncontrollably, missing an 18 wheeler truck by a hair that the truck driver was forced to blare his loud horn, which was illegal within city limits. Sofia, out of sheer panic and reflex action, tried to grab the wheel, but her body too felt weak and numb, her hands were suddenly heavy as lead, rendering them incapacitated. The car kept spinning and spinning, disorientating them in the process, and hit the center divider that separated the eastbound from the westbound freeway; two airbags immediately deployed, hitting both Sofia and Jeremy in the face and stomach. Sofia felt the bile rise up her throat before she passed out, and at that moment the vehicle spun to the right.

"Oh God!" Danielle cried out, before the vehicle capsized, and rolled the entire length of the freeway from the left to the right. When it reached the shoulder, the van tipped over and burst into flames, killing the rest of the band and their dreams instantly.

ༀ ༀ ༀ

At that very moment, Raymond Pata was in his makeshift shrine, kneeling in front of the altar, possessed. The walk-in closet was dimly lit with candles of all shapes and sizes. In both hands, he clutched the doll, and on it were strands of hair

132

from all four of the band members that he had been tugging one at a time, and when the moment came, the moment of their demise, he knew it.

"Another offering to you *Nana Buluku*, the god creator, and *Mau* goddess of the moon, and let their blood spill, and with it come success, wealth, and power that you will bestow upon me," he said softly as he again felt that same surge of power and intoxicating sense of invincibility that he felt earlier when he took the young lady's life in the mountains. It was a feeling he now felt was a part of him, and he was fully enthralled by it, not realizing that he was enslaved by it.

CHAPTER 10

BY THE TIME THE FIRE ENGINES, the police, and the medics arrived, the fire had consumed the band members' bodies to a point almost beyond recognition. The scene was so gruesome that the eastbound freeway had to be blocked off between the Sierra Madre and Baldwin Avenue exits, and with the California Highway Patrol in full command, cars had to be detoured to the surface streets and directed to join the freeway several miles away from the scene of the accident.

Luckily, because of the time of night, there were not very many cars to deal with. The westbound freeway was an entirely different matter altogether, because cars started slowing down to take a closer look at the wreckage. That was always a problem in such situations, human beings are by nature very curious creatures, and a car engulfed in flames on a freeway attracts the 'lookaloos.' It did not, however, take long for the fire to be put off; and when it was reasonably safe, the firemen from both the Arcadia and Pasadena Fire Departments first examined the carnage, and began the grisly and yet arduous task of getting the bodies out of the smoldering mayhem.

They took their time, because it was pretty much obvious that there were no survivors to be rescued. At some point they had to use the 'jaws of life' to peel off the metal that prevented them from getting to the charred remains of Danielle and Laura at the back. A forensic team was also onsite, collecting all the necessary evidence to determine if there was any sort of foul play at hand. This was just standard operating procedure. To their trained eye and nostrils, it was pretty obvious that drinking and driving was the main culprit. With this suspicion in mind, they removed tissue samples from everyone before the bodies were placed in bags and sent to the local morgue.

Through the soot covered vehicle registration plate, the California Highway Patrol was able to locate Jeremy Yee's parents who lived in Seattle, and break the devastating news to them. They promised to be on the next plane to Los Angeles. It took a little longer to identify the other three victims, because their picture ID's were incinerated in the flames. The authorities had to use dental records; but within 24 hours all the next of kin were notified, and had to make the painful trip to the Arcadia Mortuary to claim the remains of their loved ones.

It was later determined that Jeremy Yee, the driver and owner of the vehicle, had a blood alcohol level (BAL) of 0.24, exactly three times the legal limit to operate a vehicle in the state of California, and almost every other state in the union. The other victims of the crash also registered similar blood alcohol contents. The ruling was that this was a typical drunk driving accident. The driver, Jeremy Yee, was definitely intoxicated and somehow lost total control of the vehicle which ended up crushing the center divider wall of the freeway, and rolled to the other side before the fuel line broke and caught fire.

The news of this fiery crash was picked up by the local airwaves of NBC, ABC, and CBS. This was fanned further by a joint press conference a few days later from the two Police Chiefs of the Arcadia and Pasadena Police departments to announce the official findings of the deadly accident. Toward the end of the media briefing, Chief Marcus O'Reilly of the Arcadia Police Department made it a point to emphasize the dangers of drinking and driving.

"If you have to drink, please don't drive; and if you're going to drive, again I will say ... don't drink." He, together with Chief Brandon McCoy of the Pasadena Police Department, were standing in front of the Arcadia Police Precinct that bright sunny morning, two days after the tragedy, addressing the media, with Police Chief O'Reilly doing most of the talking and relishing every minute of it. "This tragedy could have been easily averted," he continued, "and again, it could have been worse because other cars could have been involved, and more lives could have been at stake. There is always a reason why it is imperative that you do not drink and get behind the wheel. Next question, please…"

The news should have lasted three or five days at the most, had it not been for a rookie writer of the *Weekly World of LA* who was desperate for a story. Her name was Maureen Webb. Fresh out of college from the University of California at Santa Barbara, like any young ambitious writer who had dreams of winning the Pulitzer someday, she knew with every story, no matter how inconsequential it may appear on the surface, there were always layers underneath.

With much digging, she found out that the fiery crash victims were members of some struggling band based in Altadena. And this is where things got a bit interesting. As she dug deeper, she found that they were actually on their way from a studio where they had just finished recording their first CD; this then led her to Chico Valenzuela the studio owner and recording engineer. When she could not reach him by phone, she decided to drive to Eagle Rock and show up at his doorstep unannounced.

It was Saturday morning, a week after the tragic accident, when Maureen Webb pulled up in front of Chico's home. It had not been hard to find, especially for a journalist still wet behind the ears, and one who was not afraid to get her hands dirty. All she needed was a name; and via all the public information readily available, if you knew where to look, in this instance the Los Angeles County Records, she was able to find his property. She even pulled out a short rap sheet that involved Chico when he was much younger, at a time when he was sucked into the wrong crowd before his true calling intervened.

So when she showed up at his doorstep, she knew a lot more about him than some of his closest friends did. She also fancied the element of surprise; this way, once caught off guard in this manner, she could gather a lot more facts. But in this case, she felt that there was nothing to hide except finding out more about the band and their premature demise.

The morning was warm, and Maureen's attire was anything but casual. She had on a nice skirt with stockings and matching black heel stilettos, and a white, short-sleeved blouse. Her brunette hair was short and her makeup was mild. She was beautiful, with stunning, hazel, inquisitive eyes. She carried with her a striped Kate Spade shoulder bag. In it, among other things, were the tools of her trade: a miniature tape recorder, notepad, numerous pens, and a camera.

She pulled out her small hand mirror from the bag one last time, before knocking, and quickly looked at herself for the hundredth time it seemed, flashing her teeth in a wide grin to make sure that none of them were stained with lipstick. Maureen quickly stroked the sides of her head to remove any hanging strands of hair, which were nonexistent.

She knocked on the door several times before it was opened by a Hispanic woman, who looked to be no more than thirty; she had long, jet black hair that crawled a little below her shoulders. It was Maria Valenzuela, Chico's wife; she instantly recognized her from the pictures that showed up during her investigation. She knew they had been together for six years – married two out of those six.

"Yes?" Maria instinctively narrowed her eyes as she regarded the pretty and petite white stranger standing at her doorstep.

"Maria Valenzuela?" Maureen Webb flashed her award-winning smile.

"Yes, and who are you?" Maria looked at her suspiciously, her guard suddenly up. She was dressed in a long summer dress, and had been in the midst of preparing breakfast it seemed, judging from the aroma of which permeated through the half-open door. She stood five feet five four and a half inches, almost the same height as Maureen. She had high cheekbones, and Maureen could tell by the shape of her face and mouth, that she was most likely Mayan. She very pretty, and Maureen wondered if Chico had met her during one of his recording sessions of up and coming musicians.

"My name is Maureen Webb; I'm with the *Weekly World of LA*." She flashed her credentials and handed Maria one of her business cards, and thereafter extended her arm for a handshake. Maria reciprocated, and then glanced at the card Maureen gave her for a moment before looking up at her.

"How can I help you, Miss Webb?"

"I'm covering a story of the band members *'Rhythm Makers'* who were killed in a car crash last Saturday on the 210 freeway, and would like to speak to Chico Valenzuela about it," she replied.

Maria Valenzuela's lower lip dropped slightly, and her eyes were suddenly moist. The news had first hit them like a tsunami when they initially heard it. She instinctively raised her hands to her mouth, and her beautiful eyes were soon filled with tears. For some reason she felt pangs of guilt for their deaths, especially after her husband confided in her after the news reached them, that he had been a bit concerned about the drunken state they were in before they left. Now, here was a reporter at their doorstep snooping around wanting to know more about what could have possibly happened.

"May I come in?" Maureen asked, still flashing her reassuring smile, which seemed to work its magic; and with that she crossed the line of bad guy to that of an average white woman.

"Oh yes, please," Maria said as she stepped aside and led the way into a nicely-furnished living room. She waved Maureen to a comfortable chair next to the couch. There was a large plasma TV on the other end of the room playing a Mexican soap opera. Maria immediately muted the volume.

Maureen looked around again. The house was immaculate — signs of a very comfortable lifestyle. Maureen had also found out that Chico's recording studio business, 'Azteca Sounds,' reported a gross of nearly $85,000 last year; that number, according to expert projections, was set to increase exponentially over next few years. Already, the city was suggesting that he move his home-based business to the more industrial side of town. It could easily sustain itself and more, they argued.

"You have no idea how shocked and sorry my husband and I are about this tragedy, Miss Webb," Maria said as she parked herself on the couch facing her guest.

"I bet, and it is Maureen, please," she said politely as she impulsively pulled out her notepad and miniature tape recorder from her bag. "The person I also would like to speak to Miss Valenzuela …"

"Maria, please," she returned the favor with a weak smile.

"Okay thanks Maria. As I was about to say, the person I also would like to speak to is your husband, Chico Valenzuela. Is he in by any chance? I'm so sorry, I should have called first."

Maria opened her mouth to say something when Chico entered the living room from the other side of the house. He was barefooted, dressed in sweatpants and a white t-shirt. He looked as if he had just woken up because he was stretching his arms and yawning at the same time. He was almost six feet tall with bushy eyebrows and a well-trimmed goatee. He regarded the stranger in his living room for a moment, and then looked at his wife questioningly.

Saving Chico's wife the trouble, Maureen immediately stood up, arm outstretched and smiled as she walked toward him. "Maureen Webb, I'm a reporter with the *Weekly World of LA,*" she said.

Chico shook her hand and looked at her suspiciously. For a moment he wondered what a reporter from one of LA's most reputable papers would possibly want with him.

"A reporter? With the *Weekly World of LA*?" he asked almost to himself, as he ran his fingers through his well-kept jet black hair that almost always had a styling gel in it. He, like his wife and most people, was familiar with this free publication that came out once every week, always filled with intriguing stories of the urban legend variety.

"Yes, the *Weekly World of LA*," she reiterated as she handed him a card similar to the one she had given to his wife.

As he took the card with both his fore and middle fingers, she noticed that his nails were beautifully manicured, which instinctively drew her to his big feet. They also had a nice pedicure. The feet were cream white, revealing the fact that they had not seen the sun in a while. They reminded Maureen of, other than what was believed about men with big feet, a pair of raw chickens ready to be purchased at a supermarket.

He motioned at her, indicating she should take a seat as he took his place beside his wife.

"What can I do for you, Miss Webb?"

"Maureen," she smiled.

"I wanted to ask you a few questions about the band that died in a car accident last weekend," she announced. She then pulled out her tape recorder and turned it on. "Would you mind if I recorded this conversation?"

Chico hesitated for a brief moment and looked at his wife, who shrugged her elegant shoulders.

"Not at all, Miss Webb — I mean Maureen," he replied.

Chico's mind was already working full throttle. This could turn out to be good for his business, he thought. If his name, and that of his studio, were mentioned constantly in an article with a large circulation, like the *Weekly World of LA*, there was no telling how many more potential clients it would attract. This was the kind of free advertising he never dreamt possible. The sky was certainly the limit, and he intended to give the woman as much information as could.

"Oh, and Maria," she looked in her direction. "Please feel free to add anything that you might feel relevant to the story, because I assume that you met the deceased right?"

"Yes," she answered, and then as an afterthought she added. "Oh, and before we begin Maureen, can I offer you something to drink? Coffee? Juice? Water?"

"No thanks," she declined with yet another smile. "Okay, shall we begin? Please take your time, I'm in no rush. Tell me all you know about this group and why they chose to record with you on that fateful day."

Chico took a deep sigh; he was more than happy to oblige. He began with when he first got a call from the supposed band leader, the Haitian, Raymond Pata. He continued on to describe the initial struggle to come up with the money to record their CD and the actual recording. He hesitated a bit when he was at the point where they voiced their concerns about Raymond's singing aptitude, the three women in particular whom Maureen was already familiar with: Sofia Keenan, Danielle Jacobs, and Laura Jaeger. He went on to state, rather more emphatically than was necessary, that he had tried to stop them from driving since they were obviously drunk, and definitely in no position to drive; but of course, it was an argument he did not win.

All the while, like the trained reporter that she was, Maureen listened without interrupting and nodded at appropriate moments to egg him on. She made a great show of taking notes, but could have easily recited the whole narrative from Chico verbatim.

Toward the end, she asked, "Can you tell me more about the surviving member, Raymond Pata? Why was he not in the car with them? Why did he choose instead to drive himself?"

Chico answered as best as he could, and mentioned that of all the band members, Raymond was the one who seemed most preoccupied with his thoughts; that several times the other band members had to snap him out of his cocoon. He ended up by saying, "One thing, though, that looked odd is that he had them sign some sort of agreement, which they all did without, as far as I could tell, even glancing at it."

This got Maureen thinking. Perhaps she had stumbled onto something big. "And do you know what that document was?" Her demeanor had not changed even though her heart was fluttering with excitement.

Chico shook his head no. She would have to try and find out from Raymond Pata when she met him, which she hoped would be soon; and after that she would decide whether to run with the story or kill it. But there were some things that were a bit fishy; some instinct inherited from some long-deceased ancestor that told her something did not gel. She smelled a rat, and that rat was Raymond Pata; but this, she had to admit, was most likely her journalistic instinct, which could be nothing – or everything. Only time would tell.

In the end, she asked Chico if he could show her around and even requested to listen to some of the songs that he had recorded for the group. She also asked if she could snap some pictures, and Chico was more than willing to do that and more. In the end, she thanked the couple for their time and cooperation, and assured them that she would keep them posted as to when the article would be published. Now was the time to prepare for the sole survivor of the 'Rhythm Makers' – Raymond Leonard Pata.

CHAPTER 11

FOR A LONG TIME, husband and wife sat in silence. They were clearly pondering the visit of the young journalist from the *'Weekly World of LA.'* They were undoubtedly astonished by it. Fatal accidents happened all the time in a big city like Los Angeles and its surrounding cities, Pasadena, Arcadia, Eagle Rock; — heck, all over the world since the invention of the automobile. What was so different about this one that a reporter would come knocking at their front door?

The answer came to Chico almost immediately. He considered the fact that the victims had been struggling musicians who had just recorded their first album and died shortly after. There was a great possibility that their deaths could very well arouse public sympathy, and spike sales of their CD. After all, this kind of thing did happen. He thought of movie stars who died after making a movie and their work became box office hits when released after their deaths, which otherwise would have been judged solely on merit had they been alive. A few names came to mind: Tupac Shakur and his movie, *'Gang Related,'* which was released a year after his death in 1996; Brandon Bruce Lee and his movie, *'The Crow;'* the iconic James Dean and the movie, *'Giant;'* and just recently, Paul Walker of *'The Fast and Furious'* movie franchise.

It happened in music, too; and for the most part, the media hype that their deaths brought was beyond price. This was the kind of thing that would have a reporter sniffing around. As the sole surviving member of the band, Chico was certain that Raymond Pata was going to reap the rewards of this fateful tragedy. He also wondered why he had yet to hear from him, and figured that in light of this catastrophe, he was most likely in seclusion, grieving in private. After all, this was more than one man could handle all at once. And as this particular thought ran through his mind, the smartphone in his pocket rang, breaking the silence. He pulled it out and looked at the screen, and his heartbeat accelerated. It was Raymond Pata.

అంఅంఅం

Raymond woke up that morning, a week after the deaths of his band members, still not feeling the gravity of the situation. He had gotten a call from the police a few days after the disaster; this after calling their homes, for the sake of keeping up appearances, to find out why they had not shown up the next day at the appointed time. He could not bring himself to attend any of their funerals, and the families understood. Besides the logistical problems posed by the fact Jeremy was buried in Seattle, Washington, Sofia in Pueblo, Colorado, Danielle in San Diego, California, and Laura in Mesa, Arizona, the families of the victims figured he could only be at one place at a time.

The main reason why he didn't go to any of the funerals was that he did not want to deal with the inevitable scrutiny and attention that was sure to come from the friends and family of the deceased, and the unspoken questions of why he was not in the car with them that night. As for their deaths, he tried not to think too much of it, because he still had his eyes on the ultimate prize. The band members happened to be casualties of war as far as he was concerned. He was so obsessed with his ambition that any feelings of guilt were quickly disposed of when he thought of what would be.

As Chico had guessed earlier, he decided to lay low for a few days. He stayed indoors, unhooked his landline and turned his smartphone off after he spoke to the police and the families of the departed. He watched the news as they covered the accident, first in full, right after it happened, and later in snippets as the story began to lose its luster and fade into oblivion. It was at this point when he decided to give Chico a call.

The phone rang at least four times before a familiar voice answered. "Chico speaking."

"Yeah, Chico it's me, Raymond Pata," he tried to add the proper pain in his voice.

"Hey, Raymond … Maria and I are terribly sorry about what happened, man. We saw it on the news. Unbelievable man; we're still in shock," Chico said. "All four of them?"

"Yes," Raymond said, still maintaining that pain in his voice, which was very convincing. "Fate can be cruel, man."

"I'm really sorry man," he said again. "As a matter of fact, I had just finished laying the tracks down just that morning. They sound incredible and I was about to give you guys a call when the news came. So given the circumstances, Ray, I thought you might need some time to yourself. I cannot even imagine how lousy you must be feeling right now."

Great as a matter of fact, Raymond thought. Aloud he said, "Words just won't cut it, Chico. When I got that phone call from the police, my whole life changed, man." He meant it in a way Chico would have never guessed.

"I hear you, man," Chicco empathized. "Perhaps this is not the best time to bring it up, but what are you going to do with the music now that you are the only surviving member of the band?"

Are you kidding me? The world is about to know about Raymond Pata, he almost said, but held his tongue instead.

"Just finish working on the tracks some more, and I will come and pick up the CDs and the master. I have power of attorney that they signed over to me. I will figure out what to give their estates if and when the CD becomes the hit that I know it will be."

You sneaky, cold-hearted bastard, Chico thought. All of a sudden, he could sense that Raymond was relishing that opportunity the untimely death of his band members had brought.

"Yeah, do so, man. I really wish they would have heard the entire album as it sounds now. It is amazing, Ray. I remastered some of the tracks … let me not say anything; you will see for yourself. So when is the best time for you to come by, all things considered?"

Raymond thought about this for a second. Much as he would have loved to have the CD and master in his hands, he did not want to sound over anxious, hard as it was, even though he knew that Chico was too much of a professional to ask too many probing questions. This, after all, was business; he had been paid in full and Raymond did not owe him a dime. All he had to do was get the products and wait for the highest bidder for the master, who was sure to be calling soon, and thereafter negotiate a three album deal with a real record company.

"I will say tomorrow afternoon," he said.

"Good, and oh, Raymond?"

"Yeah?"

"Just to give you a heads up, a reporter from the *Weekly World of LA* was here."

He could almost hear Raymond holding his breath at the other end of the line.

"A reporter?"

"Yeah, her name is Maureen Webb. She is piecing together a story about your band, and I have a feeling that she is eager to talk to you."

It was all Raymond could do from screaming aloud with joy and doing the jig right there and then. It had started. He could not believe it; his dream was unfolding right before his eyes.

"Oh, when was this?" he tried to sound nonchalant.

"She just left less than an hour ago," Chico said.

"I see," Raymond said in as calm a voice as he could muster. "I will see you tomorrow, Chico."

"Great."

There was a click on the other end of the line as Raymond hung up to forestall any further conversation. Chico then looked at his wife for a while in deep thought.

"What?" Maria asked returning his gaze.

"He made them sign over power of attorney to him the same night they were here. Think I should call that reporter and let her know about that?"

His wife's reply was, "No, that is none of your business, Chico. You've said it yourself time and again that your business is just recording the artists and not getting involved in their messy little affairs."

Chico, coming to his senses, finally nodded in agreement before saying, "You know, you are absolutely right, sweetheart." He then kissed her on the forehead. "What's for breakfast? I'm starving."

꙰ ꙰ ꙰

Maureen Webb left the Valenzuela residence with a mind too full for words. She drove through the morning streets, and instead of heading to the office to prepare for her possible face-to-face with Raymond Pata, she instead pulled into a Wal-Mart parking lot on Fifth and Figueroa. Once parked, she pulled out a miniature tape recorder from her bag, and replayed her taped interview with Chico and his wife.

The issue that bothered her most was figuring out what it was that Raymond had the group sign before their deaths. Chico also mentioned that, of the five, he seemed to be the most preoccupied, and most sober for all he could tell. That and the fact that he drove himself to the recording studio, and left soon after they had signed. Could this just have been a fantastic coincidence, or was there something more sinister behind all this?

Could Raymond have somehow sabotaged the vehicle, and in the process became the sole beneficiary to the notoriety that was sure to follow once word came out that the victims were, in fact, members of a struggling band that had just made its first album? She then pulled out the police report of the accident and read it for perhaps the hundredth time. There was no mishap as far as the car was concerned. Nothing physically or mechanically wrong, no signs of tampering whatsoever. If anything, the car was in tip-top condition and less than three years old; so foul play was definitely ruled out. As a matter of fact, the first things the investigators looked for were to see if something like the brakes malfunctioned, or if there were any loose lug nuts or anything of that nature – there were no such anomalies. It all came back to the hard and indisputable fact – the driver, Jeremy Yee, was intoxicated while operating a motor vehicle. And as such, the case — if there ever was one to begin with — was closed.

However, Maureen was not so sure. That gut-wrenching instinct, which was hard to ignore, kept gnawing at her. Perhaps it had to do with the fact that her father, David Webb, had been a top detective for over twenty-five years with the Santa Barbara Police Department, and perhaps she had inherited the investigative genes from him.

Born to a family of four, Maureen Webb was the last of the four children of David and Gloria Webb; her only other siblings were boys, so she grew up to be tough as one might expect. She was raised in the small city of Goleta, just north of Santa Barbara. Her parents were both retired now. Her mom had been a manager of a local bank from as far back as she could remember. Her older brothers, Richard, Wesley, and Jonathan, had moved to the Bay Area shortly after the dot com boom, and were all married and raising families. Maureen, whose love for writing stemmed from an early age, did her undergrad at the University of California Santa Barbara (UCSB), where she majored in Journalism and minored in Art History. Even though she graduated with honors, it had been one hell of a task securing employment with the major newspapers; she however considered herself lucky to be on the paid staff of a paper such as '*The Weekly World of LA*' while many of her colleagues barely scraped by as freelancers, and that is if they were lucky enough to even get that.

In the cold, harsh world of corporate America, the mantra was 'take no prisoners.' Competition was brutal, and that's an understatement. Demand for great stories, especially on free publications that depended solely on advertising for revenue, was cruel. And thus far, Maureen had yet to generate an article worthy of praise; especially at a paper where many of her counterparts were male, and who never stopped wondering if she got the job by merely her looks rather than talent. Because of this, she had to work extra hard to prove herself. That is why she took as many assignments as she could; even the ones deemed 'dead,' just in case there was something missed.

She always remembered hearing her father say, 'A good detective always does his homework, but a great detective, on the other hand, suspects everything and everyone. He does not see things in black and white or for what they are.' Although Detective Webb lived and worked in a city where crimes like murder and armed robbery were rare compared to Los Angeles, he was known for being a great and thorough detective on cases that landed on his desk all throughout his illustrious career. And Maureen — the apple of her father's eye and 'daddy's little girl' — was eager to make him proud.

She decided to do her groundwork on Raymond Pata before she interviewed him. She was not going to be just a good journalist, but a great one. For now, Maureen Webb had to believe that

Raymond Pata had a hand in the death of his band members. But proving that, if there ever was a need, would be a challenge. For all she knew, the man could be totally innocent; just someone who was smart enough to know that drinking and driving were a deadly — and at times — fatal combination.

It was time to prepare and find out who this Raymond Pata really was. It had only been a week since the accident and she thought, for all intents and purposes, the poor guy could be a wreck emotionally. So she decided to give him two more days before she came knocking at his door.

CHAPTER 12

THE 24-HOUR FITNESS, at the corner of the busy intersection of Woodbury and Fair Oaks in Altadena, was a sanctuary for the health nuts. Conveniently located at a mini mall in this lower middle class section of the city, there was a supermarket, a Panda Express restaurant, and a Starbucks across from the gym, and right underneath was a Subway. Since it was open all day and night, as the name suggested, close to the 210 west freeway and literally across the street from the city of Pasadena, this gym attracted all types of clientele. Many were from the nearby city of La Canada, an affluent neighborhood just west of Pasadena. A number of these health buffs came at night, and some in the early hours of the morning.

It was a state of the art gym, equipped with all the latest equipment available in the market today. Above every treadmill, flat-screen TVs kept members up to date on all the current events worldwide via CNN and other networks. There were also private trainers for hire, if needed, along with personal lockers, a sauna, and an Olympic size indoor swimming pool.

This was where Brittany Gomez, an aspiring actress and model, liked to come at least three nights a week. She lived in Pasadena and just recently had signed up for kickboxing lessons for beginners, in an attempt to burn more calories rather than for self-defense. Her big break had yet to come, so during the day she worked at an animal shelter on Marengo and Walnut, not too far from the Pasadena Superior Court House. It was a part time job with flexible hours, which was perfect because she was able to attend auditions when the need came.

Extremely beautiful, Brittany always turned heads wherever she went, and the gym was no exception. She looked stunning, especially now in her tight spandex pants and workout tank top. At five feet eight and a quarter inches, she was quite tall for a Latina woman. That, and the fact that she had a dazzling smile, prompted a lot of people to encourage her from a young age to go into modeling or acting as a career.

After securing an agent right after graduating from high school, she did a few local commercials, photo ads, and once in a while, bit parts in B movies if she was lucky enough to land a role. Beautiful and talented as she was, there were only so many roles for minorities. However, lately things started to look up. Her agent booked an audition for an independent film that was to be shot in Los Angeles. The movie was rumored to have a budget of close to two million dollars, considered 'low budget' in Hollywood, because the average picture cost at least fifty million to make and was almost always guaranteed a theatrical release worldwide. With this particular movie, at best, it would get a limited theatrical release; and based on how it fared, a national and international release was a possibility. Otherwise the picture would go straight to video, where the market was wider, though thoroughly saturated due to the advent of Netflix, Redbox, and Internet movie streaming. But it would be a great platform to finally introduce Brittany Gomez to the world.

The audition, held at a small studio in Burbank, attracted over a thousand hopefuls. The part itself was not big, but the character had more than enough lines and was memorable. She prepared for days on end, in the process working with a dialogue and acting coach and even a yoga instructor for meditation purposes so that she could delve even deeper into the character. The bills were footed by her boyfriend, Hugo Martinez, who was desperate to hold on to her even though she was what guys called 'high maintenance.' Hugo, who worked as a commercial realtor, was more than willing to meet all her needs. After all, he had just closed a few lucrative deals over the last few months, and as a result he was more than able to provide.

On the day of the audition, she did extremely well even though she was a bit nervous at first, and the sight of the many other actors vying for the same role was also somewhat disconcerting.

However, when her agent called to let her know that she was invited for a 'call back,' she had every reason to feel elated and confident that the part may just be hers. It was now down to two, she was told. Brittany and one other lady she did not know. But according to her agent, Bob Wakefield, he had a feeling the casting director was leaning toward her.

This drove Brittany to work even harder. The role was just right for her, and she believed sincerely that the part was meant for her. What was even more appealing was that after reading the entire script, which was sent to her after she earned her 'call back,' she could totally relate to the character. She would not even have to act. All she had to do was be herself, and everything would fall into place. The role called for a bit of nudity, but nothing she could not handle. In addition to preparing for the role, she also prayed just as hard to The Almighty to grant her the opportunity of a lifetime. Raised Catholic, she went to the local church for mass and Sunday service every week.

On this particular night, she was more focused as she headed to her favorite treadmill. The second audition was only two days away, and she knew she had to give more than a stellar performance.

First she had to loosen her body, ignoring the obvious stares from the guys and the envious looks from the other women. She was used to that and much more. Men were always asking her out on dates. Some would even work out some clever maneuvers just to strike up a conversation.

It would go something like, "Oh, I see you here all the time. Are you on any particular regimen?"

"No."

"Oh." This was followed by the usual, "Would you like to grab a cup of coffee when you're done?" or the old tried and tested, "Haven't I seen you somewhere before? Do you work at such and such? How about if we grab a bite sometime?"

She would, for the most part, politely refuse their advances. A few times she had to be short with one or two, who were not only married men according to the ring on their fingers, but would also not take no for an answer. There was one man in particular who pursued her with such impunity that she was forced to inform management. The patron was given a stern but polite warning that if he persisted, not only would his membership be revoked, but charges of stalking would be filed with the police; and there the matter rested permanently. Needless to say, she secretly enjoyed the attention, especially from the many admirers who would come up to her and tell her in no uncertain terms how pretty she was and walk away after giving the compliment. She wondered what it would be like if and when she became a big name like her idol, Halle Berry. Just that thought alone was enough to give her chills and drive her to push herself even harder.

On this particular night, she went through her usual routine of running on the treadmill for two miles, calisthenics, weight lifting, and later kickboxing. After two hours, she was spent. She never took a shower at the gym if she could help it; she much preferred a hot bubble bath, in which she would sit in the hot water for an hour while her muscles relaxed. Even though Hugo paid most, if not all, of her rent, they did not live together. Her strict Catholic upbringing forbade that until they were married – a subject that was broached once in a while, but they both agreed that for now, they would concentrate on their respective careers. However, Hugo was a regular at her apartment whenever possible, many times spending the night.

The car she was driving was parked in the roofed parking lot downstairs, on the eastern side of the gym. The vehicle was a blue Lexus, the very latest that her boyfriend let her borrow from time to time.

Brittany felt the exhaustion coming in full swing as she got to her car. She had disarmed the alarm a few seconds earlier by pressing a button on the remote. There were few cars at that time of the night; only a beige Toyota Camry parked besides hers. The place was well lit, and she had done this so many times that it never occurred to her that she could be in any danger.

As she opened the door, a dark figure suddenly lunged at her from behind. She saw it in her peripheral vision, and before her brain could send a signal to her body to react accordingly, it was all over. All she could do was let out a yelp, which was quickly muffled by a gloved hand that covered her mouth.

"Make another sound and you're dead!" Raymond said as he shoved her in the car.

Brittany's blood ran cold. The voice, hidden by a ski mask that exposed only the eyes, nose, and mouth, was raspy, a chilling sound much like fingernails being scratched down a blackboard. And as a demonstration of his determination, he reached over and pressed a blade so hard against her ribs that a trickle of blood was drawn just beneath her spandex tank top.

"Understood?"

"Y-yesss." She was shaking like a leaf as he forced her into the driver's seat.

"Good," Raymond said as he slid lower in the passenger seat, still keeping the pressure of the blade. "Now drive. Head toward Eaton Canyon. Don't even look sideways or at a car that pulls up next to you; and if you so much as look at your phone, you die."

She believed him.

To her surprise, even though she tried not to look, she saw him take off his ski mask and wipe off the sweat from his face. This made her wonder why he would do that, but then she realized if someone saw him in a ski mask, that would most definitely draw suspicion.

He had been watching her, stalking her for the past month to the point where he knew her routine inside-out. She was not the 'pure at heart' victim he was looking for, but a sacrifice was due and she was it. The task had been easy, much easier compared to the rest. He wore the ski mask because there were surveillance cameras around the property and it would be hours before detectives would get to them. By then it would be all over.

Frightened as she was, Brittany was forced to wonder about her assailant's display of utmost confidence. By taking off his mask, he was risking identification by her at a later time, if and when it came to that. It also occurred to her in less time than it took to think that he intended to kill her, but she had a surprise for him. The key right now was to play along as calmly as possible. The moment he let his guard down, that would be her chance. At the same time, she did not want to appear too timid. That, she knew, might arouse his suspicions even further and keep him on high alert. She said a silent prayer.

Neither of them spoke , but Brittany kept glancing at the rearview mirror, obviously hoping for assistance. Unfortunately, the streets were deserted. Raymond had chosen a route that avoided busy streets wherever possible. Throughout the drive, not for one second did he ease the pressure of the blade on her ribs.

This was until they stopped at a traffic light at the corner of New York and Altadena Drive, when headlights flooded the interior from the rear and a Crown Victoria pulled up alongside them a few seconds later. It was painted black and white, with the emblem 'Pasadena Police' printed on the sides. When Raymond glanced sideways at it with a thumping heart, he made out two figures of the officers in the front seat gazing forward, and seemingly not paying attention at the Lexus and its occupants.

Beside him, he felt Brittany stiffen and gather herself. Stealthily, the beautiful woman reached out for the door handle on her side.

"Don't, woman," Raymond said pleasantly. "Don't do it. A stab in the kidneys will cripple you instantly, and blood all over your Lexus' upholstery will ruin its resale value." The statement was delivered with such chilling calm that it scared her into complying immediately. Brittany deflated slowly. One of the officers in the car was now staring across at them. Raymond stared back, though briefly, giving him a lazy smile, and the officer looked away. At last the lights changed, and the Crown Victoria pulled forward and vanished into the night. The Lexus turned left and headed toward Eaton Canyon.

A little while later, the car pulled over at a secluded spot near the wooded area at the canyon. Raymond ordered her out; the knife was still in place.

"Look, why don't you do whatever it is that you want and leave me alone?" Brittany pleaded as calmly as she could while she tried to think of a way to thwart her assailant. She tried to think of what technique to employ, anything that her kickboxing instructor told her that she could remember. What gave her some comfort was the fact that her attacker was not armed with a gun. Perhaps she could fight her way out of this one before he tried to violate her, which is what she thought was most likely what he had in mind.

For an answer, Raymond hit her on the head—not too hard, but hard enough to let her know that he was not about to brook any argument with her. "Didn't I tell you *not* to open your mouth?" he hissed, at the same time violently pulling a strand of hair from her head.

"Ouch! Please let me go," she pleaded again as he led her along a deserted path through the forest.

All was quiet except the noises from the insect world. The moon was out, and up to the left, just at the edge of the cliff, the backs of houses were visible. Their lights were on, and Brittany prayed that someone would see what was happening and come to her aid or call the police. But she knew that the chances of that happening were close to nil. Her attacker had planned this to the last detail, leaving nothing to chance. This she could tell by the way he had her negotiate the path with ease, very much like someone who could have easily carried this out with his eyes closed.

When they reached a hidden spot in the woods, Raymond said, "Stop." He released the pressure of the knife, and in the same motion pulled out the doll that he had in the side pocket of his jacket. "Kneel down," he ordered. *But first, pull down your pants and your panties*, she expected him to say next, but that did not happen.

Brittany did as she was told. She had to make her assailant feel that he was in total control, lull him into a false sense of security. That way he would lay his guard down and that was when she would orchestrate her move. With his other hand, he took out the jute mask similar to the one he used on the first victim and placed it over Brittany's head, which made her shudder as she tried to understand where all this was leading.

"What do you want from me?" she asked, clearly confused and dumbfounded by this latest maneuver.

Raymond then placed the knife in his left hand as the other clutched the doll. He did this after making her turn her back to him.

"You see," he whispered again in that chilling voice that had a frightening effect on her each time. His mouth was just inches from her neck. "A being has to be sacrificed in order for the gods to be appeased."

Oh Lord, another one of those lunatics, Brittany thought. She now knew that she was in the hands of a madman. Any remote chance of being spared was lost—not that the thought of dying had never occurred to her, because it did the moment her attacker caught her by surprise in the parking lot. She had, up until that moment, held out hope for a dramatic rescue, just like in the movies where someone or some circumstance peremptorily decided to meddle. But this was reality. It was no movie. Brittany Gomez again said a silent prayer.

"Oh, so what is this, some kind of occult thing? Why me?" she asked, expecting to be hit again. But it was worth the risk.

Instead, Raymond again said gently as he placed both hands on her shoulders to force her to her knees, "You are the perfect offering." As far as she could tell, he seemed to be going into some sort of trance. The transformation was becoming all the more scary.

As he released his grip on her shoulders to hold the doll in both hands, Brittany sprang to her feet with lightening quickness, thanks to her training. As she did, she struck Raymond with her elbow, right on the neck. The attack was so sudden and so swift in that it staggered him, making him gag and grunt with pain. He was stunned and confused, which gave Brittany time to orchestrate yet another attack. This time it was a well-aimed front snap kick to the balls. The pain was sickening. It was a paralyzing blow, a very common self-defense technique among women.

"Take that, you psycho!" Brittany screamed as she turned to flee, and at the same moment tried to remove the hood from her head.

Raymond clutched his testicles with both hands as he slowly sank to his knees. He was finding it hard even to breathe; and in the meantime his quarry was making a run for it. If she got away, that would be the end of him, the end of his dream. She had seen him and would definitely give the authorities a perfect description of him, which would lead to consequences he could not even begin to imagine, let alone contemplate.

As Brittany ran awkwardly, she still tried to remove the hood. She was panic stricken still, which made her fumble with it a bit, momentarily blinding her and making her stumble into a thicket and fall flat on her face. By this time her attacker had gathered enough strength to recover from the assault and grabbed the doll, which had fallen a few feet away. He immediately tugged the strand of Brittany's hair tied to it. At that very moment, Brittany, who had finally taken off the hood and was already on her feet and running like a spooked deer, felt a sudden and excruciating pain shoot through her entire body. It was a paralyzing pain, like nothing she had experienced before. Her body froze like a rock as she fell slowly like a pole to the ground.

She tried to get up, but her body was numb, deprived of all feeling. She could hardly move a limb, let alone twitch a muscle. Raymond tugged at the strand again. He was at present seated upright on the ground, in full control now and suddenly enjoying the scene. The excruciating pain followed and doubled, causing bile to rise from the pit of her stomach. All of a sudden she could hardly breathe, totally incapacitated by a power she could not describe. She now knew the end was about.

On seeing her body go through the now-familiar spasms and convulsions, Raymond got to his feet. When he got to her, he grabbed her by the foot, methodically placed the hood back on her head, and started dragging her deeper and deeper into the woods. With incredible willpower, Brittany turned to face him. The light from the moon revealed her beautiful, tortured and bruised face as blood started to trickle from the corners of her mouth, ears, and eyes – it was a gruesome sight.

"B-by God I know … y-you are going to pay dearly for w-what you have … y-you have done to m-me. But … I f-forgive you because you're nothing b-but a lost s-soul …" With every word coming out of her mouth, Brittany could feel the life slowly being snuffed out of her.

Raymond gave a sardonic smile that she could almost see even in the darkness as he continued chanting incantations. He was possessed now. *How could people be so stupid,* he wondered, worshipping a God that obviously cared so little about them. His gods, the gods he offered human sacrifices to, demonstrated their power in ways he had never thought possible. He stopped at last under a tree and tugged at the strand of hair one final time, and Brittany turned her head again to face him. In that last moment, he saw the light of life die in the woman's eyes as clearly as a candle go out.

"Let the blood spill, and with it come the success, wealth, and power, for the gods have once more been appeased."

This had been a close call as far as Raymond Pata was concerned. He had become complacent and careless, and that had almost complicated things. He would have to change the way he snatched his next victim, and this one was going to be the 'pure at heart.' The method would be different. As he left the forest after the body was well hidden, he felt the now-familiar excitement and high that happened after disposing of yet another life. His ambition had blinded him to the fact that he had now become a predator. He could not wait for the next victim. He had already had his eyes on her. She was young, beautiful, and fresh. She was a high school cheerleader. He smiled at the prospect of this next one.

CHAPTER 13

Saint Vincent High School in western Pasadena, a Christian school, was also known as a college preparatory school. It was a private school and the tuition was high. Thus, it attracted children from some of the wealthiest families in the San Gabriel Valley and beyond. The campus was also breathtaking, with facilities that rivaled even the great Pasadena City College not too far off. Their football field was state of the art, with bleachers that even had a grand stand for the home fans.

September was always the beginning of football season, and it was no coincidence that Raymond Pata found himself at one of these home games, which also happened to be the opening season home game. It was here at this school that he was eager to find what would be the ultimate sacrifice. The 'pure at heart,' as Baba Brima had put it.

He began attending the football games religiously whenever there was a home game. The games always drew large crowds because this season the school's varsity team was expected to go all the way to the conference finals, and perhaps even reach the state championship game and win it all. They had recruited heavily this past summer and even appointed a former NFL great to be coach. It was easy because his son attended the school. This alone attracted many prospects who had dreams of playing in college, and even the pros—particularly from nearby John Muir High School.

Each time Raymond went to great lengths not to draw attention to himself. He never sat in the same seat twice, nor did he wear the same clothes. Each time he disguised his appearance and tried as best as possible not to be sucked into any conversation. He had learned these things over the past few months when tracking someone. A careless word here or there, or a certain look, could jog a few memories from those questioned in a police investigation that was sure to follow. He did everything to fit in without drawing unnecessary attention – he had to appear as just one of those many fans who loved watching a regular old high school game. So it was little wonder that anybody noticed or bothered him at all.

Conversely, it was not the game that Raymond was interested in but the cheerleaders, or rather one in particular, that he was fixated on. Her name was Lola Hutchinson, a vivacious senior who was also very popular among her peers at school. Raymond knew enough to know that the dark-haired beauty was from a straight-laced, wealthy family who lived in the affluent western side of Pasadena. She was never allowed to stay out later than 10 o'clock at night—except, of course, on special nights like this one. He had studied and mapped out her entire routine to the last detail over the past three weeks, just as he had with Brittany Gomez, and he was almost certain what her next move was going to be.

He left before the fourth quarter ended with Saint Vincent leading the game by two touchdowns over their biggest rival, La Salle High School. He was careful not to make eye contact with anyone for any lengthy period of time as he exited the field at the northern end and went to where he had parked his car. It was now a late model Honda Accord. The Lexus had been disposed of by Larry and his crew, and he got a great deal – four thousand dollars, cash. He drove off into the night, and when he got to Mar Vista Avenue, he turned left and then connected to Fair Oaks north, heading toward Altadena. After crossing the 210 freeway, the neighborhood changed dramatically. He was in the poor part of town.

Before reaching the intersection of Orange Grove and Fair Oaks, he turned left into the vast parking space of a shopping complex. Here there was a Vons Supermarket, a Starbucks at the far end of the northern corner, a Chase Manhattan Bank, and numerous other stores – mostly clothing boutiques, hair salons, and fast food joints.

He pulled up next to a grey 1995 Dodge cargo van and looked around, scouring the area for any suspicious activity. Not that he expected any, but he preferred to be cautious nonetheless. When it appeared that all was normal for a typical Friday night, he stepped out of the car; and, after furtively glancing around again, he walked to the driver's side of the van, pulled out a set of keys from his pocket, opened the door and got in.

As Raymond reached for the gloves from underneath the seat, he felt that familiar excitement again as his heart beat even faster. He was almost at the point where he needed to be, as far as his music career was concerned. He inspected the vehicle one last time and nodded with satisfaction. Everything was in place. He looked at his watch and was surprised at how little time had elapsed from when he left the school.

He looked around again before driving off. This time he made a right turn on Orange Grove Avenue and headed east toward Hill Street, where he made a right at the onramp leading to the 210 east. He drove for close to ten minutes before taking the Sierra Madre exit, and headed north before making a right turn into yet another parking lot of a much nicer shopping complex that catered to the wealthier class of society. He chose a parking space a little farther from the buildings and waited. In front of him was a popular grill that was open 24 hours. He sank low in his seat and waited. He was prepared for a long wait, and that did not bother him one bit. He could be patient as a vulture whenever he chose to.

Around 10:30 p.m., they started arriving. He could tell from all the chatter and banter that Saint Vincent had won the game, and tradition dictated that they all come to the grill and celebrate. They could come even after a loss; but on victory nights, especially victory over an arch rival, the atmosphere was electric.

Most of the cheerleaders carpooled with their teammates, while others rode with their boyfriends, but he knew Lola drove herself. Her car was a red convertible BMW, no doubt one of the nicest in the student parking lot. It did not take long before she appeared with two friends. They were chatting excitedly and still wearing their cute cheerleading outfits. He observed all this from where he was, and in spite of himself and his beliefs, he unconsciously prayed to God that she would come alone. A little later, they disappeared inside the grill.

Raymond waited until the car space next to Lola's was open and slowly backed into it. He made certain that the side sliding door was directly opposite her car door. This time he sank even lower. No one would have noticed that there was someone in the car, unless they looked really hard. However, this time everything happened sooner than he had anticipated. Once inside, before she could sit down and order something, Lola suddenly remembered that she had forgotten her purse in the car and told her friends that she would be right back. That would be the last anyone would see her alive again.

As she was opening the door to her car, she felt something move behind her and heard a footstep. Then a strange male voice said softly, "Hey, Lola." In a split second Lola knew she was in trouble. She turned, got a glimpse of a black handgun—a toy, really, but she had no way of knowing that—and saw a face she would never forget. She tried to scream. With astonishing speed, Raymond slapped a hand over her mouth and said, "Get in the van." The sliding door was already open, and he shoved her inside. He immediately got in after her and slammed the door shut behind, then again slapped a hand across her face and stuck the gun barrel in her left ear. "Not a sound," he hissed.

Almost too horrified to move, she did as she was told. He reached for a roll of duct tape, covered her mouth, bound her wrists and legs; and before long it was all over. The whole process had lasted less than five minutes. No one noticed anything out of the ordinary, and later when consulted, the surveillance cameras at the parking complex were too far away, out of focus, and of no benefit.

On driving back home, this time Raymond took the surface streets, avoiding the freeway just in case. The van, though, was one that could not be traced back to him. He had arranged for such a vehicle through Larry, without telling him why. It had been stolen out of Fresno California a few weeks earlier, and if anyone described the van and read the license plates, it did not matter. It was also a stolen Oregon plate, and there were over a million such vans in southern California. It had all been too easy, and Raymond could not help but smile as that feeling of euphoria swept over him again. It was nothing near the first, but it nonetheless surged through his body like a typhoon.

When he got home, he drove slowly up the driveway and parked as close to the front porch as possible. The floodlight did not automatically come on as it usually did when the motion sensor was triggered, because he had disabled it just in case someone saw him carry the teenager into his house. But he was ever cautious as he jumped out of the van, looked around to make certain that there was nobody around or lurking nearby, and walked quickly to the front door. He unlocked it and left it wide open before he headed back to the van.

He looked around again before he grabbed Lola and effortlessly carried her over his shoulder, into the house. She was still too stunned to struggle, let alone move. He took her to his bedroom, where a makeshift altar made from a trolley was ready, with the doll at the head of it. The room was brightly lit with candles. He placed her on the altar, her short skirt stretched up, exposing mini tights she was wearing underneath her cheerleading outfit. Her eyes were wide open with unspeakable horror.

She looked up with pleading eyes; he was gawking at her in deep thought. The flare from the candles reflected in his eyes. His face was the gargoyle of the devil—it was not human, and it was not sane.

"If I take the tape off, do you promise not to scream? Not that the screaming will help you, but it will only make me mad," he said in a way that made Lola's whole body shudder involuntarily. She nodded yes, still overwhelmed and stunned, wishing this was nothing but one of those terribly vivid nightmares she would soon wake up from. Tears streamed from her eyes.

"You do?" Raymond asked again, very calm. He was in his territory now, totally at ease, but his eyes were what scared Lola more than anything. Again she quickly nodded yes. He pulled off the tape gently.

"Please, mister, don't hurt me please," she managed to whisper.

Raymond smiled again. It was a chilling smile that made her teeth chatter.

"I won't hurt you," he said. It was comforting to hear, but hard to believe. This calmed Lola down, although briefly.

"Thank you, mister, thank you. Now please, let me go," she pleaded. "I won't tell anyone about this, I swear. You want money? Let me call my father, he'll bring whatever you want. Please ... my father will bring the money ... h-how much do you want?"

"I don't want your money," Raymond hissed again. "I just need an answer, and answer truthfully for your sake. Are you pure at heart?"

The scared and confused look in her eyes told him that she had absolutely no idea what he was talking about.

"Pure? Am I pure in heart?" The tears were still streaming down her cheeks.

"Yes, are you pure at heart?"

"Please, mister, I have no idea what you are talking about."

"Have you been with a man?" Raymond glared at her as he leaned closer, malevolent insanity stamped on his face. The foul-smelling incense in the room seemed to have an uncanny effect on him, and for a moment Lola thought she did not quite comprehend what he meant.

"I still don't understand what you mean."

"Are you a virgin?" he asked with a twisted brow, and a look on his face that told the pretty young girl that her tormentor was obviously in the grip of some unseen demon. She instinctively sensed that her worst nightmare was about to unfold before her eyes. She started screaming hysterically.

"Mister, please don't rape me. Please, I'm just a kid, please …"

Raymond, totally ignoring her screams because the room itself was soundproof, leaned forward and ripped the top of her cheerleading outfit, exposing young breasts. Then from the head of the altar, he pulled the doll, raised it above his head and smiled, as he was about to tug the strand of hair attached to it.

"See, I told you I was not going to hurt you, but the gods need your blood." And after a few agonizing minutes, it was all over. Young Lola Hutchinson was dead.

༺༻ ༺༻ ༺༻

The next morning, Raymond was sitting in his living room dressed in his pajamas, sipping on some coffee and making plans to dispose of Lola's body later that evening, which still lay on the makeshift altar. *Rigor mortis* had already set in. The blood from her mouth, nose, ears, and other body orifices had long stopped dripping and had dried up, and some of it had congealed on the floor right beneath the altar. Suddenly, a gentle knock interrupted his thoughts. Raymond felt his hair rising to meet in the middle of his head. Who could it be, knocking at his door so early in the morning, he wondered as he walked to the front door. His testicles still hurt from the kick Brittany had given him. It could have been worse, much worse, he kept telling himself.

He opened the door. A total stranger, a young woman, stood at the other end of the door. She was white and petite, with bright hazel eyes that had the piercing look of a fanatic and also radiated intelligence. She immediately smiled, revealing well-kept teeth.

"Mr. Raymond Pata?" she asked as she extended a handshake.

"Yeah, who wants to know?" His guard was instinctively up.

"Maureen Webb. I'm a reporter with *'The Weekly World of LA,'* and I wanted to talk to you about your band, may they rest in peace, and your music. May I come in, please?"

It's about time. All praise to you, Nana Buluku the god creator, and Mawu goddess of the moon, Raymond thought triumphantly, but his face revealed nothing. To keep up the charade, he hesitated a bit.

On sensing the hesitation, Maureen said, "Oh." She reached into her bag, pulled out a business card and handed it to him, further validating that she was who she said she was. Raymond regarded the card for a moment, as if debating with himself if now was a good time to talk to this woman. After all, there was a body in his bedroom, and the thought made him a bit uneasy. He then thought *what the heck*; there was no way on earth she would know that.

"Okay, come on in ... eh, Miss Webb," he sighed.

"Maureen," she smiled. And then she thought *what a good-looking guy.*

"Excuse me?" he asked as he made way for her.

"Please call me Maureen, as opposed to Miss Webb," she said pleasantly as she flashed another one of her pretty smiles.

"Okay. You can call me Ray, as opposed to Mr. Pata." He returned the smile.

A little later they were seated in the living room. It had been well furnished over the past few months, making Maureen wonder where the money was coming from, especially for a struggling band member; but then she quickly reasoned that he had a wealthy mother who took care of him. She had done her homework. He offered her coffee, which she politely declined.

"Okay, Maureen, what can I do for you? What is it you want to know about me and The Rhythm Makers?" he asked as he settled on his couch and at the same time turned off the television. The local news was going on and on about the disappearance of a local cheerleader the night before at a neighborhood restaurant. The police were appealing to the public for their help, while parents, friends, and the school feared the worst. Particularly now that a serial killer was on the prowl, as this news closely followed the discovery of the body of one Brittany Gomez in the Eaton Canyon forest in what clearly was a ritual killing.

The police instantly suspected foul play in the disappearance of Lola Hutchinson. According to her parents and those who knew her well, Lola had no record of bad behavior or trouble with the law. No history of drug use or eating disorders, so the thought that she could have run away was not even discussed. There had been no signs of a struggle, no sign of anything wrong, and no sign of Lola. These were the observations that authorities made when they found her car exactly where she left it. In light of all this, a search party was being organized. At least a thousand volunteers were ready and willing.

"Do you mind if I record this interview?" Maureen asked as she took out a miniature tape recorder and placed it on the coffee table between them.

"Not at all," Raymond agreed.

"Great," Maureen said. "Let us start from the beginning. Tell me about you, Raymond, and the band, leading to that tragic night?"

It took a moment for Raymond to collect his thoughts and pour out the whole story: his upbringing and his coming to Los Angeles, the forming of the band, the inevitable disagreements, and the recording of their first CD. He would delve into his monosyllable, and at times add a little drama by choking with contrived grief when he talked about the band members, wiping tears off his cheeks with the back of his hand in a way that impressed Maureen. She let him talk, not once interrupting him. And when she posed a question, particularly a hard one, he used as few words as possible. Reporters, he knew, were brilliant in taking loose words, piecing them together, and tying them around your neck.

Maureen, on the other hand, had done her research. She had looked at the police report of the accident. There had been no tampering of the vehicle whatsoever; it had spun out of control because the driver was intoxicated. She had asked people back in Jacksonville, Florida, about Raymond's upbringing but drew a blank. His mother, Jean Pata, was a self-made successful business woman who rose to the top through sheer hard work, wit, and determination, something that was very common among immigrants. She did, however, hear an unsubstantiated rumor that Jean Pata also practiced 'black magic'—voodoo, to be exact. Some neighbors suggested that was how she got to be successful.

Nevertheless, journalism was about printing facts. Cold, hard facts, not sensationalist mumbo jumbo. These were parts of the story that she could not dream of publishing unless she had the facts to back them up. Right now the death of a struggling band that had just recorded its first album and their sole survivor was, to her, the hottest issue.

In the end, she got all that she needed from Raymond and promised to let him know when the article was ready. She left, though with a nagging feeling at the back of her mind that there was something sinister hidden. Perhaps these rumors about 'black magic' were not totally unfounded. The hard part would be to uncover it. But then again, this could all be a witch hunt. She was willing to try anyway, and kept all these thoughts to herself. She would not even share her suspicions with her editor. After talking to Raymond, watching him closely, she knew he knew more—much more, in fact, than he was letting on. Something did not quite add up, especially when Chico told her that Raymond had insisted on having the band members sign everything over to him. Maureen decided right then and there to make it her life's mission to uncover the truth about Raymond Pata. She was not taken in by his charm and killer good looks; there was an unsettling evil behind him that she could not place her finger on. Maureen Webb would later write: "Watching Pata's eyes and face as he spoke, it never occurred to me, at the time, that I was in the presence of a ruthless killer, and that my life could have very well been in danger. A thought that even to this day still makes me shudder. The story that we will never know, and perhaps prefer not to know, is the suffering these poor girls had endured throughout their ordeal."

CHAPTER 14

THE *SAVE A PENNY* LAUNDROMAT, at the corner of Lincoln and Altadena drive, was run down and virtually deserted at night, even though it was open 24 hours a day. It was located in a small shopping complex with a liquor store, a dry cleaner, a thrift store, and a Mexican restaurant. While the place was dingy and a bit neglected, the washers and dryers worked well. This was where Raymond Pata liked to come and do his laundry at least once a month. Even though he had his own washer and dryer at home, there was something about this place that he was drawn to. Perhaps it was the fact that it looked very similar to the laundromat him and his mom used to frequent in Florida when he was a kid. That and the fact that at times, he preferred the solitude of the facility late at night, where he could play his guitar while clearing his thoughts as he was in the process of drying his clothes.

It had been a month since his last sacrifice. The body of Lola had been found in the Topanga Canyon Forest, with the hood still covering her face, confirming the authorities' worse nightmare.

The 'hooded serial killer,' as dubbed by the media, had struck again. Authorities were baffled as they wondered where and when he would strike again. The police were ever more vigilant; their presence was felt everywhere. The surrounding forests were now heavily patrolled by police and volunteers alike, but there was no sign of the killer. A special task force was established, led by detective Doug Willoughby of the Pasadena Police Department. They worked around the clock. A toll-free hotline was set up with a reward that was first offered as $100,000 but quickly sprang to a million. Calls flooded in, of course, but none proved to be credible.

Experts and even profilers from the FBI lent a hand, but so far they also were shooting blanks. A website was created to monitor the search for the killer and filter gossip, none of which proved effective. Doors and windows were bolted. Fathers slept with their guns on their night stands. Little children were watched closely by their parents and babysitters. Police cars were parked in front of the houses of the known victims twenty-four hours a day, ostensibly to make the families feel better. The gossip and the news seethed nonstop, and the surrounding cities talked of nothing else.

The police gave daily briefings for the first few weeks, but when they realized they had nothing to say, they began skipping days. They waited and waited, hoping for a lead, hoping for the killer to make one bad move—the unexpected phone call, the snitch looking for reward money. They prayed for a break, but none was forthcoming. All this time, police were visiting high schools and giving students lectures on safety measures. The cities of Altadena, Pasadena, San Marino and Alhambra took it a step further by enforcing a 9 p.m. curfew on all teenagers. These were dangerous times indeed.

They waited. Detective Willoughby and his partner could not remember when last they had a good night's sleep. His life's mission was now to nail the son of a bitch. All he had to go on was that the killer was Haitian; but that too could be highly inaccurate and lead to charges of civil rights violations and racial profiling. So instead, he prayed for a miracle.

On this particular night, as he was folding his clothes, there were two other patrons in the laundromat. The two were young Hispanic ladies who happened to be in their early 20s. They were also finishing up their laundry when one of them came up to him.

"Hi, do you have change for a dollar?" she asked.

Raymond looked at her for a brief moment, as if debating with himself whether to give what she asked or not, but that was not the only reason. Of late, some uncanny feeling, some sixth sense, told him that he was being watched by someone or *something*. It came suddenly and at times unexpectedly; he had felt it earlier tonight. But as always, he sought solace in the fact that he was protected by forces that defied imagination.

"I need it," he said as he snapped back to reality. "Try the change machine, they have several of them ..."

"We tried," the young lady said, flashing a weak smile. "But none of them will dispense quarters for a coin dollar."

He then made a decision. "Well, in that case, here you go." He reached into his pocket and gave her four quarters.

"Thanks."

"Don't mention it." He smiled as he turned to attend to his clothing.

A little later the two women were gone. He placed his last load into the dryer, and after putting a couple of quarters in, he watched the machine spin and the clothes tumble. He stood in front of the dryer for almost a minute before he went back to the chair that his guitar leaned on and then placed it across his lap. His back was turned to the entrance as he started fiddling with his instrument, trying to come up with a new soft tune.

Things were moving quite well for him. After the newspaper article was published, his phone started ringing nonstop. Producers, both fake and real, were seeking him out. Though the offers were not that enticing, there were one or two who were willing to put something concrete on the table. Case in point, one independent label that claimed to have ties with Warner Records was willing to distribute the album worldwide, give it serious airtime, internet exposure—and most importantly, sign him to a one-record contract with an advance of $25,000. They would also set him up with one of their more popular groups that would first tour the US; depending on how successful that tour was, they would shift to parts of Europe. From there, anything was possible. The offer was pretty generous and almost unheard of in the indie circles, especially for a virtually unknown group whose rise to fame was their tragedy.

Raymond counter offered by saying that he wanted a two-record deal instead, and a $50,000 advance with guarantees of a solo act between performances of the new group he would be a part of. After all—and this he told the young executive in no uncertain terms—he was the next big thing out of Haiti since Wycleaf Jean. The young executive at the indie label wanted to tell him otherwise, but held his peace instead. In this industry, people like him had been known to make mistakes that had cost them their careers, simply because they failed to recognize genius through their own arrogance and lack of foresight. So he told Raymond that he would discuss his counter proposal with his other partners and get back to him in a week. After all, the CD had a lot of potential, and marketing Raymond as the sole survivor could sure bring in sales. He secretly wished, though, that he had discovered the act before their premature demise.

So it was now with a happy heart that Raymond was now playing his guitar. He was convinced that he would hear from them in less than a week. In hindsight, he wished he could have pressed them more on the advance, because doing his own research later after that meeting, he found that the record label *Phoenix Records* had netted a gross profit of over $5 million in the last year alone. Raymond Pata, the self-titled 'Haitian Sensation,' had arrived at last—or so he told himself.

As these thoughts flashed through his mind, he stopped suddenly and turned around. He was sure he heard something, a sound that came from behind like soft footsteps; and again felt that uncanny feeling that he was being watched. He quickly stood up, guitar in hand, and looked around. The place was empty. Everything was quiet except for the sound from the machines. He then dismissed it as a figment of his imagination. Perhaps he was just being paranoid with all this publicity going on, he thought before he sat back down and tried to concentrate on his instrument— which was suddenly no easy matter. There was a sinister chill at the back of his mind, telling him that all was not well.

A little later, he was again engrossed in his guitar when suddenly a soft voice interrupted him from behind. "Hi." It was so sudden and so unexpected that he almost jumped from his chair as he quickly turned around to see who it was. He was not imaging things this time. The voice was real.

A stunningly beautiful and exotic-looking Asian woman stood behind him. It was as if she had appeared from thin air. She looked to be in her early 20s, with high cheek bones and shiny skin that seemed almost pale, as if she had not been in the sun for a while. She also had slightly almond-shaped eyes, not entirely slanted as one might expect. There was a presence about her that somehow radiated a mysterious and uncanny glow. She was smiling, but it was her eyes Raymond seemed lost in. They were dark brown and stunning. She wore a light brown dress that crept a little above her knees. Her legs seemed firm and strong, and her long, dark hair fell a little beneath her shoulders. Raymond Pata had never in his life seen a creation so beautiful and so gorgeous that his heart gave a painful lurch. He wondered what she could possibly be doing in a place like this, and at this hour of the night.

"Oh … hi," he managed to say as he unconsciously sat his guitar aside and slowly stood up. He had been clearly hit by a thunderbolt!

"Is it always this empty at night?" she asked, smiling. Her teeth were perfect white.

"Pretty much," he said. "That's why I prefer coming at this time of the day." He was still battling the effects of the thunderbolt, and the stranger picked up on what he said quickly.

"Oh, so do you live in this neighborhood?"

Raymond's antennas were immediately up. He sensed that this was by no means an idle question. He stared at her for a while. There was something about those gorgeous eyes, something mystical about them, that he could not place a finger on, but he was totally mesmerized by them. Nonetheless, something did not seem quite right about this woman.

"Are you a cop?" he asked before he could stop himself. And when she did not answer right away, he pressed on. "You are, aren't you? What's with the thousand and one questions, lady?"

She looked at him in astonishment, as if not knowing what to say next. "Of course not," she said. "Look, if you don't want to talk to me, that's fine. Sorry I bothered you." She turned to leave.

Raymond sighed, cursed beneath his breath and quickly went after her, arm stretched for a handshake. "Look, I am sorry I was rude. It's not often that you see a pretty woman at this time of the night, in a dingy place like this," he said pleasantly.

"It's okay," she said taking his hand in hers for a brief handshake. It was cold.

"And yes, to answer your question, I do live in the neighborhood," he said. "Are you new around here?"

"You could say that. I'm just looking for a decent laundromat, and I guess this is it," she said. The woman's aura was so intoxicating that Raymond could not help but smile.

He deliberately enunciated his next response in an attempt to raise his charm. "That is correct."

"Do I detect a slight accent? Where is it from? I totally love it," she said, truly intrigued.

Now we're getting somewhere, Raymond thought. "I'm originally from the Caribbean, Haiti to be exact, but I grew up in Jacksonville, Florida. That's where the rest of the family is."

"What brought you to southern California? I'm Geraldine Chung, by the way. And you are?" She stretched her slender arm again for a handshake.

"Ray … Raymond Pata, but you can call me Ray. Everyone else does. Wow, your hand is cold. Where did you live before you came here?"

For the briefest of moments that he held her soft hand in his, he felt a sensation that sent goose bumps along the back of his neck. He had never in his life been overwhelmed by the presence of another being as he was just now, not even the great Baba Brima. He wondered why.

"Some place far, and let us keep it at that for now." She was coy with her answer and this puzzled Raymond for a bit. But he recovered in time; just to keep up appearances, he turned around to start folding his clothes. He was still keen to continue the dialogue, and she could tell.

"Oh, I see. No biggie. Why tell a complete stranger your whole life story anyway, right?"

Geraldine smiled again. Her mysteriousness was overwhelming, and that only seemed to add to her magic. "Trust me, Raymond, I feel as though I have known you for years. So you're no stranger to me."

The statement was flattering to the ear. Little did he know that someday in the future, he would grasp its true meaning. "Oh, and how so?" He grinned from ear-to-ear. "Do I remind you of some friend ... or boyfriend, perhaps?" He was almost hoping that she would say that she had seen him in the 'Weekly World of LA.' After all, his picture had been flashed purposefully.

"Oh no, no, nothing like that ... you just look very familiar, that's all."

Under normal circumstances he would have reminded her that it was because he was on his way to becoming very famous, but he bit his lip instead. Even a fool would know that such a line would be fatal to a woman he was trying to woo. He had to be modest, even humble. He could not even mention that newspaper article. All this was new to him, and he knew he had to learn fast. Blowing your own horn could definitely be a turn-off.

Instead he said, "Oh ... I see." And then he decided to press his luck. "So, is there a boyfriend in the midst?"

She looked up to the ceiling and rolled her eyes in a suggestive manner. "Maybe, maybe not. Like I said, I'm new to this part of town."

That was the answer Raymond was hoping for, or at least it was as close as it got. "Good, and since you are new to this area, would you allow me to buy you a cup of coffee from next door?" The Mexican joint was the only one open in the mini complex this late.

"No thanks, but I wouldn't mind chatting for a bit while you fold your clothes. That is, if I am not imposing on you."

Imposing? Far from it, fame truly has its rewards. "No, no, I don't at all." *Are you kidding me?* "It's not every day that you get a chance to meet a lovely lady in a place like this." He had been there so many times, and this definitely was a first.

She smiled again. He could not help but wonder how she looked naked.

"Why thanks, Raymond," she blushed. "It's just that sometimes I get a bit restless when in a new environment, and I don't usually get much done the first day. Even sleep becomes elusive. That's why I decided to go for a night walk."

That explains it.

"I'm glad," he blurted out; a response that earned him a strange look. "Oh, what I mean is that I am glad your walk led you here. A guy just feels lucky when a chance meeting like this happens, especially when there is no woman he can share a conversation with while folding his clothes." He left the last statement open to interpretation, hoping and willing that she would swallow the bait. She did.

"And by that, it is safe to assume there is no woman in the midst?"

He thought of Sofia, their brief and at times passionate affair—but all the same, full of friction. "Not anymore," he said.

"Oh," Geraldine said.

"That's the way it is with men and women, right? It never lasts."

The beautiful stranger gave a long sigh before saying, "I agree."

Raymond seized on it as he looked up at her. "Really, you do? Why?"

She looked at him for a moment. Again he was lost in her eyes, and there was something about them that he could not quite yet grasp – captivating as they were.

When she did not answer him right away, he egged her on gently, "No, I'm interested, really."

"I was just being agreeable," she said, flashing those white teeth. It was almost inconceivable that someone could be this beautiful and totally captivating at the same time. In the brief moment that he had come to know her, Raymond Pata was awed by this woman; she conjured feelings in him that had been dormant for a long time. Dormant because he was chasing his dream with impunity – regardless of who he harmed along the way until he reached the top, which now seemed very much within his grasp. All of a sudden he felt he needed to be with a woman on his side when he 'arrived,' and he had come to the conclusion that this stranger was that woman, even if he had to employ all the powers bestowed on him by the gods.

"I see," he said. "Having said that, though, I believe one woman is always enough," he continued.

"Oh, so you are a one-girl guy?"

"That's right," he affirmed with no hesitation whatsoever, in a way that even impressed her.

However, when she responded with, "Right," her tone implied that she did not believe him.

He then decided to push his luck even further. "Actually, I am looking for her right now, and who knows? You just might be her." He smiled hard, but inwardly winced, not sure if he had scared her with that statement. Still, he knew this might be his only chance to lay his cards on the table.

"Do you say that to every girl you meet, Raymond Pata?"

He loved the way his name last name rolled from her mouth. It was sensual, damn near erotic.

"No, Geraldine, I have always believed in forgetting your head and following your heart. If you haven't loved, you haven't lived. Always stay open, because you never know when lightning will strike." He had heard or read that somewhere, but made it his own nonetheless. She was impressed.

"Wow. Poetic, but I see what you mean." She then paused and added, "It's nice to meet a man who can express himself." There was no doubting her meaning, and Raymond's heart soared.

A beautiful woman had practically appeared from the dark shadows of the night and availed herself to him. He could not believe his good luck. Luck he immediately attributed to the all-powerful gods he worshipped with a zeal that would even shame Baba Brima. In his heart, he said a short but powerful entreaty, thanking them mightily.

"You know, you never gave an answer to my first question," she continued.

For a moment Raymond was at a loss, wondering what the question was. "And what was the question, by the way?"

"What brought you to southern California?"

"Oh, opportunity. See I play a little music, and I came out here almost two years ago and formed a band." He was somewhat convinced that she knew all this, but at the same time he had to sadly admit to himself that not everyone read 'The Weekly World of LA.' Chances were that she did not know about Maureen Webb's lengthy article about him and the deceased members of 'The Rhythm Makers,' and that he had been the sole survivor.

"Band? Cool, how do you like it? I have always wondered what it's like to be a part of something like that." She was intrigued, very much like a groupie that followed bands wherever they toured.

"It was great while it lasted," he said with just enough in his voice to sound sad.

"While it lasted?" The smile was now replaced with a look of curiosity.

"Yes," he said without looking up.

"What happened? Everyone went their separate ways, is that it?"

He did not answer right away, deliberately sparking her interest. "No, tragedy," he said, as if words were suddenly hard to come by.

At this she raised her eyebrows. "Tragedy?" she asked almost in a whisper.

"There were five of us, and we had just finished recording our very first CD. Right after the celebration that night at the house of the producer, my friends were involved in a terrible car crash. The driver, Jeremy Yee, bless his soul, who was also our drummer, somehow lost control of the vehicle and it hit the center divider of the freeway. It capsized and then caught fire – everyone perished in the flames. It was, terrible Geraldine, terrible," he said with sadness in his voice. He forced a tear, mainly to invoke sympathy from her and to show that he was a man also very much in touch with his feminine side. It worked, because she was visibly moved.

"How awful. When did this happen?"

"About six months ago." He wanted to add that it was all over the news and in the papers, but again, he held his tongue. He hoped he would tell her in the very near future, after a night of heated passion. The thought alone inflamed his erotic imagination to a point that he felt his manhood stiffen. "But it feels as if it just happened," he continued.

"I bet."

"You know, I keep asking myself, why wasn't I in the car with them? Why was I the sole survivor of the group? I mean, I should have …"

"Oh no, Ray," she interrupted tactfully, sensing that this could lead to a total breakdown over a tragedy that happened so recently. "You can't blame yourself for what happened. There was nothing anyone could have done," she added kindly as she patted him on the shoulder.

Raymond pretended to consider this for a while, and slowly nodded—as if he'd finally understood the full import of her words and had at last found serenity.

"I suppose you are right, Geraldine. I never really thought about it that way."

She looked at him with pity, and again he was lost in those deep brown, mysterious eyes.

"I really hope that you will find peace within you, Raymond, and know that fate took a stand against you in the most surprising manner. It was death, the grim reaper himself, who betrayed you." At the mention of the word 'death,' her face took on a menacing intensity, but it lasted less than a split second. Enough for Raymond to think that he had imagined it. He digested her words for a moment.

To find safer and more comfortable ground, Geraldine asked, "You mentioned that you guys recorded a CD, right?"

"That's right." Raymond's face beamed once again, and his eyes sparkled, still glassy with tears.

He went on to tell her about the possible deal currently being negotiated with a reputable label. He was prudent enough not to disclose the monetary figures involved, at least not now, but she was impressed all the same. Even though it must be said that he embellished the whole thing, to a point where it looked as if all the major labels were tripping all over themselves for his signature.

"Wow. That is a great accomplishment, Raymond," she said.

"Thanks."

"I would like to hear it. Is it something I can download? Oh, I forgot—it's not out yet."

"I can give you a signed copy," he said eagerly, already anticipating another meeting, which hopefully would lead to a date where the deal would be closed with her.

"Really? That would be neat. How much do you want for it?" She was intrigued as she clasped both hands and looked him in the eyes.

"Are you kidding me? Nothing, just consider it a gift." He smiled. It was a wide and inviting smile. She was already living and breathing in his wildest fantasies.

"That's so sweet, Raymond," she said softly.

"Oh it's nothing, Geraldine." By this time the clothes were long forgotten. In fact, everything was—the sacrifices, the media, the hopes of superstardom, time. Everything had come to a standstill in the presence of this woman. She had to be his, and his alone. *Totally*.

"What was the name of your group, by the way?"

"*The Rhythm Makers*," he said with pride. After all, the group's name was his idea. Some of the members, like Sofia of course, thought the name was tacky and on one or two occasions told that to Raymond in no uncertain terms. In hindsight, he realized that was where the tension between them had started. And her orchestrating the move to strike '*Caribbean Rose*' off the track list of the album sealed the deal. It was the last straw that broke the camel's back.

"Nice name."

Now here was someone who appreciates genius, he smiled inwardly.

"So what was it? Raymond Pata and '*The Rhythm Makers*'?" Again his name rolled off the tip of her tongue in a way that gave him nice chills.

"No, just '*The Rhythm Makers.*' Wish it was that though, with my name," he admitted with a laugh. He had really wanted to have his name come before the title of the band, much similar to greats like *'Bob Marley and The Wailers'* or *'K.C. and The Sunshine Band..'*

"I know, I was just teasing. And what is the title of your CD?" she wanted to know.

"Caribbean Rose." Of course, he had the title changed after the death of the other members; even the agreement they signed without reading through had stipulated that. However, he had made sure that it was in fine print. "It happens to be the name of our favorite song," he lied with a straight face.

"Now I can't wait to listen to the entire CD."

"Don't raise your expectations," he cautioned. "Because you may find that it totally sucks and you'd be disappointed, and we wouldn't want that now, would we?" It was a great attempt in an area he was not used to – modesty.

"You're just saying that, Raymond," she smiled. "And you wanna know what's exciting about all this? For me, at least."

"What?" he asked, anxious.

"You're the first musician I have ever met with a CD to his name."

He was instantly and truly flattered to hear that. "No way ... really?"

"Yeah. Are you embarked on a solo career now?"

"Trying," he replied with the twisted brow of someone in deep thought. "I do sing once in a while at *'The Dug Out.'*"

"The what?"

"The Dug Out," he answered, and when he saw the blank look on her face he went on to say, "Oh, it's a popular club in Old Town Pasadena. But it's been hard without a band."

Shortly after the newspaper article was published, he also got calls from many bands similar to his willing to offer a helping hand, or so they alleged, by having him join them. The truth really was that Raymond Pata was the man of the moment, and having him be a part of their singing group would be great for publicity on their end. In this industry, publicity was gold, but he was smart enough to know their true intentions and so declined their offers one after the other. However, he did perform with one particular group that he rather liked. It was according to him 'on a trial basis,' when truth be told he just wanted to make a grand public appearance after the tragedy. What better way to do it than at a popular nightclub? He was invited again by the same group, but lately he had been putting them off with one excuse after another.

"I can imagine that," she said.

"But the new album I'm working on is proving to be the therapy I need, and I will be dedicating it to them," he lied again. He wanted them forgotten, erased completely from his memory as if they had never existed. To him, they were simply a means to an end.

"Now that's awesome," she said.

Raymond snapped his fingers, as if an idea had just struck him. "I tell you what, how does your day look like tomorrow?" he asked, anxious to get a response that would make his heart soar once again.

"Pretty open," she said with no hesitation. "Why?" Raymond's guitar by the chair suddenly had her full attention.

"Farnsworth Park is not too far from here," he said quickly. "We can meet there tomorrow, and I can bring you your signed CD." *And after that, we can go out for dinner.*

"How nice. What would be the best time for you?" She finally took her gaze off the guitar and faced him.

"Say late afternoon, around five, does that work for you?" It was fall, and in southern California at that time, dusk set in quickly.

Again she answered with no hesitation. "Absolutely."

All this was going smoothly –too smoothly, in fact. Raymond Pata could not believe his luck, and the most gratifying feeling about all this was that it was just the beginning. He said another silent prayer to the gods.

Now that they were certain to meet again, Geraldine looked around, and then at her watch. It was time to leave apparently. "Oops! Gotta go, my time's up. It was nice talking to you, Ray," she said, once again showing those healthy and beautiful white teeth.

"No, no, no, the pleasure was all mine." As he said this in the most sincere tone, he gently took her arm and kissed her hand, like a servant kissing the hand of a queen. "Wow, are you feeling cold, Geraldine?"

She smiled and said, "No, I guess I'm just cold-blooded."

They both laughed as they appreciated the joke. She turned to leave, but halfway across the laundry room, she turned back.

"Oh, I forgot something. Got a pen?" she asked.

Raymond always had one in his pocket. That and a note pad. He kept them in case he needed to jot down crucial information about a possible victim, or if he was hit by a sudden jolt of inspiration strong enough to write the lyrics of a song that suddenly came to mind. He quickly got the pen out of his pocket and handed it to her.

"Here you go."

"Let me see your hand," she said somewhat mischievously.

He did not even dare to ask why as he simply complied. She then wrote a number on his arm. The touch of the pen on his skin gave him another rush of goose bumps.

"That's my number. Call me anytime," she said. This was incredible. She was now his; he was convinced.

"Thanks, Geraldine," he managed to say. This move had taken him by total surprise, and he found himself almost gasping for air.

"You're welcome, Ray. Just don't forget our date tomorrow." Would he ever? She was already leaving again.

"Appointment," he managed to blurt out.

"Excuse me?" she turned around quickly.

Raymond was smiling. "It's an appointment. There's a difference, you know."

"Gotcha," she smiled back. She was so damn beautiful!

And just like that, the flirtation was over. He watched her as she left, and then turned to get the miniature notepad he'd placed on the chair. He turned again to take one last look; but she had already left, making him wonder if she had practically run out of the place.

"What a woman," he said to himself.

The task of folding clothes, which not too long ago had seemed very important, was now insignificant. He just stood there fixated, staring at the entrance where she'd walked through. He finally sighed and started putting the clothes in his laundry bag, not even bothering to fold the rest. Then suddenly, as if on an impulse, he rushed to the door, obviously going after Geraldine as if there was one more thing he wanted to say to her. Mainly it was for another look at the woman who had so viciously swept him off his feet.

There was no sign of her. Not even a car pulling out of the premises, even though he recalled that she said she'd walked. He looked this way and that – nothing. He even rushed to the back of the laundromat, hoping against hope that he would see her. It was not to be. It was as if she had simply vanished into thin air, the same way she had appeared to him. Disappointed, he headed back inside the laundromat. At least he had her number, and the plan was to wait at least an hour or two before calling her. However, he had to admit to himself that this was not going to be an easy thing to do. He *had* to see her again, or at the very least speak to her, keep the conversation that he had enjoyed going. He almost forgot that they were set to meet again in less than 24 hours, but that now seemed like an eternity.

After stuffing all the clothes in his bag, he did not leave right away. Instead he kept glancing constantly at the number she had written on his arm. He was debating with himself whether it would be a good idea to call her so soon after meeting or not. Finally, he could no longer resist the urge. He could say he was making sure she got home all right. So he pulled out his smartphone and started dialing. There were eight or nine rings before a generic answering service came to life.

'No one is available to take your call right now, please leave a message after the beep.'

He did not leave a message after the beep. He hung up, grabbed his clothes and the guitar, and headed to his car. He looked around again in a desperate attempt at a chance to see her. *This is insane,* he thought. *I will see her tomorrow. Why the hell am I tripping like this over a girl I just met?* He knew these were just thoughts to console himself. He was sprung in a way he never could have imagined.

Later when he got home, he went straight to his bedroom and lay on his king-size bed, smartphone in hand. He was not tired, but still felt the need to lie on his back and gaze at the ceiling in deep thought. Who was this woman, this Geraldine Chung? And why had she had such a profound impact on him, in a way that no other woman had before in the past? He realized this was no coincidence that just as he was on the brink of superstardom, a beautiful woman—a woman more stunning than a vision, at that—had literally walked into his life. *How many such women existed out there*, he wondered. He could only come to one conclusion: They were destined to meet at this juncture of his life. It was fitting that he shared his success and glory with a woman of Geraldine's stature. One thing hinged on the other. He *had* to make her his.

He dialed her number again, which he had already put on speed dial. He made a mental note to take a picture of her when they met again. Not that one was necessary, for he was already obsessed with her; that much was clear. The thunderbolt that struck him was still in full effect. Again he was met by the generic answering machine.

He cleared his throat before speaking in a well-rehearsed tone. "Hi Geraldine, this is Raymond Pata. Sorry to call you so soon, but I must say what a real pleasure it was to meet you this evening, and I look forward to seeing you tomorrow. Nothing will give me greater joy. Take care, and don't let the bedbugs bite."

He hung up and lay on his bed in deep thought. What was it about this woman that had him so twisted? He tried to recall every detail about her, however minute. She was petite, but athletic looking at about five feet four and a half inches. She had an immediate impact far greater than her size or appearance could explain, as though she were clothed not merely in a long dress with spaghetti straps on her elegant shoulders, but in some powerful magnetic field that bent the world to her.

Her soft voice had been musical, and the mere thought of it brought back the goose bumps all over his body. Each time he touched her, albeit briefly, he felt an almost supernatural quality to the moment that half-convinced Raymond *she* was some sort of apparition, that her touch had been achingly gentle precisely because it was a barely real, ectoplasmic caress. The woman herself, however, was too powerfully present to be a heatstroke illusion. Petite but dynamic. More real than anything in the day. No! He had to see her again, and this time he would never let her out of his sight.

He dialed her number again, and like before had to endure the disappointment of listening to that damn answering machine.

'No one is available to take your call right now, please leave a message after the beep.'

Once more with well-rehearsed speech, he said, "Oh hi, Geraldine, I just remembered that I did not give you my number when I left my message a few minutes ago. My home phone is 6265551255, and my cell phone number, which you can probably see on your screen, is 6265552295. Take care now, and good night once again."

He hung up, and for a very long time he looked at the phone hopefully, willing it to ring. He was in turmoil now as it looked like insomnia was going to set it. After ten minutes, which to him felt like ten hours, he redialed her number and again the generic answering machine greeted him. *This is ridiculous; why am I behaving like this?*

"Geraldine, one last thing. So sorry for being a complete nuisance, really, but you can also friend me on Facebook. While there you can visit our band's page, which in turn will connect you to our website, and you will know all about our songs and *'The Rhythm Makers.'* Well that's it, I suppose, and I look forward to tomorrow. Remember, you can call me anytime."

He put just enough emphasis on the word 'anytime.' He meant it that way, twenty-four-seven. Things would not snap back until he touched her again. It was not until a few minutes before 5 a.m. that he finally fell asleep.

CHAPTER 15

MAUREEN WEBB WAS A WOMAN on a mission. Yes, the Raymond Pata story and the demise of the band was now old news as far as the paper was concerned; this was the general consensus following the publication of the article, a week after her face-to-face with Raymond. She was objective as she was sympathetic, especially when covering the lives of the deceased and the careers that ended before they even began. She kept her personal opinions to herself, even though she periodically fought the urge to spice it up a little, so to speak. It was after the publication of this story when Raymond Pata's phone started ringing off the hook.

It was naïve, she knew, to think that Raymond Pata had a hand in the deaths of his band members, but the nagging thought at the back of her mind would not go away. This was amplified when she finally met him in person. In some cases, he was evasive in his responses, especially about the contracts he had them sign before the accident. Did Raymond know that they were going to die? And if so, how? There was only one way to find out, and to do that she had to head to Jacksonville Florida, and dig into Raymond Pata's past.

She kept all these thoughts to herself. When she asked her boss for a few days off, he did not ask her why but only when she thought she would be back; and when she stated that she was not sure, he just told her to keep him in the loop. With her father's help, she managed to get all the assistance she needed from the Miami Police Department, and also from the Jacksonville Police. She got to know more about Jean Pata, a self-made successful business woman who owned a cleaning business, now estimated to be worth 2.5 million dollars. She was a legal resident now and ran a legitimate business, so the file on her was thin. She had no criminal record, save for a few parking citations and fines that occasionally came with the cleaning business. She also paid her taxes.

There was, however, no file on Raymond Pata, for the simple reason that he had never been in trouble before. She wondered if she'd made a mistake coming to Florida, and assuming the worst of a man who really just happened to be lucky or smart enough to not be in a car full of and driven by drunks. She could not fault him for that. She understood this had been nothing but a witch hunt. She had *wanted* there to be something sinister, so she could unravel a story sensational enough to merit a Pulitzer. Maureen Webb had been blinded to the truth by her own burning ambition.

Beaten and discouraged, she packed her travel bag in the motel room she had rented close to the airport. On her desk were scattered papers, all public records, about Jean Pata. She was planning on tossing and then burning the file, as she now had no use for it.

As she started putting the papers in a folder one at a time, she stumbled on a piece of information that she had overlooked. It seemed as if Jean Pata's cleaning business had skyrocketed after the death of one Erlinda Ramos—who also had a cleaning business, but on a much larger scale than one run by Jean Pata at the time. Upon digging further, she found the cause of her death – car accident. With a thumping heart, she started making the necessary calls. An hour later, she could not believe what she had stumbled on.

After reading the accident report some clerk at the county office was kind enough to fax to her, she immediately drove her rented Mercury Coupe to Jean Pata's old neighborhood. With much prying, under the pretext that she was an IRS tax auditor, she was able to jog a few memories. After Maureen showed a picture of Erlinda Ramos, a neighbor confirmed that the deceased woman had a quarrel with Jean. It was Erlinda doing all the jawing one morning when she drove up to Jean's house threatening to turn the Haitian woman over to the authorities and have her deported for among other things, operating a business without a license. Not too long after that, Erlinda died in a car wreck on the Miami turnpike. Maureen did not even have to look closer to notice that there were deadly, if not identical, similarities to that crash and the one suffered by the band. The neighbor even half-jokingly added that it had been a closely guarded secret that Jean Pata practiced voodoo, and that she had cast a spell on the Ramos woman.

Maureen was still shaking with excitement when she boarded the last plane to Los Angeles later that night. She had to ask herself a very difficult question that went beyond her professional training and personal beliefs when it came to the occult. Did she believe in this voodoo gibberish? And could she bring herself to accept as true that Raymond Pata had learned this from his mother, and had in fact cast a spell on his fellow band members? Could she really write such a story and not get laughed out of town? That was the question.

She would have to dig even deeper to get to the truth, and she knew that was not going to be easy. She ordered a martini to calm her nerves and thought about what to do next. Added to this, she had personal concerns that plagued every young woman in Los Angeles – there was a serial killer on the prowl; one who targeted young women, it seemed.

CHAPTER 16

FARNSWORTH PARK, a beautiful place, is located at the very northern part of Altadena, just at the foot of the Mount Wilson mountain range up on North Lake Avenue. It features cinder pine trees, park benches, tables, and a few tennis and basketball courts, as well as the William H. Davies Recreation Hall. It was built in 1934 during the Great Depression, and includes a breathtaking outdoor theater and stage. Many hit movies, including the cult classic *Dirty Dancing*, were filmed here.

This was the setting where Raymond Pata chose to meet the woman who had struck him with that thunderbolt and subsequently swept him off his feet – Geraldine Chung. Even though he was casually dressed in khaki pants and a white polo t-shirt, he looked and smelled good, eager to make a good impression again. That was assuming he'd done so the first time, which was why he believed she'd chosen to initiate a conversation in the most unlikely of places, at that time of night. He'd brought a box of chocolates and a bouquet of flowers—not roses, but the type that conveyed he had serious intentions of pursuing a relationship with her. He had spoken at length with the young store clerk at the flower shop. He also made sure to bring his guitar and the signed CD he had promised. He had already rehearsed, in earnest, the song he was going to sing for her. He was in very high spirits.

It was almost 5 p.m. and the winter sun started slowly setting. Very soon it would be evening, a great time to ask her to join him for dinner at the nearby *'El Patron,'* which was a popular Mexican restaurant at the corner of Lake and Altadena. In great anticipation, he'd already made a reservation for two.

He sat on one of the park benches after carefully placing the bouquet of flowers and the box of chocolates on the side. He then placed his guitar on his lap, ready to play it the moment she came. He smiled to himself in anticipation of the arrival of the beautiful woman.

The wait proved to be a nerve-wracking affair. He kept glancing at his watch time and again. He looked around—there were people engaged in all kinds of activities, playing basketball, tennis, exercising; and parents with their children, watching them as they played on the swings and slides. There was no sign of Geraldine.

After an hour, darkness began setting in rapidly. *Where* was she? He stood up for perhaps the hundredth time and looked around, searching desperately, wondering what could have possibly happened. After all, meeting today was perhaps her idea just as much as it was his.

His thoughts were interrupted by a plastic ball that rolled to his feet, coming from behind. This was shortly followed by a little girl dressed in jeans and a sweater. She had long brown hair and looked to be about 11 or 12 years of age. He bent over, picked up the ball, and handed it to her with a forced smile on his face.

"There you go, little one," he said, glad to divert his attention away from the thoughts that were clouding his mind right now.

"Thank you, mister," she said as she picked the ball. She looked bright and full of life, beaming with all the innocence of a child.

She was about to take off when Raymond Pata, with a complete lack of sense or thought, asked, "How long have you been playing in the park, little one?"

Maintaining a safe distance, the child looked at him for a while before giving an answer. "My mommy told me not to talk to strangers."

To put the little girl at ease, he gave her one of his best smiles, one that he had been practicing on the mirror all morning and afternoon. He then looked past her and at the lamp that had finally lit up, spreading part of the park with its glow. He knew he had to appear normal. In this day and age of child molesters and kidnappers, one could be arrested for just looking at a child funny.

"Well, mommy is right, but I need to know something."

"What's that?" Her eyes were now suddenly focused on the guitar that was still resting on his lap.

"I'm waiting for a friend of mine. She has long hair like yours, maybe a little longer. She is Asian and really pretty. Have you seen someone like that around here?" He was desperate and he knew it.

"You said she was Asian? Like Chinese?"

His heart began to soar. Forgetting that this was southern California; there were millions of women who fit that general description.

"Yes, absolutely. Have you seen her?"

She paused for a while as if in deep thought. This kind of reaction was unusual for a child her age, he thought as he waited patiently for an answer.

"No," she said and ran off, disappearing into the night to reunite with her parents and possibly siblings, he assumed. He gritted his teeth in frustration.

"Phew! That went well," he muttered to himself as he once again pulled out his smartphone, checking if there were any missed calls or text messages. There were none.

It was a little after 8pm when he finally clued in to the fact that Geraldine had stood him up. He stood up, quaking in every bone; he got his guitar, and the chocolates and flowers, which he soon tossed in a trash bin. Perhaps there was a reasonable explanation to all this. She probably had an emergency of some sort and thus could not make it to a phone. He also knew these were just thoughts to console himself. The truth—the naked, ugly, messy truth—was that he probably would never see her again. She was one of those types of women who flashed brilliantly into someone's life like a meteor, and then vanished. He understood immediately that Geraldine was that kind of woman. The hard part would be forgetting all about her.

෴ ෴ ෴

When he got home later that night, the first thing Raymond did was down two stiff vodkas before he settled on his couch to check his messages and missed calls – again, nothing. There was one message on his landline from the record producer. He was still eager to sign the deal, and from what Raymond could sense, he was willing to meet all his demands if they could meet soon. But all that was not important at the moment.

He wondered what could have gone wrong. He had her in the palm of his hand, already fantasizing about the great life they were going to have; and like a puff of smoke, all that fantasy was just that—a fantasy. Another long slug at his drink, and the phone rang. He had left it on a small table a little out of reach, and almost knocked over the bottle of vodka as he grabbed it. He did not even bother to look at the screen to see who the call was from.

"Hello … hello … G-Geraldine?" he suddenly was out of breath.

It was a gruff male voice at the other end. A voice he did not want to hear at the moment, because it meant trouble.

"Geraldine? Raymond, it's me." It was Larry Allen.

Shit, Raymond thought to himself. He tried to adopt the proper tone in his voice. "Oh, yeah? What's up, Larry, how have you been?"

"Never mind the formalities, Ray. Why haven't I heard from you in a while?"

He tried to think of something sharp to say. "Well, I have not found the car you need just yet." The car he was supposed to deliver was a white 2006 Range Rover.

"It's been over a month now and the guys are on my back, getting a little antsy. They want the car now, as in yesterday."

"Tell them to relax, Larry. I will get it soon." The truth was, at the moment all of this was far from his mind. In fact, he had totally forgotten that he had a job to do for Larry. Lately, he had set up a lucrative syndicate with some South Americans. There were cars that could not be stripped and sold for parts, but they could be put in a container and shipped south through a very sophisticated and profitable system. Larry was determined to keep his clients happy. They were the ones who paid the most money, and at this rate he figured he could retire in less than three years.

"When?" Larry wanted to know. He could not help but wonder what had gotten into Raymond lately. He seemed distracted, not enthused like he normally was. He had become sloppy. Worse, Larry had relied on him heavily in the past, because he always delivered on time with as little trouble as possible, considering everything that could go wrong in this type of business. This was not like him, and Larry was determined to find out sooner rather than later.

"I said soon," Raymond snapped.

"No, no, that's not good enough, Ray. I need a definite answer. I mean, after all, you were paid in advance." It was true. Conversely, Raymond wanted to tell him where to shove it—after all, he was about to hit it big—but he knew he could not easily walk from this. The excitement, the 'juice,' as some people called it, was never easy to let go.

He decided to bluff instead. "Oh, you don't like the way I'm doing my job? Hell, I'll give you your money back."

Larry chuckled, not for a moment calling him on the bluff. "Knowing you like I do, Ray, I know you done spent it by now."

Raymond could feel his blood boiling, and the vodka. "I said I'll get it, dammit!"

"Easy, now. A deal is a deal. They need the ride by Friday."

"Hey, man, that's the day after tomorrow."

"You've been paid, Ray; it's time to deliver."

Raymond paused as he thought about this for a moment. "Sunday ... that's the best I can do," he said at last.

The line was silent for a while as Larry thought about this.

"Okay, Raymond," he said at last. "I can hold them off until Sunday. But if you don't have the ride by then, they're gonna want to smell blood or money – it's your choice."

"Is that a threat?" Raymond was reeling now. Everything seemed to be going wrong, and he could do nothing to arrest the avalanche.

"Take it any way you wish, Ray. Their words, not mine, partner." To preclude any further conversation, he unceremoniously hung up on him. It also indicated that he meant business. A bad day had just become worse. But it was not Larry's implied threat of imminent danger that had his mind fixated as he poured himself another drink. He was still wondering how that beautiful woman could have slipped through his fingers. At that moment, the thought of never seeing her again was far beyond the limits of his imagination.

There was something else on his mind, too. The new moon was almost out, and he needed to perform another sacrifice. It had been three months since the last one, but now things were getting a little harder. The police and the public were more vigilant, aware now that a serial killer was on the loose. Much as he hated to admit it, in a way the urge was getting stronger every day. He needed to kill again. But just as they'd been for the last 24 hours, his thoughts were on Geraldine.

He took another sip at his glass, pulled out his smartphone and checked again for missed calls, messages, or even a text – there was none. He looked at his home phone. The screen on the answering machine read 0:00. He finished the strong liquor in his glass and stood up to go to his bedroom. At that moment, something strange and bizarre happened. The nearly empty glass he had been drinking from, which he had left on the table, tipped over from an impossible angle, spilling the small amount of liquor that was still in it. Soon thereafter, a book fell from the bookshelf and onto the floor. Raymond felt the little hairs at the back of his neck rise.

Such a thing was impossible, Raymond knew that. And yet his brain was reacting to what his eyes were showing it. His bowels turned to water as he looked around in sheer terror and recalled Baba Brima's warning. *Because if we do this, Raymond, there is no turning back – ever! We are unleashing mysterious powers that we have no control over, and the consequences could be dire!"*

He looked around, and then at the ceiling. "Bear with me," he managed to say beneath his breath as his teeth chattered in horror. "A sacrifice is forthcoming." He could almost feel the walls closing in on him. Now more than ever, he needed to find that woman—not to kill her, but to have her complete his life.

Once in the bedroom, he logged on to the internet on his laptop and checked his email. He had already done that on his smartphone, but for some twisted reason he hoped this time, the result would be different. There was no email from Geraldine. Raymond Pata was a tormented man as he stepped into the shrine.

He looked around before falling on his knees as he clutched the doll close to his chest; this after taking it from just above his head where he'd placed it in a sitting position. The hair strands of all his victims were still tied to it.

"Hear me now, *Nana Buluku* the god creator, and *Mawu* goddess of the moon. Lead me to the woman I have fallen head over heels for, the woman they call Geraldine Chung. For that, and for your protection, I shall spill more blood for you before the next full moon. I know I have been lacking of late, but I promise you this will *never* happen again, so long as you can help me find this woman."

CHAPTER 17

OVER THE NEXT FEW DAYS, Raymond Pata's behavior became more bizarre. Food suddenly lost its taste; colors, the fresh smell of flowers, and the outdoors seemed nonexistent. The only way for things to snap back would be if and when he saw the mysterious woman again, and made her his for all time.

For this reason, he would periodically take long drives along the freeways and drive through nearby cities. He spent the nights roaming the city, loitering around shopping malls, cinemas, boutiques, and any of the other places where women liked to gather. He was often seen at Fawnsworth Park, and at times at the laundromat—gazing at places from a distance, lost in another world. He knew it was irrational. He knew it was almost inconceivable that he would run into Geraldine this way. She would not be found unless she wanted to. Nevertheless, he kept up the search, watching faces. He couldn't quit. He had to do something.

One Sunday morning, he walked aimlessly on Ventura Boulevard in Sherman Oaks, an affluent city some 15 miles west of Altadena, off the 101 freeway. He walked past a beauty salon, one of many he had passed by over the last few days. Why and how he ended up in this city, not even he could tell. As he walked slowly, hands in his pockets, he glanced rather absentmindedly inside the salon. Several women were having their hair done, and some were getting a manicure.

He had barely walked past the business when he suddenly stopped dead in his tracks. His brain was frozen in shock, and his heart gave a painful lurch. He felt as if he free-falling inside an elevator. There was a woman in the salon he'd glimpsed, but it did not hit him until a few seconds later that she looked very familiar. *It was Geraldine*!

Raymond quickly backtracked, and without another thought rushed into the beauty salon. He was almost out of breath when he walked, or rather stumbled in, startling the women in the process. There were several of them, and two men working at their booths. They all stopped what they were doing and stared at him. His gaze was aimed at the woman sitting at a booth at the very end of the store, near the back door. He then quickly realized his mistake. The woman was not Geraldine.

Her name was Brenda, a young, attractive woman with long dark hair who looked to be Persian and in her 20s. The woman who was working on her hair was short and stout. She was the owner, and her name was Natalie. Like the others, she immediately stopped what she was doing and studied Raymond for a moment.

"Yes, may I help you, sir?" Natalie asked with a smile.

He studied her for a while, slightly embarrassed. She was light-skinned with a round, happy face that she always wore for clients and potential customers.

"Eh ... pardon me, ladies. It's just that when I saw you," he nodded at Brenda, "I thought you were a friend I hadn't seen in a long time."

Natalie smiled and said, "I see. Well, no sweat, sweetie, it happens."

"Sorry for the mix-up." He forced a smile; his eyes were still fixed on Brenda.

"No problem," Brenda said as she flashed her teeth.

Raymond turned to leave as he briefly wondered if he was losing it.

"If you don't mind me saying," Natalie said, "those are some pretty neat dreads you've got going on."

Raymond turned around and gave her a wide and inviting smile, which was genuine this time. A smile he always flashed whenever his ego was stroked.

"Thank you … thank you very much," he said.

"How long did it take you to grow them?" It was Brenda who asked this time.

"These took seven years. The ones I had before, I had since I was four."

"Really? Wow." Natalie was impressed.

"What made you cut them the first time?" Brenda wanted to know.

Natalie looked at Brenda, and then said, "Brenda, that's kinda personal, don't you think, girl?"

"It's okay. Well, the truth is that I wanted to see how I looked without them."

He was trying to keep appearances when he was really itching to bolt and resume his search, futile as it was. But the women would not let him be.

"Liked what you saw?" It was the Persian woman again.

"I would say the answer is pretty obvious now, don't you think?"

"Brenda," Natalie intervened. "All these questions. What's up with that? Can't you see that you are bothering this nice gentleman?"

For an answer, she looked at Natalie and then said, "Come on, Natalie. I'm just curious, that's all."

It was obvious by the way they spoke and interacted that they were friends, besides being customer and client. They both smiled at him, and he could not help but reciprocate. He was starting to warm up to them at last. For a moment, they did take his mind off other matters.

"Nice talking to you, ladies. I have to get going." At that moment he got the feeling he'd outlived his welcome.

As he turned to leave, Natalie's voice stopped him in his tracks. "Who does your hair?" she asked, obviously fishing for a new customer.

"Excuse me?"

"What I mean is … do you have a personal hair dresser?"

"No, I don't think I need one. I do it myself." At least for now, but soon I will even have a personal manicurist.

"Well, you never know. Let me give you one of my business cards … just in case."

Raymond was about to protest, but then he thought better of it. Natalie searched first in her apron pocket, and then looked around for one. She looked over to one of her male colleagues, who up until then, besides a brief nod when Raymond walked in, did not seem to have acknowledged his presence. He was a young black man who also looked to be in his 20s.

"Hey Joey, you got one of my cards?"

Joey placed the hair trimmer he had been using on a small glass table next to his booth and searched his pockets, but like Natalie, he came up empty.

"Sorry, Nat, I ain't got one," he said.

Natalie looked at another woman who was also busy with a customer.

"How about you, Alicia?"

The young white woman shook her head 'no' and said, "Sorry, Nat."

She looked at Raymond, raised her index finger and said, "One second, please."

Her pace was fast and brisk for someone her size as she pulled a key from her pocket. Raymond walked with her and stopped at the entrance, watching as she headed to the cars parked by the cab on Ventura Boulevard right in front of her store. He froze again, not believing what he was seeing. Natalie was walking straight toward a white 2006 Range Rover—the exact car he was looking for.

Serendipity, Raymond, you lucky son of a gun, he thought to himself as he was engulfed by a wave of euphoria. He watched her deactivate the alarm, open the door, and from somewhere in the glove compartment pull out a box of new cards, two of which she handed to him as she walked back into her place of business. This was going to be too easy, he thought as a smile crept to the corners of his mouth.

"Thank you very much," he managed to say, still finding it hard to keep his eyes off the vehicle. How could he have missed it? Right away, he had to admit that it was not the car he was looking for, but the woman who in that one brief encounter had managed to divert his focus from everything else, including a potential deal of a lifetime which was the key to making him '*The Haitian Sensation*.' The intricate task of finding that particular car had suddenly become a piece of cake.

All he had to do now was move his car to an all-night parking place, come back and wait until night fell. As an added bonus, he could even offer Natalie, who had led him to the car, as a sacrifice to the gods. Again he was impressed by their awesome power. He already had all the items he needed, including the doll and a hood for his next victim, hidden somewhere in his car.

"You're welcome," Natalie said as Raymond was ready to leave at last. "And like I said, you never know. Our rates are competitive, and I can personally give you a great discount."

I'm sure you can, Raymond thought as he forced himself to focus on one of the cards she had given him.

"Thanks again," he said and left.

The woman watched him until he disappeared out of sight. They were silent for a while before Natalie broke the ice. "Cute, isn't he?"

Brenda smiled mischievously and said, "Not bad at all. Nice butt, too." They both giggled.

"Did you detect an accent?" Natalie asked?

"I sure did. I was trying to place it, and when I couldn't, I thought of asking him, but then you interrupted me."

"Even though he sounded American, I could notice what I thought was a Jamaican accent."

When Brenda answered, she mimicked the Jamaican accent. "Yeah *mon*, I think he's from Jamaica, *mon*."

"I hope he comes back," Natalie said.

"I bet you would." And they both chuckled.

Meanwhile outside, after reaching a safe distance, Raymond pulled out his phone from his pocket and dialed a number after making certain there were no missed calls or text messages. It was Larry's number he had dialed.

"Hello," Larry said.

"Larry, what's up? It's me, Ray." He could immediately hear the other man sigh on the other end.

"Ray, I thought I told you that ..."

"Shut up and listen," Raymond snapped. "You said your guys are looking for a white 2006 Range Rover in mint condition, right?"

"Yeah," Larry concurred, and Raymond could almost hear the other guy stiffen at the other end of the line.

"I may have just found one for you, so call off the dogs, and tell them I will have it in no time."

It took a lot restraint for Larry to keep from shouting with joy and relief. His top performer was back at full throttle. "That's wonderful news, Ray," he said. "I knew I could count on you."

"The hell you did, you son of a bitch." He laughed, and so did Larry. This time it was Raymond who had the pleasure of hanging up on him.

Now all he had to do was wait until dark to take the car. There were quite a few places in the area where he could sit and wait. He did this by not staying in one place for too long, and even at some point bought a hat, which he later discarded.

⸎ ⸎ ⸎

It was already dark when Raymond decided it was time to make a move. He was well prepared. He had his black hooded sweater and a black pair of jeans to match. His car, the Toyota Camry, was parked at a 24-hour parking structure. He had already paid for three days in advance, so he was not worried about it being towed away. He would come for it after delivering the Range Rover.

He had all that he needed with him for this exploit: the hood, the doll, leather gloves, and the tools to bypass the alarm system. He felt and welcomed that familiar excitement he always experienced whenever he was about to pounce on an unsuspecting victim. He felt alive again. This feeling momentarily took his mind off Geraldine. He waited from across the street, keeping his eyes on the vehicle and immediate surroundings. Because it was a Sunday evening, there was not as much traffic on Ventura Boulevard as there normally would be on a weekday. He could not believe his luck. The gods were once again smiling at him.

When traffic cleared, he looked around one last time before he quickly crossed the street and hurried to the car. He glanced around again; there was no one in sight. Good. He attached a magnet to the driver's side door, took the slim jim from inside his sweater, and he quickly opened the back passenger door. In no time he was in the back seat and immediately lying on the floor. This was done with all the finesse and expertise of a pro who'd done this type of thing on more than a dozen occasions.

Some 45 minutes later, the door to the salon opened and the unsuspecting Natalie came out, after she'd turned off the lights and closed the drapes to her windows. She was done for the day. There was a bag strapped to her left shoulder, and she had the keys in her right hand as she pointed the remote at the car and pressed the button on it to deactivate the alarm. She was forced to press it several times before it finally deactivated. Natalie found this to be a little odd, but did not give it too much thought when it finally worked.

Meanwhile in the car, watching her like a hawk, Raymond got ready. He had the blade and hood in position. She did not glance at the back of the car, even for a second. Raymond was about to pounce when suddenly the door to Natalie's beauty shop opened again, taking him completely by surprise. He could have sworn that Natalie was alone all this time.

Out came a tough-looking young black man he had not seen before. He was in his late 20s or early 30s. It was Jamal, Natalie's younger brother. He was using the restroom while Natalie was getting ready to close. Raymond's heartbeat accelerated as he ducked even lower to the floor of the car. He had not anticipated the presence of another party.

Just as he was getting ready to bolt out of the car, Natalie and Jamal got inside. The passenger door to his right was locked, and he knew any movement from him would most certainly give him away. He was trapped, and the opportunity to bail was lost the moment the car started moving. He laid even lower, his dark clothes giving him cover. He had his knife ready just in case he needed to fight his way out. He chided himself for not bringing the toy gun that looked like the real thing. Dreading the idea that Natalie might see him, he controlled his breathing—something that was suddenly very hard to do—and waited for his chance to escape undetected. He dared not think of the repercussions if he was discovered.

"Really appreciate you waiting on me, sis," Jamal said. He was breathing heavily, something that was common with people his size.

Raymond heard Natalie say, "This is the last time, Jamal, I mean it. Why couldn't you have Hannah pick you up?" Hannah was Jamal's on-and-off girlfriend.

"We got into a fight, remember?"

"Yeah, you and her always getting into fights. And then I gotta clean up your mess."

They were heading east, and Raymond's plan was to quickly unlock and open the door on his side, and then disappear into the night the moment the car stopped at a traffic light or intersection. He could not wait for any other opportunity, because for all he knew, they could be heading to the 101 freeway. Once there, that would make things even more complicated. He clutched tighter at his blade and kept wincing with pain every time the car hit a bump.

"You think Bobo is gonna like sitting in the back?" Jamal asked.

"He's a dog, Jamal. I don't think he'll mind at all."

"It's just for a couple of days, you know, right?"

Natalie sighed before saying, "That's what you always say, and then I end up keeping him for a month. And just when he starts getting used to his new environment, you yank him away."

"He's my baby, Natalie. I think he prefers to be with me."

"Yeah, right," Natalie laughed. "Have you taken him to obedience classes yet? Because he's a bit vicious for my liking. Not toward me, of course, but to anyone outside the family."

"He's not that vicious, Natalie. It's just that, as you say, he prefers family members. That's all," Jamal said.

All this time in the back, Raymond's heartbeat accelerated with every passing minute. *Wait a minute*, he thought. *Are they talking about picking up a vicious dog?* It was time to bail, and soon. What had looked like a routine cinch of an exploit was turning into something he could not even have imagined in his worst nightmare. At that moment the vehicle slowed down, made a turn and came to a complete halt. *Perfect.*

"Why are you stopping?" Jamal asked.

"I got to pick up something from Alicia. I'll be right back."

"Who?"

"Alicia, one of my girls," Natalie answered.

"The white girl?"

"Yeah, and what does it matter?"

"Nothing," Jamal smiled. "Just wondering. Don't take too long."

She opened the door to her car and stepped out. They were parked in front of an apartment building at the corner of Ventura and Vincent Street. Skyline Apartments, where Alicia lived, were not too far from her shop.

It was Raymond Pata's best chance to skedaddle, and he intended to do just that. He could always come back for the car, or find another. Jamal leaned his massive body forward and reached for the controls to change the radio station. His sister liked the soft type of music, since she found it relaxing after a long day at work. Her brother preferred rap and hip-hop, the type of music you would find on stations like Power 106.

As Jamal was searching for the station, Raymond saw his opportunity. Slowly and carefully, he stretched his arm and reached for the handle. The door was still locked. He moved his hand until he was able to touch the knob that unlocked the door and pushed it. There was a snapping sound, which startled Jamal.

"What the hell?" he said as quickly turned around, just in time to see Raymond opening the door. "Hey!" Jamal shouted. "What the hell are you doing?" He lunged at him, moving incredibly quickly for someone his size, and grabbed Raymond by the arm—who stabbed Jamal on the hand. This forced him to release his vice-like grip. Jamal managed to rip part of Raymond's sweater, but he was able to make his escape after falling knees-first to the pavement. He got up quickly and vanished into the night.

Jamal jumped out of the car, gun drawn, but his nimble quarry was nowhere in sight. He cursed loudly as he looked this way and that. His hand was on fire; blood was already dripping from the wound. The cut was not deep, but it hurt badly. At that moment Natalie came rushing toward him from the front entrance of the apartment building, closely followed by Alicia. Natalie was horrified.

"I heard you shouting. Jamal, what's going on?" she asked, her eyes wide open.

Jamal was breathing heavily; still searching the surroundings with his eyes. He went to the back seat of the car, discovered the hood that Raymond had left behind, and showed it to his sister.

"Look," he said, still breathing hard.

"What the hell is that?" Natalie wanted to know.

"There was a man hiding in your car, Natalie."

For a brief moment his sister thought she had not heard him correctly. "What? You're lying." She was shocked beyond reason.

"No, I'm not. He left this behind," he said as he waved the hood in front of her face with his good hand. "And look at my hand."

Natalie unconsciously took a step back and clasped her mouth with both hands. It was all she could do to keep from screaming in sheer terror. The situation appeared more dire than she had originally thought.

"Oh my God, Jamal, are you okay? What happened to your hand?"

"I'm fine. The bastard stabbed me before I could tackle him. That's how he managed to get away."

"Did you get a good look at him?" Natalie wanted to know.

"Not really. I was gonna, but that's when he stabbed me."

Natalie thought about this for a moment, and then she suddenly gasped. "Oh my God, Jamal ... you don't think it was him, now do you?" she asked as she unconsciously lowered her voice to a harsh whisper. Her heartbeat gathered speed.

"Who?"

"Him," she said as if her brother could read her mind. "He's been on the news, but not as much lately."

"Who, dammit?" Jamal took a step forward.

"The hooded serial killer," she replied.

Jamal looked at her with a twisted brow, as if trying to make sense of what she was talking about.

"The hooded serial killer?"

"Yeah, don't you read the papers, or at least listen to the news?"

Jamal was starting to get a bit agitated. It was just like his sister to make him feel as if he was out of touch with life's important events.

"Obviously not," he snapped.

"Well, there's been a string of unsolved murders in the valley and far-off places like Altadena and Pasadena over the past year or so. All connected, the authorities say. They say this creep, whoever he is, targets young women in dark alleys and parking lots or something like that, and then takes them to the mountains or another secluded place for some ritualistic killing," she said.

Her brother gave her a strange look. "Ritualistic killings?" he asked incredulously.

"Yes, because all the bodies they found have had a hood on their faces, and according to the cops, the victims die a horrible death of choking on their own blood and vomit."

Jamal winced at the thought. "Jesus H. Christ! What kind of sick bastard does stuff like that? And how in the hell do they know they're ritual killings?"

"Because of the way the bodies are found, and the fact that their faces are covered in a strange hood."

"Goodness gracious!" Jamal exclaimed. In spite of himself, he wondered how on God's green earth he could have missed hearing about such a killer lying in wait; especially in this day and age where news travelled faster than the speed of light.

Natalie came closer to her brother and hugged him, making certain not to inflict further pain on his injured hand. She was overcome with emotion as she rested her head on his massive shoulder. There were tears rolling from her eyes.

"Oh my God, Jamal," she said. "You saved my life. The psycho was waiting in my car for me, and he couldn't act on his intentions because you were there," she continued. "I'm so glad you and Hannah had a fight, I really am. Otherwise I would have been dead."

In contrast, Jamal gritted his teeth in anger—not only because the near-victim was his sister, but he had missed his chance of catching a high-profile killer, the most wanted man in California today. He would have been a hero, most definitely. The media, the newspapers, the magazines, they would have sought him out. Even the police and the mayor would have wanted to make his acquaintance, no doubt, and all his past troubles with the law would have been forgiven and forgotten. Damn!

Aloud, and before his imagination got inflamed even further, he said, "Man, I would have given anything to lay hands on that fool for trying to hurt my sister. He done crossed the line now." He punched his fist into his open palm, ignoring the pain it caused to his injured hand.

"How do you think he managed to get into the car without setting off the alarm? I always activate it, you know," Natalie wondered aloud.

To this, Jamal said, "Trust me, Natalie, these idiots know how to bypass any alarm system. I saw how they do it on the *Discovery Channel*. This scumbag is obviously a pro."

His sister twisted her brow as a thought came to her. "No wonder the alarm was acting a little funny," she said.

"What are you talking about?"

"When I tried to deactivate it when I got off work, it wouldn't respond as it normally does."

Jamal nodded with comprehension as Natalie reached into her bag and took out a headscarf that she used to gently cover the wound on her brother's hand.

"You know what?" Jamal snapped his fingers as a thought came to him.

"What?"

"This is something we must report, like right away. Much as I don't like them cops, I feel they should know about this," he said.

"So we should head to the station?" Natalie wanted to know.

Jamal shook his head. "I say we call and tell them what happened. Maybe they'll send some detectives and forensic experts, or some shit like that, to come look at the car. You just never know. He could have left fingerprints or anything that may help them in tracking this guy down."

"You're right," Natalie agreed, silently impressed with her brother's mode of thinking. She pulled her cell phone, and after making certain she had done an adequate job on his hand, she dialed 911. Afterward they waited for the police to arrive, something the 911 operator promised was going to happen very shortly.

ৼৢৢ৾ ৼৢৢ৾ ৼৢৢ৾

Around the same time, Raymond Pata was on his way back to Altadena—grateful for the narrow escape, but reeling over the missed opportunity. The encounter with Natalie's big brother had shaken him. He would have to be extra careful next time. Perhaps he was becoming complacent again, and that very well could be his undoing. But he knew he had to find another car similar to Natalie's... and soon. After all, he had promised Larry that he was going to deliver it. To admit failure right now was something he was not willing to do. It was bad enough that he was thwarted by Natalie's brother, but telling Larry that was tantamount to being emasculated.

However, as it had succeeded in doing over the past few weeks, the image of Geraldine flashed before his eyes, making him forget the urgency and the possible danger of his situation with Larry. He had to find that woman somehow, but he had no idea how he was going to accomplish that.

When he arrived home, he was still breathing hard, obviously dazed by the near miss. To calm himself, he rushed to the liquor cabinet—something he was doing more and more lately—

and slugged at a bottle of brandy straight without bothering to pour it in a glass. Within a minute, he was calm again. He walked over to his landline; there were no messages. He then went to sit on the couch, bottle in hand, and was soon lost in thought as he gazed at the ceiling.

CHAPTER 18

DETECTIVE DOUG WILLOUGHBY was a very troubled man. He could not remember when he'd last slept. The 'hooded serial killer' case was wearing him down, both physically and emotionally. Hard as he tried, even with the help of the Feds, he was getting nowhere. There were no leads and no trace of the killer – nothing. Meanwhile, more bodies had been found. Worse, the father of one of the victims, Lola Hutchinson, was a friend of the Pasadena mayor. The father had been leaning hard on the mayor to find the perpetrator, who in turn raised holy hell with the Police Force.

People were questioned. Known criminals, even those with no history of violence, were hauled in for impromptu interrogations. In some instances, individuals' civil rights were blatantly violated, all in search of the killer. The cities of Altadena, Pasadena, and South Pasadena clamped down hard on the mandatory curfew for teenagers to be in their homes by 10 p.m. Other nearby cities, like Alhambra, Monrovia, Arcadia, Glendale, and Eagle Rock, followed suit.

Neighborhood watches were intensified. The police department's tip line, which had been established after the first victim, was inundated day and night with calls, all of them bogus. An FBI profiler was consulted again and again. Detective Willoughby and his partner, Detective Jen Russo, worked to a point past their mere physical limits. They also hoped and prayed for a miracle—something, anything to crack this thing wide open. The task force worked around the clock as well, and for the moment the cities seemed to be in a state of emergency, ready to blow up if that call did not come.

The call did finally come, and it was from a woman named Natalie Anderson in one of the unlikeliest of cities – Sherman Oaks. The moment Natalie dialed 911, after stating what her call was about to a now very alert operator, she was patched through to the lead detective on the case, a certain Detective Willoughby. He had insisted that such calls, no matter how frivolous they may seem, should be forwarded to him. Soon thereafter he was talking to Natalie at length.

He asked her all kinds of questions, first to establish if she was for real and not one of those nitwits who just called for the sake of garnering attention of some sort. He'd had his fair share of those. He instinctively pressed the 'record' button the moment the call was connected.

Even though Detective Willoughby would later replay the tape over and over again in the next few days, weeks, and some say years; he could recite the conversation verbatim right after he hung up.

Detective Willoughby: Willoughby speaking, how may I help you?

Natalie: Yes, hello, this is Natalie Anderson. I was told you are the detective in charge, is that right?

Willoughby: Yes, that's right. How can I help you, Miss Anderson?

Natalie: Well, sir, my brother and I may have had—let me rephrase. I think we may have had an encounter with someone we believe may be the hooded serial killer.

Willoughby: Okay, you've got my undivided attention, Miss Anderson.

Natalie: It was my brother, actually, detective.

Willoughby: And what's your brother's name, if I may ask?

Natalie: Jamal.

Willoughby: Okay, tell me exactly what happened, Miss Anderson. I want to know why you think it is the man we're looking for.

Natalie: (sighs) Fine. And please, detective, it's Natalie.

Willoughby: Okay Natalie, I'm all ears.

Natalie: I own a beauty shop in Sherman Oaks on Ventura Boulevard. I had just finished my day at around 7:30 this evening, and I left with my brother. I had to stop by one of my employees' apartments, she lives just a few blocks away. I left Jamal in the car. It turns out that all this time, there was someone hiding on the floor in the back of the car. He tried to make his escape, and that was when my brother saw him. When Jamal tried to grab him, he stabbed his hand and then took off.

Willoughby: Okay, this could have been some bum high on something and trying to find a place to crash for the night. How could you be certain that …

Natalie: No, no, detective, it was nothing like that. He left some things behind that made us believe it was him.

Willoughby: (heart racing) What kind of things?

Natalie: A hood for one, and items my brother believes were tools he used to break into the car.

Willoughby: Now Miss Anderson, I mean Natalie, I want you to think carefully about what I'm going to ask you. At any time during the day, did you see any suspicious-looking person hanging around or maybe walking around your shop?

Natalie: Eh, I would have to say no, detective. But there was a guy who walked into my store this afternoon. Just a case of mistaken identity, I guess, because he thought one of my clients, Brenda, was an old friend. It turned out she was not. Other than that, there was nothing out of the ordinary.

Willoughby: (heart racing even faster, but his voice calm as snow) This guy, can you describe him?

Natalie: (chuckles) Of course. About six feet tall, give or take, very cute with dreadlocks.

Willoughby: Anything else?

Natalie: Brenda and I thought he might originally be from the Caribbean. Jamaica, to be exact.

Willoughby: (keeping his euphoria in check) What makes you say that? Is it because he had dreadlocks?

Natalie: No, he had a slight accent, which we could only guess was Caribbean.

Willoughby: Did you get his name?

Natalie: Come to think of it, he did not give a name and I did not think to ask. But I gave him one of my business cards in case he needed my help with his hair. Come on, detective, don't tell me you think it's him. He is definitely not the type.

Willoughby: Oh no, not at all, Natalie. We just have to cover all bases, that's all. Now, do you have any surveillance cameras in your store?

Natalie: No, I never had a need for them.

Willoughby: Oh, okay. Now, you mentioned Brenda, who is she?

Natalie: Oh that's my friend and client, Brenda Hussein.

Willoughby: Any chance I can speak to her, too?

Natalie: I don't see why not. We can come to the precinct together if you like and give a statement, but I doubt if she can help much.

I will be the judge of that.

Willoughby: Okay now, listen to me carefully, Natalie. A squad car should be there any minute now to secure the car and the surroundings. Please don't touch anything, even the doors, until our crime scene unit is done. You think you can do that?

Natalie: Yes, but does that mean you are going to impound my car?

Willoughby: If we do, it will be for no more than a couple of days. And not to worry, we will take care of you and your brother.

Natalie: Okay, do you still need to speak to Brenda?

Willoughby: Yes, that would be great.

Natalie: I'll try and get her here as soon as possible.

Atta girl. If only witnesses were as cooperative as you, the world would be a much better place and our jobs much easier, he thought.

Willoughby: Very nice of you, Natalie. Now just hang tight. I'm coming from Pasadena, so I should be there inside an hour.

Natalie: Okay, I will wait … oh, and two squad cars from the Sherman Oaks Police just pulled up.

Willoughby: Great. Would you kindly hand your phone to the first officer who comes up to you? I would like to speak to him.

Natalie: Sure thing, detective.

Willoughby: Thank you, Natalie. My partner and I are on our way. See you soon.

And there the conversation ended. The detective thereafter replayed the tape over and over, before he called his partner to come into the office they shared. Jen Russo walked in, stirring coffee in a paper cup. She too was exhausted and had also not slept much over the last few months. But Willoughby had to admit her stamina was compelling, even though this case was threatening to bury them both.

"What is it?" She stared into the older man's eyes, searching.

"I have just been informed that the hooded guy may have been spotted in Sherman Oaks, about twenty minutes ago," he said.

Russo maintained her cool demeanor, even though her hands were on the verge of shaking with excitement and euphoria.

"By whom?"

"I just got a call from a Natalie Anderson." He was already reaching for his jacket, which concealed the firearm strapped to his waist, but his badge was still visible. "Apparently he was hiding in her car, and got into a scuffle with her brother, a kid named Jamal."

"How do they know it was him?"

"He left a hood behind, and a few other goodies. Let's get moving. I'll play the recording for you on the way."

"Great. And if he left any salvageable DNA, we can see if it matches the one we got from the first murder and hopefully nail the son of a bitch," Russo said excitedly.

"That's assuming he's in the system," Willoughby said.

"At this point in time we can only hope and pray. And while we're on it, let's get a sketch artist to meet us there."

"Already done. Also, what was that thing about Professor Duncan saying this type of ritual killing is common in Haiti?" Willoughby wanted to know.

"Yeah, that's what he said," Jen Russo answered. "Why?"

Doug Willoughby said, "The lady said they spoke with someone today who came to their store, and that someone might have had a Caribbean accent."

"You think that could be him?"

"I don't know. It's all conjecture at this moment, but I will take anything. For months we've been clutching at straws. This might be the log we've been waiting for," he said as they hurriedly walked out of the Pasadena Police Precinct and toward their car, a late model unmarked Crown Victoria.

"By the way, have you had any luck finding Haitians here in Pasadena?" Willoughby asked his partner.

"Quite a few," she replied. "Even one who performs once in a while at the *Dug Out* in Old Town. He was part of that band that died in an accident not too long ago."

"I see," Willoughby said thoughtfully.

He had already opened the passenger door of the sedan, something he did out of sheer habit, and a little while later they were on their way to Sherman Oaks to meet Natalie Anderson and her brother. Both of them were silently wishing that this was the lead, the miracle, they had been praying for.

֍ ֍ ֍

On the other side of town, in a single bedroom apartment in the city of Burbank, the reporter Maureen Webb was packing a suitcase getting ready to head to the Los Angeles International Airport. Her destination: Port-au-Prince, Haiti. She was on an undertaking to find more about the voodoo occult and its connection, if any, to Raymond Pata and his mother, Jean.

CHAPTER 19

THE NEXT DAY AT TWILIGHT found Raymond Pata in Farnsworth Park yet again. Like before, he was seated on the same bench and facing east, guitar in hand, playing softly and absentmindedly. Wondering where the woman was, and how his burning ambition could suddenly have been pushed so far onto the back burner. Sean Miller, the young executive at the *Phoenix Records* indie label, had called again that morning. The eagerness in his voice was all the more evident now; he was willing to set up a meeting with Raymond the day after next. After consulting with the other partners, they had agreed to Raymond's demands. Sean wanted to sign the contract as soon as humanly possible and start, as he put it, 'raking in the money by the tons for both of them.'

This was great news, of course, but until he tracked down that woman and made her his, all this seemed pointless. Raymond Pata could focus on nothing else. His heart was still aching – where on earth was she? At the moment, that was the million-dollar question.

"Hello, mister," a shrill voice interrupted his thoughts.

Raymond quickly lifted his head and saw a little girl gawking at him. He had not heard her approach. When he took a closer look at her, he realized she was Natasha, the same little girl he'd had a brief encounter with a few days ago. He was amazed.

"Hi," Raymond said as he quickly looked around to make certain there were people around. This was to reassure them he was harmless, in case any one of them thought otherwise.

The next words from the bright-eyed little girl's mouth almost made him spring to his feet, but through sheer force of will he managed to stay put.

"I saw your friend," she said easily. Like before, her eyes were focused not on Raymond, but on his guitar.

Raymond gasped, his heartbeat accelerating to what he would later describe as 110 miles per hour, but he was careful not to startle the kid.

"You what?"

"I saw Geraldine," was the bombshell from little Natasha.

Raymond almost dropped his guitar, but he fought to maintain his cool. "What did you just say?" His voice was almost hoarse.

"That's her name, right?"

At that very moment, another voice interrupted. "Excuse me, sir, did you say something?" a man walking a white poodle close by asked Raymond. He had a strange look on his face; a look normally reserved for those who were mentally unbalanced.

"No," was the curt reply from Raymond.

The man hurried away, but Raymond's attention was too focused on Natasha to give the matter any thought. "That's right." His eyes were almost bulging with fascination.

"Can you play that thing well?" Natasha asked, still gawking at the guitar. Her eyes would momentarily flicker from the instrument to his face, and then back to it again.

"Yes I can, as a matter of fact, little one. But tell me again how you know Geraldine." He was anxious to keep her focused at the matter at hand and not be distracted by the musical instrument. She could damn well have it, for all he cared.

"My brother and sister got to meet her as well."

"When was this?"

"The other day, she came right after you left," Natasha said with no hesitation. This was unbelievable. Here he was, suffering over the last few days when in fact they had just missed one another on the appointed date. And to think he had been coming to the park ever since, and only today did he discover that. If only he had run into this kid—or rather, she'd run into him—the next day, maybe he would have been spared the crushing pain. He did wonder why Geraldine had not bothered returning his numerous calls. There had to be a logical explanation to all this; there just *had* to be.

"Wow, this is unbelievable," he muttered to himself.

"What was that?" Natasha asked.

"Oh, nothing. Are you sure it was her, little one?"

Instead of answering, Natasha suddenly faced the other way and called out, "Xavier! Edith! Come here."

Two other kids, a boy and a girl who up until then he had not noticed, came running toward them, giggling. They had apparently been playing tag and seemed out of breath when they got to them. They looked to be no more than ten years old, very much like fraternal twins. They both had curly hair, obviously biracial, and were stunningly beautiful children.

Xavier was the first to ask, "What is it, Natasha?"

"I was telling this man that we saw Geraldine," Natasha said.

"Who?" Xavier wanted to know.

Natasha said, "The woman with long hair, remember her?"

Raymond could barely conceal his delight.

"Eh, mom said we should not talk to strangers," said Edith. All three children looked so much alike, it was almost uncanny.

"Your mommy is right," Raymond said quickly, in a way that was placating. "But don't worry, you are all perfectly all right, because I will not hurt you," he reassured the kids.

When he looked around, he saw an elderly white couple who at first were going to walk past him and the kids. Then it appeared as if they made a conscious decision to take a different path. Upon glancing at them again, Raymond thought they wore the same strange look as the dog walker earlier on. They old couple quickly turned the other way when he made brief eye contact, but as before, none of that was the least bit worrisome to him. These kids, strange as it seemed, held the key to his total happiness—as if they linked him to Geraldine by fate.

He looked at Xavier and then at Edith, and asked them gently, "So, did you see my friend?"

"The woman with the long hair," Natasha said before Raymond could put a word in.

"You mean *that* woman, the Chinese woman we saw the other day?"

"Yes, her," Raymond said quickly. He could hardly contain his excitement. Though they did not know it, they were subjecting him to torture the way only kids had the unwitting ability to do.

"Oh, I remember her," Edith said.

"You do? You do? You saw Geraldine?" Raymond was beside himself with joy and exhilaration.

"Yes, we saw her," Edith confirmed. Like her sister before her, she was now eyeing the guitar.

Xavier added, "I remember her, too. She asked us if we saw a man with long hair waiting around here." He was also gawking at Raymond's guitar. He continued by saying, "She also said he might be carrying a guitar with him."

Smiling widely, it was all Raymond could do to stop himself from hugging the kids outright. But he knew that was out of the question. "Thank you, guys," he said instead.

"So she was talking about you," Xavier said with a smile.

"Yes, it sure was me."

"Can you play that thing too?" Edith asked, pointing at the guitar.

"Absolutely."

"Can you play something for us?" Natalie asked.

It was the least he could do, even though he was now itching to rush home, stay there, and wait for her call – however long that would take. He played a few tunes—nothing spectacular, but the kids seemed entertained judging by their faces. He tried very hard to ignore the strange looks he was getting, especially when he would look at them and say, "Oh, you like that? Want me to play it again?" It was over at last, some thirty minutes later. They thanked him and then ran off. It was already getting dark as the winter sun started its early setting.

Soon thereafter, guitar in hand, Raymond Pata left with the springy steps of a happy young man slowly approaching his prime.

"My goodness, she was here. My baby was here," he kept muttering to himself as he practically trotted down Lake Avenue toward home. As far as he was concerned, in his mind the futile search was over.

෴ ෴ ෴

The landline was ringing when he entered his living room. An imperceptible frown crept over his face, momentarily dimming the euphoria that had so engulfed him for the past half-hour or so. That was the time it took to walk from the park to his house. He immediately snatched the receiver, ready to spew venom, for he knew who it was.

"Look, Larry, I told you to relax. You will get …"

Instead, a soft feminine voice that sounded as if it came from some dark corner of the galaxy interrupted him. It was a voice that froze him dead in his tracks. It was the sweet and melodious voice of Geraldine Chung.

"Ray, hi. It's me, Geraldine ... remember me?" she teased.

Raymond had to bite his lower lip hard, almost drawing blood, to keep from screaming with joy.

"Of course, Geraldine ... is it really you?" his voice was croaky. He fought to keep it steady, but it was useless and he knew it. So he gave up trying to mask it.

"Yeah ... it's me." She chuckled at the effect she sensed she was having on him.

Raymond sighed with relief and said, "Hey, are you all right? When I did not hear from you, I was worried, thinking that something terrible might have happened."

"I'm fine," she said. Her angelic voice floated through the receiver. "Sorry to have kept you in limbo. Some things came up and I had to leave town immediately. Anyway, I'm back now, and just checked my messages. Sorry to not have made it to the park on time the other day." She did not mention anything about returning his calls, and he didn't ask. None of that mattered now.

"Hey, don't worry about it. As long as you're okay, that's all that matters," said a very relieved and excited Raymond Pata.

"You're so sweet." That angelic voice gave him goosebumps. "But I would like to make it up to you. Would you mind if I came over tonight?"

Would I … tonight!

His heart gave another painful lurch, and right away he had an erection. He was fighting just to breathe. He expressed gratitude to the gods again.

"Absolutely," he grinned from ear-to-ear. "I'll tell you what," he continued. "I'll make you my famous Haitian cuisine, what do you say?" His mother had taught him well.

"Mmm! Sounds exciting. Would you like me to bring something, or perhaps help you with the cooking?"

"Gee, that's a really tempting offer, Geraldine. But I would rather you walk in and find the table set." He was not lying about the 'tempting' part. He wanted to see her, to hold her, and never let her go. As such, he was ready to prepare a romantic dinner for the both of them.

"You sure?"

"Positive."

"How much time are you gonna need, Raymond?" His knees buckled at the sound of his name from her lips. He could almost see them, moist and sensual.

"Let's see." He turned to look at the clock on the wall of his living room, forgetting that he had a wrist watch. "It's about six-fifteen right now, so let's say eight-thirty."

"Sounds good."

"Great, I'll see you then." There was a wide smirk on his face as he was about to hang up.

"Ray?"

"Yeah?"

"It will be kinda difficult getting to your place without the address, don't you think?" He could almost feel her smile across the line.

"Oh," he chuckled, at the same time feeling silly. And then he gave it to her.

Thereafter he raced to the kitchen to prepare for this momentous occasion. As for food, it had always been in the fridge, ready to be cooked in great anticipation of this particular date. How simple she had made it all for him! He did not even have to ask her. The cake, the proposed record deal, was baked and ready; the icing was Geraldine. How blessed could a man be? A part of his dream, that had at one point seemed to fade away, was now alive as a roaring flame.

CHAPTER 20

THE AROMA IN THE KITCHEN was exquisite as Raymond put the finishing touches on the meal. There was a table for two in the dining area, with a bottle of wine and two candles ready to burn. He had dimmed the lights, and in the background there was soft music—oldies, actually, romantic ballads from the Commodores. He'd had enough time to take a quick shower and freshen up.

At precisely 8:05 p.m., the doorbell rang, and in great eagerness Raymond made certain that his breath was fresh by exhaling on his palm and smelling it. The doorbell rang again, and this time he sniffed at his armpits one at a time. The intoxicating fragrance of his cologne still held on strong, and he was glad, because he'd paid a lot of money for it. He opened the door at last, and there she was, standing behind it with that smile he'd seen many times over in his dreams, dazzling on her beautiful face.

He was tongue-tied as their eyes stayed locked on one another. His throat was dry as sandpaper, completely at a loss for words. The woman was simply spectacular.

"Hi," she said.

"Oh … hi," he managed to say. This was followed by an awkward pause.

"Well, aren't you going to invite me in?"

Fighting just to breathe, Raymond said, "Oh … yeah, absolutely. I'm sorry. It's just that you had me worried, girl. For a while I thought I would never see that pretty face again." He was not lying. The thought did cross his mind, scary as it was, on more than one occasion.

"Oh, stop now, Raymond," she smiled as he ushered her in.

Once in the living room, she turned to face him. What he did next, he did out of sheer impulse. He hugged her long and hard, and she did not seem to mind at all.

"Well, here I am. You don't have to worry about never seeing me again."

For a moment he was at a loss for words as he finally let her go and led her to the kitchen. He slid back one of the chairs at the table and sat her down. The aroma of the food still hung in the air.

"Anything to drink before we have dinner?" he offered.

"Just water for now." She smiled again and looked at him intently as he brought her a glass of water.

"Here we go," he said as he gently placed the glass in front of her with a napkin on the side.

"Thank you very much." She barely took a sip as she studied the lavish dishes on the table. The candles were lit, giving the atmosphere a passionate feel, since the lights were dimmed. "You made all this?" She was intrigued.

"Yep," he said as nonchalantly as he could, at the same time taking a seat on the other side of the table.

"Amazing. What do you call this?" She pointed at one of the dishes.

"This is what we call *Polet le Manrango* – baked chicken legs and wings coated with tomato paste and parmesan cheese."

Geraldine was impressed. "Wow, and this?" She pointed at another with a long, delicate, and well-manicured finger.

"That is known as *Diriak Jonjon-Riz Noir au Champions.* In other words, black rice with mushrooms," he said.

"What's with the French names, Ray?" the beautiful woman wanted to know.

For an instant, Raymond Pata was transformed from a somewhat bumbling milquetoast with a huge crush to a brilliant chef. "Well, you see, the cuisine of Haiti is influenced in large part by the French gastronomy, as well as some native staples originally from African food, such as cassava, yams, and maize—what you people in America call corn. Haitian food, though unique in its own right, shares much in common with the rest of Latin America."

Geraldine smiled; she was totally awed, "Are you some kind of chef, Raymond Pata?" she asked. He could not help but smile, flattered that she still remembered his last name, which rolled so perfectly from her tongue.

He smiled. "Nothing of the sort, Geraldine. I've always liked cooking. I learned that from my mother."

"Quickest way to a woman's heart, right?" she said slyly, and they both laughed, their eyes locked on each other.

At last they started eating, although she barely ate, and he did not seem to notice. They spoke, even though it was Raymond who did most of the talking. He practically told her his life story; he felt that comfortable, and he talked about his dreams, and the impending record deal, making it bigger than it really was. He of course could not, and would not reveal his deepest, darkest beliefs, or the fact that he was a wanted, cold-blooded serial killer. After they had their dessert and Raymond was sipping at his wine, he noticed that he'd done the most talking. She merely sat there and listened in silence, nodding, grunting her approval, and smiling at the right moments. And as the night wore on, he felt he was being drawn to her mysteriousness with every passing minute.

"There," he said. "I have told you all about me, and yet I don't know anything about you."

She smiled again. Ahh, that disarming smile! "There is not much to know, Raymond, except that I'm just a regular girl," she said.

"Come on, tell me."

"Not now," she said almost curtly.

He decided to pry a little further without pushing his luck. "Where are you from? I know you just moved out here, but from where? It's okay, you can tell me."

"None of that matters, Ray. For now, I just want to know more about you."

They looked at each other for a while. He was lost in those luminous brown eyes. There was something about them; something mystic or exotic that he could not readily place a finger on, but they were captivating. He felt sparks flying between them. He decided not to question who she was any further. He was scared of losing her again. Once more, she stared at him with an intensity that made him wonder why she was looking at him that way.

"What?" he asked, almost blushing.

"I just love those pink lips of yours," she said in a seductive tone. "And if you want to make love to me, Raymond Pata, you'd better come hold me now."

Raymond was stunned and impressed by her bluntness; at the same time, he felt a jolt of electricity run through his body. He stood up, and so did she, arms outstretched. Within moments they were kissing passionately as she felt his mouth on hers. They backed to the kitchen wall, and the moment they did, she felt his warm hand between her legs, ripping aside her thong to caress her vulva. She put her arms around his neck and hung there as he opened his trousers. Then he placed both hands beneath her bare buttocks and lifted her. The butt cheeks felt cold in his palms, but he knew that would change in a moment. She gave a little hop in the air so that both her legs were wrapped around his upper thighs. His tongue was in her mouth and she sucked on it. He gave a savage thrust that banged her head against the wall. She felt something pass through her thighs. She let her hand drop from his neck and reached down to guide him. Her hand closed around an enormous, blood-gorged pole of muscle. It pulsated in her hand like a wild animal. Groaning with grateful ecstasy, she pulled it into her own wet, turgid flesh. The thrust of its entering, the unbelievable pleasure, made her gasp. She brought her legs up around his, and then like a quiver, her body received the savage arrows of his lightning-like thrusts, innumerable, almost torturing; arching her pelvis higher and higher until she screamed as she reached a shattering climax. She felt his hardness break, and then the crawly flood of semen over her thighs. Slowly her legs relaxed from around his body, slid down until they reached the floor. They leaned against each other; he was out of breath, but surprisingly, not her. And this was just the beginning. A while later they were both naked and beneath the sheets in his bedroom, continuing their lovemaking.

In the living room, the TV was on and the volume was low, but neither heard or noticed it. The newscaster was saying *'The police finally have a composite sketch of the suspected hooded serial killer ...'*

The sketch was posted on the bulletin, but other than the dreadlocks, it bore no resemblance. It was obvious that the witness, Jamal Anderson in this case, did not have a clear look at the perpetrator. But at least the cops had something solid to work with, as far as they were concerned.

'... If you have any information,' the broadcast continued, 'about this suspect, you are urged to call the local police, or the Pasadena Police, or the Altadena Sheriff's Station at ...'

What the bulletin did not mention was the fact that Detective Doug Willoughby was also in search of the stranger who'd walked into Natalie

Anderson's place of business for questioning to see if he had seen anything suspicious around the beauty salon. He was prepared to tread delicately. So many innocent people's civil liberties had been violated in search of the killer, simply because they happened to be from the Caribbean.

The ecstasy continued in the bedroom, and when they were finally all spent, Raymond was able to reflect in the dark over the torment he had recently experienced. She had been worth the trouble, no doubt—the frustration of calls never returned, the wandering around searching for her like a lunatic. But now, here she was. *His* forever. And he was never going to let her go . . . not now, not ever! He was going to convince her to move in with him the next day and thereafter sign the contract with *Phoenix Records.* Once the tours began, he would take her with him, never to leave his sight again. He fell into a deep sleep with a smile on his face. She was an animal; something he never thought he would experience from a woman again. Even Sofia was no match. Now he wanted nothing more in life than to hold onto this woman.

༺ ༻ ༼

A cold, lethargic feeling woke Raymond with a start from a deep sleep the next morning. What was odd was that he had his pants on, even though he had fallen asleep stark naked. He could only construe that he had sleepwalked, or had put them on when he went to relieve himself sometime during the night. He smiled thinly as he stretched his arm to reach out to Geraldine. To his surprise, his palm felt nothing but the cold sheets and pillow, suggesting that no one had laid there in a while. He quickly turned, only to realize that she was not there. He figured that she had gone to the bathroom and would soon be back. In his mind, he had already started preparing a hearty and sumptuous breakfast for her. After the night they had, he was certain her appetite would be huge. The ingredients were already in the fridge.

The moment when he realized to his utter dismay that she had probably left, he noticed a note she had left on the dressing table. He snatched it and read it quickly at first, and then slowly. The message was brief, basically apologizing for having had to leave earlier than she had anticipated, but to his delight she mentioned what a great night she had and was looking forward to more nights like that. He was 'what women called a stud.' His ego was stroked once more as he sat up smiling on his king-size bed.

Most importantly, she'd left her home address, stating that if he wanted to visit she would be home later that afternoon. The salutation was a kiss mark from her lips. She lived in nearby San Marino, the note stated. It never occurred to him that the first night when they met, she had mentioned that she'd just moved into the neighborhood near the laundromat—at least, that was what she'd implied. His spirits were too high to note that minor inconsistency in her story. None of that mattered, so long as she was his.

CHAPTER 21

SAN MARINO, a city that boarders the southern part of Pasadena, was less than 7 miles away from Raymond Pata's house. Incorporated on April 12, 1913, the affluent city was designed by its founders to be uniquely residential, with expensive properties surrounded by beautiful gardens, wide streets, and well maintained parkways. In 2010, *Forbes Magazine* ranked the city as the 63rd most expensive area to live in the United States. There are little to no houses priced under $1,000,000, with the median list price of a single family home at $2,159,000.

Because of its beautiful and mostly breathtaking scenery, the city has played a prominent role in many movies and television shows, like '*Father of the Bride*' with Steve Martin. Scenes from the movie 'Mr. and Mrs. Smith' were filmed in San Marino, as were scenes from many other movies, including '*Memoirs of a Geisha*,' '*The Holiday*,' and '*Men In Black 2*.' The hit TV show '*The Fresh Prince of Bel Air*' was also filmed in San Marino and Pasadena.

At precisely 3:00 p.m., Raymond pulled onto a secluded street and parked near the sidewalk, next to the gate leading to an imposing mansion that he could only guess was the residence Geraldine directed him to, because the address was a spot-on match.

He stepped out of the car, note in hand, and looked around to make certain he was at the right destination. And also to check his reflection in the car window one more time. He was dressed to impress. He had on a tight-fitting pair of jeans with flat dress shoes, a navy blue polo shirt, and a black jacket, and he masked it all with one of his most expensive perfumes, bought exactly for this occasion.

As he walked along the sweeping curve of the driveway toward the double front door made of oak, he could not help but look around in awe. The place was magnificent; the driveway curved around a waterfall surrounded by a *koi* pond, and in it were the fish. Around and inside the pond were exotic flowers and plants. All this spelled immense wealth, and all of a sudden Raymond's thoughts turned selfish. If his new girlfriend came from what for all intents and purposes looked like great wealth, and he was just on the verge of hitting the big time and being 'the Haitian Sensation,' this affair could turn out to be a match made in heaven (*his* version of heaven was different). These were the thoughts in his mind as he approached the door.

He also had a box of chocolates, and a bouquet of long-stemmed roses this time. That was the least he could do after the wild sex they had the night before. The thought alone was enough to give him a hard-on as he felt the familiar bulge in his pants. She by far was the most wild and fervent lay he'd ever had, and again he vowed that he was going to pull all the stops to make her his forever. After all, he had the power from the gods.

He smiled in great anticipation and cleared his throat before ringing the doorbell. He had to ring it a couple of times before the door opened, and Raymond Pata's smile vanished almost immediately. Instead of Geraldine ready to fly in his arms, it was a middle-aged Asian woman whose features suggested that she was Korean standing behind the door. She was slightly puzzled at the sight of a tall, black, well-dressed stranger with dreadlocks standing at the doorway.

"Yes, can I help you?" Her name was Seung Hee. Her skin was smooth and well kept, and as such she looked much younger, but her eyes that told the whole story. They looked sad and tired.

Before answering, Raymond quickly consulted the note Geraldine had left him, just to make sure that he had knocked at the right door. It was indeed the right address, but something was missing. The kiss mark she had left him was gone, making him wonder if he had imagined it. He assumed, and correctly so, that the woman before him was

Geraldine's mother, and this was most likely her parents' house. He recalled the conversation they had at the laundromat on the night they met. Geraldine had mentioned that she was new to the area, making him wonder if that meant she had moved out on her own and had found a new place in the Altadena area.

"Oh, hi, my name is Raymond Pata. I'm looking for Geraldine Chung," he said.

Seung Hee suddenly looked pale as she took a step backwards, totally flushed.

"G-Geraldine?" she gasped.

What's the matter with her? Raymond wondered.

"Yes, Geraldine, ma'am. Excuse me for asking, but am I at the right place? Because this is the address she gave me last night."

The lady was totally spooked now. "Did you s-say last night?" Her voice was a hoarse whisper.

What the hell is going on here?

"Yes, ma'am, last night. That's why I got her these." He motioned at the box of chocolates and the expensive roses. "Is everything okay?"

She started trembling as she turned around and called into the house.

"J-James ... James!"

"What is it?" a man's voice from inside the house answered.

"Could you come out here for a second?"

"What for?" James, or whoever the hell he was, seemed irritated.

"Just come here, will you?" There was a sense of urgency in her voice.

A middle-aged, slender, and handsome Korean man with silver grey hair on the sides soon appeared. He had been reading the day's newspaper, which was in Korean, and had his reading glasses perched a little below his eyes. He looked the type who hated to be interrupted, hence his annoyance. He looked first at Raymond, who was growing uneasy with every minute, and then his wife.

"Yes, what is it, Seung Hee?"

"This here is …" she looked at Raymond for help.

"Raymond Pata," he said quickly.

"Yes, Raymond Pata, and he says he is looking for Geraldine," Seung Hee said. The puzzled look was still plastered on her face.

"Now, why bother me when you know perfectly well the answer to that question?" James said irritably, and was just about to turn around and head back into the living room. But Seung Hee's next words stopped him dead in his tracks.

"Well, this may sound strange, but this young man is certain that he was with Geraldine last night."

This information suddenly had James 'Jimmy' Chung's full attention. In fact, it startled him to a point that he almost dropped the newspaper he was holding.

"Yeah, what is ..." Raymond did not get to finish what he was saying, because Jimmy's eyes were suddenly blazing.

"What?" he barked, taking a step forward. "What in the hell are you trying to pull?"

Raymond was now startled and confused. The situation was becoming more and more bizarre. He fought to maintain his cool, which suddenly was no easy task; because the last thing he wanted to do was create a bad first impression. Especially in the eyes of the parents, he assumed, of the woman he was planning on making his forever.

"Fine," Raymond said, trying to sound reasonable. "She came by my house last night and left this morning, and when I woke up I found this," he said as he handed Seung Hee the note Geraldine had left.

She took a closer look at it and suddenly shrieked, covering her mouth with both hands. Tears welled in her eyes. She had recognized the handwriting instantly. "Oh my God! ... Jimmy, look." She handed the note to her husband, who looked at it and remained surprisingly calm.

"Come inside," he said to Raymond as the couple made way for him to enter.

He was led to the spacious living room, and once again Raymond could not help but gawk in awe. The floors and wall were made from marble, the ceilings were way up high, and the most expensive rugs money could buy seemed to be everywhere. The furniture looked to be specifically designed for this home. He sat on the couch; husband and wife parked themselves at the opposite side of the room. There was a large fireplace in front of him with framed pictures that he did not notice at first, since his eyes were fixed on the couple.

James 'Jimmy' Chung broke the brief silence by saying, "Young man, this is peculiar, to say the least."

"And how is that, sir?"

Jimmy heaved a long, heavy sigh and looked up at the ceiling for what seemed like a minute or two, before he leveled his gaze again at his guest.

"There is no nice way of putting it but to say that our little angel and only child, Geraldine, was murdered almost a year ago ..."

"By the hooded serial killer, investigators believe," Seung Hee added quickly, "who to this day has not been found." The tears were now flowing freely down her cheeks.

"So whoever you say you saw, it was not our daughter," Jimmy said.

"It was *not* Geraldine!" Seung Hee emphasized on behalf of her husband.

At first it seemed as if Raymond Pata did not quite hear them. He felt as if he had been hit with a sledgehammer right across the chest. He looked up, and as he did, he saw a framed picture of Geraldine, the woman he had fallen head over heels in love with. In the beautiful picture, she was wearing a pair of sexy white shorts and black stiletto heels, and seated on the floor. Her feet were parked on a flower pot, her hair was curly, her face was slightly averted from the camera when the picture was taken—but even from that profile, he knew it was her. He recognized her instantly. The picture suggested a lively, chirpy, and beautiful young woman enjoying life to the fullest; the picture seemed to be pulsating with existence, as if she would turn around and step out of the frame.

"That's her," he said as he stood up quickly, pointing at the picture. "That's Geraldine Chung, the woman I was with last night. Actually, I met her close to two weeks ago at a laundromat, prior to last night." He was convinced this was all someone's idea of a sick joke.

"But we're telling you that she's dead, and what you are implying is impossible. Better yet, there has to be some kind of mistake, young man," Seung Hee said.

For Raymond Pata, the room was beginning to spin out of control. He found it hard to breathe, but the full import of what he had been told had yet to register.

"If … if she is dead, right? T-then who … what was … oh God … no … nooo!" In spite of himself, he was reaching a point of hysteria.

The couple exchanged a quick glance, trying to make sense of what was developing right before their astonished eyes. Jimmy Chung stood up, walked toward Raymond and put his hand on his shoulder, and said in an almost soothing voice, "What's the matter, Raymond? I'm sure there's a logical explanation for all this."

The shock was finally setting in, and it looked as if he would break down any minute. Without warning and in total confusion, he tossed the roses to the floor and ripped the box of chocolates open. He saw it clearly now as it flashed in front of him, like a movie in slow motion. Geraldine, the woman he had fallen for, was in fact the young lady in the Jaguar, his first victim. He remembered how she begged him to spare her life, how he saw her as nothing but a means to an end. The realization that she had come back from beyond the grave to torment him was, at this moment, far beyond the limits of his imagination. She had led her killer straight to her parents' house. What else did she have in store for him? Only the devil knew. He was sweating bullets now, terrified beyond reason. He shook so violently with renewed dread that his knees began to buckle underneath him.

"No," he said in a croaky voice that was almost unrecognizable. "T-the logical explanation is that … I – I have to go." He had to get out of there before they figured out who he was—that *he* was the killer of their only daughter. He was preparing to practically run to the door, but his legs felt weak.

"Are you on some kind of medication, young man?" Seung Hee asked, her brow twisting in concern.

"No, I'm not, b-but I'm sorry. I'm truly sorry to have bothered you nice people," he said quickly. His face was flushed with sweat.

He left quickly, not for a moment glancing behind as he hurried toward his car, which in his haste he almost walked past. He got in and sped off. The couple stood in the doorway, their mouths slightly agape, each wondering what in the hell just happened.

"Poor thing," Seung Hee said at last.

"He's a freakin' nut case, if you ask me," Jimmy said dismissively as he turned to pick up the items Raymond had scattered on the floor. Seung Hee did not comment right away, as she normally would. She was in deep meditation, obviously trying to make sense of everything.

She looked at her husband, her eyes wide again—this time in shock. "Oh my God, James," she said in a whisper. Whenever it was 'James' instead of 'Jimmy,' it only meant trouble.

"What is it now?" he asked resignedly. He'd had enough drama the past half hour to last a week, if not more.

"The soothsayer."

"What about him?" Jimmy wanted to know as he exhaled deeply. now holding the flowers and the chocolate Raymond had discarded.

"Remember we went to the soothsayer, shortly after Geraldine's funeral?"

Jimmy's eyebrows were suddenly raised in recognition as he looked his wife straight in the eye. "Seung Hee," he said almost in a whisper. "Could this be? No!" even he could not believe what he was suddenly thinking,

CHAPTER 22

JAMES AND SEUNG HEE CHUNG were childhood sweethearts who both grew up and met in Fresno, California. They were third-generation Koreans in America, whose ties to tradition were still as strong as they were in their country of origin. They both attended Fresno State University. Seung Hee was a pre-medical student major and later transferred to Johns Hopkins University in Washington, DC, and James studied international business at the University of Delaware.

They got married soon after earning their respective degrees, and then moved to southern California, where they rented a small one-bedroom apartment in Koreatown while Seung Hee did her residency at the University of Southern California County Hospital. James started his import-export business, which soon flourished. And before long, Seung Hee, now a full-fledged gynecologist, opened her own practice in the city of Alhambra, a venture that also prospered. With their combined incomes, they were able to amass a fortune, which even to James Chung still seemed obscene after all these years.

It was at this time they felt was the moment to start a family. After many attempts and two major miscarriages, it was later diagnosed that Seung Hee had early stages of ovarian cancer. However, after one of her ovaries was removed, her chances of conception were forfeit. That was why Geraldine was a gift sent from heaven.

One of Seung Hee's regular patients was a Vietnamese couple, Tuan Pham and Mai. They were what people called Vietnamese 'boat people.' They had survived the communists in Vietnam after the fall of Saigon, and then the pirates at sea, and even a typhoon. They arrived in the US and life was an even greater struggle, compounded by the fact that much later, they had an unexpected baby they could not care for. Later they gave up that baby for adoption to Mai's gynecologist, who happened to be Seung Hee.

The baby was a miracle maker, a joy, a wonder in the Chung household. The couple had never known so much happiness, and they showered the child with so much love that to many, including Geraldine when she reached the age of understanding, the knowledge that this was not their biological child was eroded from everyone's memory—or at least to those who knew the full story. She was sent to the best schools, took horse riding and piano lessons, and learned to play chess at age five. In all, she enjoyed the best life had to offer for those privileged. After graduating from high school, a prestigious private one at that, her present from her parents was a brand new Jaguar F Type V8 Convertible – the same car Raymond Pata took from her that fateful night. Of course, it was never found. At the time of her death, she was a sophomore at the University of Southern California. Her major was still undecided because she intended to travel the world after graduation, particularly to the downtrodden countries of Africa and the Far East.

Being active members of the community, the Chungs were, among other things, boosters of the local high school program, members of the Huntington Library Society, supporters of the neighboring law enforcement, including the Pasadena Police Department, and various other organizations that brought them to prominence.

That was why after their daughter was found murdered in the way she was, with her killer still at large, there was extra pressure on the authorities to find the perpetrator. However, days turned to weeks, and weeks to months. Every lead led to a dead end, and meanwhile the suspect known as the 'hooded serial killer' had struck on several occasions, leaving investigators totally bowled over.

It was at this time Seung Hee convinced her husband to do something completely out of character. Having being raised by families rooted in tradition and the old ways, they decided to seek the help of a soothsayer. These were spiritual men in their community who were a liaison between them and the world of the dead, the recently and even the long departed.

There were such people in Koreatown. One man in particular they knew of who came highly recommended by friends was a man named Hwang Jang Park. Koreatown is located west of downtown Los Angeles, between Hollywood and West Los Angeles. Known primarily for its many businesses, the area also contains apartments and high-rise buildings, which house Korean TV studios and other such entities. Because many of the residents are Korean, it is normal to see billboards, advertisements, and other such things displaying the Korean language. In a way, one would think he was right in the middle of Seoul, Korea, when visiting the area. So, after the necessary phone calls, the couple found themselves in a small backroom of an apartment in Koreatown, where Hwang Jang Park met his clients. This happened two weeks to the day after Geraldine was found murdered.

It was late in the evening, a time spirits were believed to be active, when the Chungs were finally ushered into the soothsayer's room. Hwang Jang Park was a dignified man in his mid-60s. He was dressed in an orange robe and sitting on the floor. Seung Hee and her husband were required to take off their shoes and sit on the floor as well. The room was lit with candles, and incense was burning everywhere. The room itself gave an eerie feeling of being a gateway between this world and the spiritual one. Park had a long necklace made from beads in his right hand, at which he pulled one bead at a time with utmost patience. He was seated in front of the couple at an elevated position. His eyes were shut, and when he spoke, he did so in Korean, a language in which all three were fluent. Seung Hee could not stop the tears from flowing ever since she'd learned about the death of her daughter—and worse still, that her killer had yet to be found. Who could have done it and why, in the name of Buddha? That was a question no one could answer.

The older man's eyes were still shut when James Chung broke the ice. "Divine soothsayer, as you already knew even before we mentioned it, we came to seek your help in tracking down our daughter's killer. The police have no suspects, no leads, nothing. It is as if our daughter's murderer left no footprints and vanished like a spirit."

A now sobbing Seung Hee added, "She was our only child, divine soothsayer. To us, the sun and moon rose and set on her, and it has been tough dealing with her untimely death."

"You have brought the necessary items?" the soothsayer asked, his eyes still closed.

They were required to bring the clothes Geraldine was wearing at the time when she was killed. No easy task, because the police department's forensic unit was still trying to find any trace of

DNA from the killer on her clothes, but James's influence within the police department prevailed.

"Yes, O divine one. These were the clothes she was wearing when she was killed," Seung Hee said, feeling as if these were the hardest words to have ever come out of her mouth, as she was still struggling to come to grips with her daughter's death.

She produced a bag beside her, and from it took out the clothes, including a pair of black thong panties, and spread them on the floor in front of the soothsayer—who up until then had not opened his eyes. Park picked up a lantern with incense burning in it, made a circular motion above the spread clothes, and put it down. When he did that, a sudden gust of wind came into the room. It was so unexpected that it took the couple by surprise; and for a moment it looked as if the candles were going to be put out. But just as suddenly as it had come, it stopped. It was a strange occurrence that scared the couple, for there were no windows in the room where the wind could have originated. The soothsayer finally opened his eyes, and Seung Hee gasped.

"Yes, I can feel Geraldine with us right now," he announced at last. "And what I feel from her is that her killer invokes powerful spirits through another medium, and these spirits come from across the ocean. He believes that these spirits will bestow him with wealth, power, success, and happiness by sacrificing young women like her."

"Are these demonic spirits, O divine one?" James 'Jimmy' Chung wanted to know.

"Yes, and the big mistake he makes is that this is a doorway of evil he has opened. He cannot appease all the diabolical spirits that he invokes, and that has turned him inside out. They have turned him into a predator that cannot stop, and perhaps sooner if not later, they may come back to demand their dues."

This was an interesting piece of information that the couple picked up on. It seemed as if the soothsayer knew the identity of Geraldine's killer, and Seung Hee followed up on this quickly.

"How can he be caught, so other families will not have to suffer like we are right now?"

"Only time will tell."

"What is he like, O divine one, can you see him?" Seung Hee pressed on.

"Not very clearly, but he is foreign born. Keep your eyes and ears open; that much you should know."

"One last thing, O divine one," James Chung said, "Will our little angel find peace?"

The soothsayer took a deep sigh as he once again closed his eyes. "That is one question I was afraid you were going to ask," he said softly.

Husband and wife exchanged a quick glance, wondering what pronouncements the spirit man had in store for them.

"How is that, O Divine one?" James wanted to know, already dreading what he was about to hear.

"Because Geraldine's life was cut short so brutally and painfully, before her last breath she vowed to herself that she would not rest until she sought her killer out, in this world or the next. Your daughter loved life to the fullest. She loved her family, she was vivacious and privileged, she was grateful for all those things, and she did not want to leave them behind so soon," was the chilling revelation from the profound soothsayer.

On hearing this, Seung Hee let out a loud, uncontrollable wail as she imagined her daughter's last desperate cling to life while being claimed by the chief of traitors known to men – death. Her husband tried his best to comfort her, but it was all in vain; the grief was just too tough to bear. Even he could not fight back stinging tears. All this time the soothsayer kept his eyes closed, muttering to himself as he communicated with the spirits.

"Take comfort," the soothsayer said at last. "Geraldine will eventually find peace, and that is all I can tell you now. But keep your eyes and ears open for any sign."

And the couple did. Little did they know that the sign Hwang Jang Park had warned them about would come knocking at their front door almost a year later—and it came in the form of Raymond Leonard Pata.

CHAPTER 23

JAMES AND HIS WIFE STAYED ROOTED in the doorway for a moment longer. It was obvious that Raymond Pata's visit had sparked some very interesting questions in their minds.

"Seung Hee," James said carefully. "The soothsayer said Geraldine's killer was foreign. I don't know much about black people. Even though he sounded American, I thought I detected a slight accent. Didn't you?"

Seung Hee thought about this for a moment before she gave an answer. "So he is a foreigner."

"And he is adamant that he saw Geraldine last night, and even before that."

Seung Hee's eyes were suddenly wide open. "Could it be him, James? Could it be that the killer of our daughter was right in our house, and we let him slip through our fingers just like that?"

James did not answer right away. He was obviously in deep thought, digesting what his wife had just said. By this time, they were in their living room. Seung Hee picked up a cordless phone and started dialing. This maneuver was not lost to her husband.

"Seung Hee, what are you doing?"

"Calling Detective Willoughby," she replied as she pressed the phone to her ear.

"What are you going to tell him? That some psycho kid was just here claiming to have seen Geraldine last night?" His eyes were wide with disbelief.

"He said to call him if we heard of anything, no matter how bizarre, minute, or twisted it may be. And here is one on a platter," she said.

"Seung Hee, you are talking ghost stories here. He'll probably laugh in your face."

"I don't care," she said. "I owe it to my little angel to do everything in my power … to bring killer to justice even if I look like a fool in the process … so be it." She already knew the detective's number by heart and had finished dialing, and was waiting for an answer.

"I suppose you're right," James Chung conceded. "We owe it to her. Oh, Seung Hee, I miss her so much."

"So do I, Jimmy, so do I," she said softly, and gave a mirthless smile as the memories came flooding back. She pressed the phone to her ear. "The name is Raymond Pata, right?"

"That's right, Raymond Pata. It's a name I will *never* forget."

At that moment, Seung Hee raised her finger at him to indicate that she had connected with a live person. "Oh yes, hi," she spoke into the receiver. "Can you connect me to the homicide division, please? I would like to speak to Detective Douglas Willoughby, please … thank you very much."

Even though it was a Sunday afternoon, Doug Willoughby was in his office. He had no day off. His whole life now revolved around the 'hooded serial killer' case. The sketch of the supposed suspect had not yielded the desired results, because the 'star witness,' Jamal Anderson, had not given a clear and proper description. It had happened all too fast, he had said. It seemed now as if he was back at square one. If only he could find the mystery visitor who had walked into Natalie's store that afternoon, maybe he would find his man. But that afternoon, everything changed. It started with listening to voice messages from a phone in his office he almost never used, and just as he was trying to make sense of it, the call from Seung Hee Chung came. His heart pounded with excitement.

"Doug Willoughby, homicide," he said formally.

"Oh, Detective Willoughby, good afternoon. This is Seung Hee Chung," came the voice at the other end of the line. She needed no introduction; he could recognize that voice in his sleep.

"Seung Hee?"

"Yes, I'm Geraldine Chung's mother, the girl who was murdered …"

"Oh yes, of course, Seung Hee. I've been meaning to call you, as a matter of fact," he said as he wondered how to delicately break the news of what he had just heard to her.

"Really?" the woman was stunned.

"Yes. Ever heard of a Raymond Pata?" Willoughby asked carefully. He thought he could almost hear Seung Hee freeze at the other end of the line. There was an awkward silence that seemed to Doug Willoughby to last more than five minutes. It sounded as if the woman was struggling to breathe. "Seung Hee … Seung Hee … are you there?"

"Y-yes, I'm here, sorry," she said at last,

On the other hand, Willoughby wondered if perhaps it would have been better if he had driven to the Chung residence instead, and told her what he had just heard in person. But it was too late now.

"Not a problem, Seung Hee," he said. "But like I said, I've been meaning to call you and your husband, because I just now found out that I've been receiving strange messages I was not aware of on my other office phone that I almost never use."

"What kind of messages?" she asked, at the same time bracing herself for the worst. Her heartbeat started beating wildly.

"This may sound a bit off the top, Seung Hee, but apparently there is a Raymond Pata who has been leaving messages on this phone I was telling you about, asking Geraldine to call him. Do you by any chance know anyone by that name?"

A horse kick to the groin could not have hit harder. If Detective Willoughby had been having a face-to-face conversation with Seung Hee, he would have realized that she had turned pale and was on the verge of collapsing to the floor as she clutched the living room couch to keep from falling. Her husband, who was watching all this, quickly came to her aid.

"What's the matter, Seung Hee? Are you okay?"

She was speechless.

Over the phone, Detective Willoughby said, "Stay right where you are. My partner and I will be on our way." Following that, he hung up the phone with a mind too full for words.

ᏊᏊ ᏊᏊ ᏊᏊ

Bizarre did not even begin to describe what was happening with this case, as far as Doug Willoughby was concerned. After interviewing Jamal Anderson and posting the sketch he had given, it was enough to trigger a series of phone calls from every nut job who claimed to have knowledge of the suspect's whereabouts. But of course, none of them proved to be reliable, even from those who had full control of their senses. It seemed as if a breakthrough, if there was one to hope for, was far in the future if at all.

It was when he listened to the messages Raymond Pata left when trying to call Geraldine that he finally got a name to work with. But why had this man, Raymond, called this phone numerous times, asking to have the dead girl call him? From what he could deduce from the calls, this Raymond, whoever he was, seemed convinced to have had contact with the deceased recently, like they had something going on. This sure was preternatural. Such a thing was not possible, unless this Raymond Pata was someone who should have thrown himself at the mercy of a good psychiatrist. But then, why call the number of the lead detective on the 'hooded serial killer' case? And for that matter, on a phone that he almost never used? *Where* did he get that number? But most importantly, he had to find out exactly who this Raymond Pata was and speak to him.

It did not take long for the detective to find out who he was. The file on him, just like the one the reporter Maureen Webb had pulled on him in Florida, was about empty because he had never been in trouble – there was no arrest record or any negative report on his public record. The only thing newsworthy about him, in a manner of speaking, was the fact that he was the surviving member of an unknown band that had perished in a car crash. And now these strange messages? Interestingly, his name had come up in their investigation of possible Haitians living in the Pasadena/Altadena area.

He would first have to speak to the dead girl's parents, and thereafter pay Mr. Pata a visit to get to the bottom of this. Right now Raymond was not a suspect, but a person of great interest in breaking this strange case wide open. A little later, he and his partner were headed to the Chung residence, a place very familiar to the detectives. Thereafter he was going to Raymond Pata's last known address; he already had an unmarked squad car sent to lay surveillance on the premises. It was parked half a block away with instructions to the two junior officers to report any unusual activities, if any, at Raymond Pata's residence, including his comings and goings—and, most importantly, to not let him out of their sight until he had a chance to talk to him.

The detective did not have probable cause to arrest him, let alone serve a search warrant, but he could question him in a way that wouldn't arouse his suspicions. That was, if he had anything to hide. He'd also find out if Raymond fit the description of Natalie's would-be attacker. The fact that he was Haitian and had dreadlocks, just as Natalie had described him, was not lost to him. But so far the information he had on Raymond did not in any way suggest that he was mentally unbalanced.

CHAPTER 24

IT WAS ALMOST DARK when Raymond Pata burst into his living room. He was dazed as he tripped on the coffee table. He was fighting just to breathe. Upon hitting the floor, his legs did not have the strength to carry him, so he remained seated on the floor next to the couch. He took off his jacket and practically ripped off his shirt. Thoughts were rushing through his mind as he suddenly developed a severe case of nausea. He quickly stood up and rushed to the bathroom.

When he got there, he stooped in front of the toilet, still on his knees, and started throwing up violently. He felt a little better as he slowly got up, washed his face in the wash basin, and then looked at himself in the mirror. The image looking back at him revealed a very frightened man indeed, but the shock had yet to wear off, let alone run its full course. He could not believe all this was happening. It *had* to be a dream, a terrible nightmare from which he would soon awake.

"You're losing it, man," he said to himself.

At that moment, his smartphone, which he had left in the living room on the coffee table, started ringing. The mere sound of it, and the suddenness with which it came, was enough to startle him to a point where he almost jumped out of his skin. He wondered who it was, or if it was Geraldine. He went to the living room, looking at the phone as if it were a ticking time bomb. He dreaded to answer and yet he knew he just had to. There was no name on the caller ID, which made him even more apprehensive, but curiosity matched his fear.

"Hello," he said softly.

It was the voice of a very irritated Larry Allen on the other end.

"Raymond! ... Are you still home, man? We're waiting for you. The boys are getting edgy 'cause we've been here over three hours now."

"What the hell for?" Raymond wanted to know, confused.

"Now ain't the time to be playing games, Ray. It's Sunday, remember? And we're expecting a delivery from you."

Raymond seemed not to hear what the other man was saying. "Look, Larry ... some weird stuff's been happening to me, I don't have the time to ..."

"I don't wanna hear it, man," Larry interrupted. He was practically yelling now. "The product, or the six grand we paid your sorry ass." In his anger, his street burr had returned.

"Larry, listen to me. Do you remember almost a year ago when I delivered that Jaguar, you mentioned something about some young, hot but nosy detective who gave you the creeps?"

"What the hell does that have to do with anything, man?" Larry was still agitated.

"What did she look like?"

"You still have not answered my question, Ray. What the hell does that have to do with anything?" he asked instead.

"Larry, listen, there's been …"

"Like I said, I don't wanna hear diddly, man. We're coming, and I hope for your sake you got the vehicle you promised, or the cash we gave you … plus interest!"

This was unbelievable. "H-hey, what the hell interest are you talking about?"

"We're on our way. No more games. And let me tell you something, Ray, and listen good 'cause I'm only gonna say this once – there's no place to run to, Haitian boy. So if you don't have what we seek, you better start digging your own grave. Literally. Remember, Ray, I told you a long time ago not to *ever* fuck me."

Before Raymond could respond, the line went dead. He was left staring at the phone dumbfounded. The lines were drawn, and his life had just been threatened. Everything was falling apart, his whole world. A life that had looked promising and bright literally that morning had taken a turn for the worse. Beads of sweat appeared on his brow as he ran to the bedroom. There was only one thing left to do, and that was run home to Mama. Only back in his mother's arms, he thought—he *knew*, would he find refuge.

He quickly grabbed a small suitcase, and just as hastily started shoving some clothes into it, along with other important things he could get his hands on. Larry and his goons were going to be here any time, so he would have to make it quick. He would not even use the front door when he made his escape. He could go through the back, jump the fence, catch a bus to downtown Los Angeles, and from there rent a car at an Avis or somewhere and take the 10 freeway all the way to Florida. He still had some cash stashed somewhere. Not much, but enough to get him where he needed to be.

"Oh no, that's it," he said to himself. "I'm getting the hell outta dodge." He rushed to his place of strength – the shrine.

The ghastly room was always lit with candles, and today was no different. He got a garbage bag, collected all the items in the room, and put them in it. There was something significant missing, though, and he did not realize it until he looked at the place where he always left it. *The doll.* When he finally noticed it was not there, he let out a wild, panic-laden shriek as he began searching frantically.

"Oh, *Nana Buluku* the god creator and *Mawu* goddess of the moon. Where is it? Without it, I'm powerless. Oh help, *Nana Buluku*," he ranted

Suddenly, a voice not of this world sounded. It was so powerful, so frightening that it seemed to make the very walls of the room resound. "Are you looking for this?"

He turned around and tried to scream, but terror took the sound away. He stood rooted in one spot, paralyzed. For a moment he thought he was going to literally drop dead from fear. Geraldine was standing in the doorway behind him; she'd just appeared, seemingly out of thin air. Scary did not even begin to describe the way she looked now.

"No … no … Geraldine!" he managed to utter the words with immense difficulty.

She had the doll in her hand, her face was pale and horrifying, and he now realized why he always seemed lost in her eyes – *the eyes*! They never blinked. She advanced toward him, but she was not walking. It seemed, she was floating.

"Raymond … Raymond," her voice echoed, and he felt as if the sound itself would burst his eardrums. She shook her head from side to side slowly as her eyes shone brightly. He tried not to make eye contact, but it was impossible.

"Why would you be such a monster?" she said, her eyes piercing him. The greatest love of his life was suddenly his greatest curse. "What were all those killings about? Wealth? Power? Some kind of twisted high that your sick mind dreamed of? And look what the coyotes did to me!" she screamed as she lifted her dress. The sight was gruesome. Her bare torso, perfect when he first saw it, was covered with fresh bite marks from animals, coyotes, some of which were dripping blood. One of her young breasts was chewed off. Raymond screamed in terror yet again. This was not his Geraldine, this was something else—a devil, or rather the devil's concubine, who had come to torment him from beyond the grave. It never occurred to him that he could very well be the devil, taking into account that he himself had made a deal with Lucifer and his minions.

"No ... t-this is not happening to me. It's a dream. I touched you, Geraldine ... the kids at the park saw you." He had found his voice at last, and the shock in it had reached new heights.

"What kids, Ray?" she asked with a mirthless smile.

Things he had not noticed before suddenly became plainly obvious—like her dress, for instance. It was the same one she was wearing when he first met her at the laundromat, and the other night when she came over for dinner. She was still wearing the same dress even now, but he was too blinded to have perceived that. He realized it was most likely the dress she was wearing when he killed her. Even though he was still trying to come to grips with that fact, he could never accept the verity that she had died by his hands. No, it was all a dream. It *had* to be, one long terrible nightmare from which he would soon awake, he kept telling himself.

But then he started having flashbacks. "T-the kids at the park ..." He was going to say more, but the flashbacks intensified. His encounter with first the little girl, Natalie, and then later her siblings. He saw it all now. He was reliving the moment as clearly as if it was just happening, but this time in slow motion. He understood now that he had been talking to himself; there was nobody there. Little wonder he was getting strange looks from people, like the man who was walking his poodle, and the old couple who suddenly changed direction and started walking the other way. They were all looking at him as they would someone with a few loose marbles in his head. He then knew that his encounters with Geraldine as well—the kissing, the lovemaking and all—had not been real.

"Those kids were sent by the angel of death. They were not real, they were just like me. Spirits. Such a pity I couldn't stop you from killing those other innocent girls," she said, still floating toward him, holding the doll.

He was immobilized by fear like never before. She crossed the legs of the doll, and in the same instant, Raymond's legs also crossed. The pain was unbelievable as he fell flat on his face. He tried to scream, but then she placed her finger on the mouth of the doll and his mouth was shut for him. She rolled the doll, and on the floor Raymond did the exact same thing. In his view, which was fast becoming hazy, he noticed that a strand of his dreadlock was tied to the neck of the doll, which meant the torture had not even begun. That was enough to overwhelm him with a despair that he knew would crush him far more than death ever would. He could not even cry out, for the pain was out of this world. She then made him strip to his underwear, and rolled him into the living room.

"You know," she said in her terrifying voice, "had you not snuffed my life away, there's a lot we could have done with that body." She was mocking him now. The torture had yet to start, let alone the nightmare, and in all this turmoil Raymond wondered if he would ever see the light of the next day. His dreams had gone up in smoke, and he knew it.

At that moment, an unmarked Crown Victoria sedan pulled up outside in front of Raymond Pata's house. When it finally came to a stop,

Detectives Douglas Willoughby and his partner Jen Russo stepped out. They had come to question Raymond. They walked to the front door, and Doug Willoughby knocked real hard.

"Raymond Pata, police, open up!" It was a demand.

There was no response, but they could hear a deadly commotion in the living room. This prompted them to draw their weapons.

"Raymond Pata, open the door right this instant. We need to ask you a few questions," Willoughby said.

There was still no response, but the commotion continued, along with what sounded like muffled screams. They considered their next move, which involved breaking into his house. Normally such a move would require a search warrant signed by a judge. But in light of what was going on inside the house, they had probable cause to force their way in. At that moment, Mrs. Barnard, the landlady, appeared.

"Hi, can I help you?" She regarded the two detectives suspiciously. Straight away, the badges came out. Her eyes were fixed on their guns.

"I'm Detective Doug Willoughby, ma'am, and this is my partner, Jen Russo. We're with the Pasadena Police. And who are you, ma'am?"

"Oh, I'm Katherine Barnard, the property owner. Thank God you're here."

"And why is that?" Russo wanted to know as she took a small step forward.

"I was just about to call the police."

"Why?" Jen Russo asked again.

"Well, there's been a lot of screaming coming from the young man who lives here," she said. "I also saw him humping against the kitchen wall last night when I went to throw the trash."

"You mean Raymond Pata?" Jen asked, missing nothing.

"Yes, him."

Willoughby started thinking fast. "Do you have keys to his house? We need to get inside now." The tone of his voice outlined the urgency of the situation.

With no hesitation, Mrs. Barnard pulled out a bunch of keys from her apron pocket, picked one among many, and handed it to Detective Willoughby. He immediately unlocked the door. His gun and that of his partner were still drawn.

"Stand back, Mrs. Barnard," Willoughby barked.

The older woman retreated to a safe distance as the two detectives charged into the living room, where they were treated to a very strange sight.

The living room that not too long ago was spotless was now a complete mess, and looked as if it had been hit by a bomb. There were all kinds of things, including furniture, strewn all over the floor. And as if that was not enough, they saw Raymond Pata being tossed all over the place like a rag doll by some invisible force. He was not doing this to himself, that much was clear, but still it was enough to freeze the detectives in their tracks and gawk in astonishment. None of their training had prepared them for what they were seeing.

"What the hell?" Willoughby was the first to recover from his shock.

Raymond Pata was ranting as he frothed from the mouth. "P-please … get her off me … stop, Geraldine … please stop …"

Detective Willoughby quickly placed his Police Special firearm in its holster, rushed toward Raymond and grabbed him to prevent him from hurting himself even further. It was no easy task. This also compelled Detective Russo to jump in and give a hand. When they finally managed to subdue and handcuff him, Jen Russo immediately pulled out her smartphone, which also acted as a two-way radio.

"Officers at scene need backup, and send in the medics now!" she shouted.

There were deep cuts all over his bare torso, and his face was a bloody mess. At first glance, the wounds seemed self-inflicted, but what the detectives couldn't see was Geraldine continuing to do a number on him nonstop.

A little later the house was swarming with cops, as well as members of the Altadena Sheriff's Department, as Raymond Pata was being led to an ambulance strapped in a straitjacket, still ranting. The medics in charge had a difficult time with him until they injected him with a strong sedative, which finally calmed him down. As far as they were concerned, he had lost his mind and was delirious at the same time—or psychotic. At that moment, a car pulled up at a safe distance. In it was Larry Allen and two tough-looking hoods. They had come for Raymond just as they had promised, and were puzzled by these new developments. They did not linger around for long, because they took off a little later. Larry had new concerns now and had to make his own escape, in case Raymond spilled the beans on him. For all he knew, his own liberty could be in jeopardy, and waiting to find out would certainly not be the smartest thing to do.

As Raymond was being led away by the medics to the waiting ambulance, watched by his landlady Mrs. Barnard, among others, the two detectives and a few of the cops who were now in the house gathered all kinds of incriminating evidence that pointed at Raymond Pata as the dreaded 'hooded serial killer.' He took one last look at his house and saw Geraldine Chung smiling at him through the bedroom window. Her striking features had returned. She was oh so beautiful, and like the ghost that she was, her image dissolved.

Raymond Leonard Pata later confessed to the murders of Geraldine Chung, Brittany Gomez, Laura Hutchinson, and many others. He escaped the gas chamber because he was deemed mentally unfit to stand trial, and was sent to spend the rest of his life at an institution for the criminally insane somewhere in Northern California, where he continues to receive visits from supernatural beings.

A year later, a book called '*Anatomy of A Killer: Inside The Mind of One Of California's Most Notorious Serial Killers*' by Maureen Webb was published. It stayed on the top of the bestseller lists for a little over five months, making her a wealthy woman and an expert on the subject—but most importantly, she got her Pulitzer Prize.

The End

AUTHOR'S NOTE

The Devil's Concubine started off being a screenplay titled *'Geraldine.'* With the help of great friends Jana Baroga, Erik Hudson, and others, we managed to shoot the entire screenplay on something that was less than a shoestring budget. I was attempting to follow the footsteps of Robert Rodriguez, a filmmaker I admire a lot. But considering I had many personal demons I still had to conquer, the main one being alcoholism, a lot of things were missed—like the preparation of the necessary paperwork with the Screen Actors Guild (SAG). So the movie, or whatever you want to call it, was shelved, with hopes of reshooting it with a bigger budget in the future. But in the meantime I felt the need to share the story with the world somehow, and thus the novel version.

The Devil's Concubine is entirely a product of my imagination, so mistakes and inaccuracies in covering aspects of voodoo are mine and mine alone. Any resemblance to actual people, locales, buildings, and events are purely coincidental and unintended; I just like running amok with my imagination and seeing where it takes me. Many times it takes me to places I never thought possible. Save for obvious historical facts and the names of places and people, this is an entire work of fiction. And really, I want to take this moment to thank you from the bottom of my heart for taking the time to read my novel. There are many more exciting ones, I know, but the fact that you took the time to read it and hopefully enjoy it is what inspires me to try and get better with every project I engage in. Thank you so very much.

81363575R00188

Made in the USA
San Bernardino, CA
07 July 2018